THE
LAST
SUMMER
OF THE
GARRETT
GIRLS

JESSICA SPOTSWOOD

sourcebooks
fire

Published by Sourcebooks Fire, an imprint of Sourcebooks, Inc.
P.O. Box 4410, Naperville, Illinois 60567-4410
(630) 961-3900
Fax: (630) 961-2168
sourcebooks.com

Library of Congress Cataloging-in-Publication Data

Names: Spotswood, Jessica, author.
Title: The last summer of the Garrett girls / Jessica Spotswood.
Description: Naperville, Illinois : Sourcebooks Fire, [2018] | Summary: Told
    through four viewpoints, sisters Des, Bea, Kat, and Vi, aged nineteen to
    fifteen, are each transformed, especially in how they see one another, in
    the last summer before Bea leaves for college.
Identifiers: LCCN 2017061763
Subjects: | CYAC: Sisters--Fiction. | Orphans--Fiction. | Dating (Social
    customs)--Fiction. | Grandmothers--Fiction. | Family
    life--Maryland--Fiction. | Maryland--Fiction.
Classification: LCC PZ7.S7643 Las 2018 | DDC [Fic]--dc23 LC record available at
https://lccn.loc.gov/2017061763

Printed and bound in Canada.
MBP 10 9 8 7 6 5 4 3 2 1

THE LAST SUMMER OF THE GARRETT GIRLS

ALSO BY JESSICA SPOTSWOOD

Wild Swans

THE CAHILL WITCH CHRONICLES

Born Wicked

Star Cursed

Sisters' Fate

For Steve, who read every single draft,
and for Tiffany, who answered all my flailmails.
You are this book's fairy godmother.

CHAPTER ONE

DES

Des has a morning routine. Des *likes* her morning routine. Her sisters slamming doors and screaming at each other is not part of that routine. Neither is the broken dishwasher, being out of sugar for her tea—she grimaces as she takes another still-scalding sip—or sleeping through her alarm.

"Des!" her youngest sister, Vi, screeches. "Kat locked me out!"

There's a loud thumping as Vi pounds on the bedroom door that she and Kat share. A moment later, she rushes into the kitchen, her auburn hair still tangled from sleep, her freckled face flushed with anger. "Did you hear me?"

"I'm *busy*," Des snaps, reaching into the sudsy sink. She

needs to call Mr. Stan to come take a look at the dishwasher. And of course no one bothered to touch last night's dishes. It's Kat's week, but it's easier for Des to do it herself than to nag her sister.

"I got up to go to the bathroom, and Kat locked me out, and now she's FaceTiming with Pen about what to wear to their audition," Vi fumes. "Tell her to let me back in! I was *sleeping*!"

"Why don't you go sleep on the couch?" Des suggests. She isn't sure when she became the arbiter of all her sisters' squabbles. They used to go to Gram with every skinned knee and hurt feeling, but lately—especially since Gram's knee replacement a few weeks ago—it's been on Des. It's *all* been on Des: shopping for groceries, picking up Gram's prescriptions, cooking supper, washing the dishes, and doing the laundry—all that on top of running the bookstore. She thought things would go back to normal once Gram was home from the rehab center, but they haven't.

Maybe this is the way things are now. Forever. Dread washes over her at the thought.

"Why do I always have to give in?" Vi demands, twisting her hair into a ponytail. "You just don't want to fight with Kat."

There is some truth there. Kat has been extra venomous since her breakup. "I don't have time for this right now, Vi." Des tosses the clean silverware into the dish drainer.

"I have to leave in five minutes if I want to open the store on time."

"Okay, okay." Vi yawns. "Where's Gram?"

"Miss Lydia picked her up and took her out for breakfast."

Vi points at the baking dish next to the stove. "Is that a strawberry crumble?"

Des nods. That's why there's no sugar for her tea. Des woke up when Bea came to bed at two in the morning after her late-night stress baking. That's been happening often enough lately that Des is starting to worry. She thought after Bea's acceptance to Georgetown—or at least after being named valedictorian—Bea would be able to chill out a little. She hasn't. If anything, she seems more tense than ever.

Des feels stretched in so many directions right now and inadequate in all of them.

Vi grabs the strawberry crumble and a clean fork. "Yay, breakfast!"

"Use a plate. And wash it when you're done." Des drains the sink, gulping down the rest of her bitter tea. God, when did she become their mother?

Footsteps pound down the wooden stairs, and then Kat saunters in, wearing high-waisted white shorts and a black *The Future Is Female* T-shirt. "What do you think? Do I look like a modern-day Jo March?"

"That's my shirt!" Vi protests.

Kat smirks. "It looks better on me."

Vi plants her hands on her slim hips. "You're going to stretch it out! Des!"

Des closes her eyes. Maybe if she closes her eyes, they'll go away.

"You're calling the sister with the eating disorder *fat*?" Kat scowls, tossing her red curls over her shoulder. "Nice, Vi."

"I was talking about your ginormous boobs, and you know it," Vi retorts.

"Okay, no talking about Kat's body." Des frowns. She's been worried about Kat relapsing since her douchebag boyfriend broke up with her last month. Is Kat's lack of appetite normal teenage heartbreak, or does she think Adam would still love her if she had a thigh gap? Des isn't sure.

"Fine. Wear the shirt. But you are my *least* favorite," Vi spits. It's their worst sisterly insult, ever since Gram banned them from saying *I hate you*.

Vi's right. She *is* always the one to give in. It's not fair, but at the moment, Des is grateful for it.

"It's your turn to clean the bathroom, Kat," she says. "Today, please. It's gross."

Kat doesn't even acknowledge her. She's too busy squealing and fending off Vi's attempts to stab her with the strawberry-stained fork.

Des grabs her tote from the back of a chair and whirls around the kitchen for her phone, planner, and keys to the store. "I've got to go. See you two later."

There's probably a better way to handle this, but it would take time and patience and an authority she doesn't have. She's only nineteen; she's not their mom.

Lately, she really misses their mom.

The purple-haired waitress is back.

Des watches as the girl outside paws through her enormous black leather bag. She pulls out a sketchpad, a pair of headphones with three colored pencils caught in the tangled cords, a bottle of Diet Coke, a wallet, and a set of keys. The bottle falls to the brick sidewalk, followed by the keys. The girl drops her bag and cusses. Des can't hear the words from inside the store, but she can read the shape of the girl's dark-lipsticked mouth. The girl looks up and down the street hopefully. The past two days, she's bummed change from kind passersby.

That's how people in Remington Hollow are: kind. And curious, especially about strangers.

Des is no exception. She doesn't have any customers, so she grabs a dollar in quarters from the register and strolls outside.

"Hey," she says. "Do you need change for the meter?"

"Oh my God. Yes. Thank you so much." The girl takes the quarters from Des's outstretched hand. "Why can't I pay with the app on my phone? What kind of stupid hick town still requires actual *quarters* for parking meters?"

Des laughs. "Welcome to Remington Hollow. We peaked during the Revolutionary War."

"Ugh." The girl leaves her stuff splayed across the sidewalk and starts feeding the meter next to her beat-up silver Hyundai. "I guess. I have to remember I'm not in the city anymore."

"Where are you from? Annapolis? DC?" Des guesses.

"Baltimore," the girl says. "I go to MICA. Maryland Institute College of Arts?"

Des hasn't heard of it, but she feels as though she should have. She's an artist too, isn't she? That's the kind of thing she should know. Her not knowing feels like proof that Remington Hollow *is* a stupid hick town and, having lived here all her life, having no real plans to go anywhere else, she is a stupid hick too.

Of course this girl is an artist. She looks like one, with her vivid purple hair and mouth and the bright tattoos spiraling up and down her pale arms. Des feels embarrassingly plain in her ripped blue jeans and faded, worn-soft *Pride and Prejudice* T-shirt. She's not wearing any makeup, and her red curls are pulled back in a simple ponytail. Everyone in Remington Hollow already knows how she looks—how she looked at four and nine and fourteen too—so there's usually no point in trying very hard.

"I'm here for the summer. Staying with my grandmother." The girl confesses it like a prison sentence.

Des looks at the bookstore on the corner, at Tia Julia's next door, at the SunTrust and the pharmacy farther down Main Street. At the wooden benches spaced along the uneven brick sidewalks, and the U.S. and Maryland flags flapping in the wind outside the post office. Down the hill, four blocks away, the river sparkles in the sun. The briny scent of the water carries on the breeze, hidden beneath espresso beans from the Daily Grind and the fragrant blue hydrangeas in Mrs. Lynde's window box.

Des loves Remington Hollow. Yeah, it's small. But she has never been desperate to escape, to get away for college like some of her classmates. Like her best friend, Em. Like Bea and Kat and sometimes even Vi.

It's a good thing Des doesn't want to escape, because Gram is counting on her. Most people are retired at seventy, not running their own business and raising four teenage girls. Gram needs Des, and honestly, Des has always liked being needed.

She looks up. The girl is watching her. She's pushed her sunglasses to the top of her head, revealing smoky eyes and long, black lashes. Des flushes, knowing that she's going all blotchy-pink from the vee of her V-neck all the way up to her cheeks. It's the downside of being a fair-skinned, freckle-faced redhead: she can never hide her mortification.

"I'm Paige," the girl says, holding out a hand with lavender nails.

"Des. Desdemona, but everybody calls me Des."

"Desdemona?" Paige raises two perfectly winged dark brows.

Des winces. She's not used to having to explain. Everyone in Remington Hollow already knows the Garrett sisters and their tragedy.

"My mom really loved Shakespeare," she explains. "My sisters are Beatrice, Katharina, and Viola. She named the bookstore too." She gestures behind her at Arden Books. "As in the forest of, from *As You Like It*."

"That's some serious literary devotion. So your mom owns the bookstore?"

"My grandmother." After the accident, Gram remortgaged the house, quit her job as an English teacher up at the middle school, and devoted herself to the store. She thought it was important for the girls to have that part of their mom. Maybe it was important for Gram to have it too.

Thankfully, Paige doesn't press. "Are you working here for the summer? I'm waitressing next door. Grandma Lydia got me the job."

Des isn't a college student home for the summer, working at Arden to pay for books and extras; she's been working there full-time since she graduated last June. Even before that, she worked after school and every weekend.

Arden Books is her past, her present, and her future. She'll take over when Gram retires.

But she decides not to get into all that. "Grandma Lydia? Lydia Merrick?"

"Oh my God, does everybody in this town know every-body else?" Paige crouches on four-inch black heels and starts tossing everything back into her bag.

"Pretty much, yeah. My gram is friends with yours."

Paige covers her face with one hand. "Grandma Lydia is the most—she's so—I mean, I love her, but—"

"She's a character," Des agrees charitably. Lydia Merrick is one of the town matriarchs, owner of the Tabby Cat Café, and an enormous gossip. "Why aren't you working for her?"

Paige's big gray eyes dart up and down Main Street like she's checking for spies. She lowers her voice to a husky, secret-telling whisper. "I told her I'm allergic. Have you been inside that place lately? I loved it when I was, like, *five*, but as a grown-ass adult, it gives me nightmares. Those porcelain plates are going to come to life someday. And all those cat figurines? They're going to form an alliance with the real cats and organize a mutiny and take over the town."

"You don't like cats?" Des asks dryly.

"I think Snowflake is their general," Paige whispers.

Des throws her head back and laughs. Snowflake is Mrs. Merrick's finicky, long-haired Persian. "Not Cinnamon?"

Cinnamon is the original tabby the café was named after. He's fat and affectionate and super spoiled.

"Oh my God, you know all my grandma's cats. This town is so *small*!"

"Haven't you ever visited?" Des doesn't remember her, and she feels like she would. Even without the purple hair, Paige stands out in Remington Hollow.

"Not since I was ten. Mom and Grandma had a falling-out." Paige turns toward the river. "Last time I was here, we went to a Fourth of July raft race. Do they still do that? And the reenactment on the old ship?"

"Definitely." The Fourth of July is a huge deal in Remington Hollow. Townspeople reenact the Remington Hollow Tea Party, a smaller and less publicized version of the Boston Tea Party, in which a group of intrepid citizens boarded the ship anchored at the town dock and dumped crates of tea in the river to protest the British tax. Remington Hollow was kind of a big deal in colonial times. Now, men dress up in Revolutionary War–era costumes and march with old muskets down Main Street. The high school band plays, and the color guard twirls red, white, and blue flags. After the parade and the reenactment, there's music and food and vendors in the park. Then, the next afternoon, everyone watches the big race across the river on homemade rafts. People get extremely creative—and extremely competitive. Last year, Bea's team built the raft that won, and Kat's raft sank but got the most applause, because she and her drama club friends were singing songs from *Hamilton* as it went down. "That's *tradition*. Remington Hollow is very big on tradition."

"Oh wow."

Des can't tell whether Paige means *wow* as in *cool* or *wow, what a totally stupid tradition.*

"Yeah." Des doesn't say that it's her favorite weekend of the whole year. "So, how come you're staying with Miss Lydia for the summer?"

"It wasn't exactly my decision," Paige explains, winding her purple hair into a neat bun and checking her phone. "Damn. I'm going to be late—I've got to go." She flashes Des a dark-lipped smile and hurries toward Tia Julia's. "Thanks again for the quarters. See you around, Desdemona."

Des doesn't correct her, even though literally no one else calls her Desdemona.

It's the third week of June, and the whole summer stretches out before her, lonely as hell, except for her endless to-do list. Her best friend—former best friend?—is too cool for watching old British murder mysteries or decorating their planners or anything else they used to do together. She's barely texted Des since she's been home from college. What is there to look forward to? Everything—all the work at Arden and at home—will keep falling on Des, at least until Gram can get around better.

Des bites her lip, remembering the conversation they had about Gram's living will and her funeral wishes. *Just in case*, Gram had insisted. The doctor and the physical therapist say she's making good progress. But Des can't help worrying. Gram has always seemed young and strong and indomitable. It's been hard to see her weak, in pain, looking…old. It hurts Des's heart, and it makes her wonder how their family will function, moving forward.

What if all her new responsibilities *aren't* temporary?

The Garrett girls' roles have long been established among themselves and around town. At fifteen, Vi is the sensitive, bookish one. At sixteen, Kat is the diva: emotional, theatrical, and never afraid to make a scene. Eighteen-year-old Bea is the brilliant, ambitious one, off to Georgetown in the fall. And Des? At nineteen, Des is the oldest. The responsible one.

The boring one, maybe. Next to glamorous, artistic Paige, she felt hopelessly dull.

But Des wants things for herself beyond running the bookstore. Beyond taking care of her sisters. Maybe she needs to try to carve out more time for her illustrations. For making new friends. For figuring out who she is now, a year after high school graduation.

What if she *isn't* boring, responsible Des this summer?

What if she tries being *Desdemona*? That's what Mom named her, after all. Maybe it's past time she tried it on for size.

CHAPTER TWO
BEA

Dread slows Bea's footsteps as she approaches the Daily Grind. She scuffs her sensible black flats against the brick sidewalk, glancing in the window of the Tabby Cat Café to see how many cats she can spot. It's a game she plays with herself on anxious days; if she sees five or more cats, it's good luck. It means that whatever she's worried about will work itself out.

The original tabby, Cinnamon, is snoozing in a puddle of sunshine on the flowered love seat, flanked by pillows bearing his likeness. Snowflake, the floofy Persian, is perched on a bookshelf like a watchful sentinel, tail twitching. A small black cat is in the process of batting a figurine off a high café table. Two calicos are curled together on the back of an overstuffed armchair. One, two, three, four, five. Bea takes a deep breath and waves at Mason Kim, the sulky fauxhawked waiter, who's messing around on his phone behind the counter. Mase waves back half-heartedly.

"Bea! Yoo-hoo! Bea Garrett!" Mrs. Lynde calls down Prince Street. "That was a real nice story in the *Gazette* yesterday!"

Bea considers pretending that she didn't hear her. Maryanne Lynde is a talker, a notorious busybody, and this short walk—the five blocks between the offices of the *Gazette* over on Queen Street and the Daily Grind—is the only time Bea will have to herself all day.

Instead, she takes a deep breath and heads down the street toward Mrs. Lynde. That is what's expected of her, after all, and that's what Bea does: she takes what is expected of her, and then she exceeds those expectations. She pokes her rectangular black glasses back up her nose and gives the older woman a practiced, polite smile. "Thank you, Miss Maryanne. I'm really grateful that Charlie gave me the column. It's a great opportunity to spotlight local women-owned businesses."

"Well, you earned it, didn't you? It's about time you got to do more than book reviews," Miss Maryanne says, and Bea feels a rush of satisfaction. She *did* earn it. Unlike *some* people. "So Charlie's treating you all right?"

Charlie—Charles Lockwood, the editor of the *Remington*

Hollow Gazette—is treating Bea just fine. He's a great boss, encouraging but challenging. His daughter Savannah, home from Vassar for the summer, is another story entirely. She's a gossipy, entitled, brat who's writing the *Gazette*'s new *Around Town* blog and competing with Bea for features.

"Charlie's great." Bea keeps the smile on her face. *Nepotism aside.*

"How's Helen?" Miss Maryanne stretches out one thick leg, clad in purple linen trousers, and massages her knee. "Dr. Kim says I might want to start thinking about a knee replacement myself."

Bea smooths her gray pencil skirt. "Gram's better, thank you. Still having a little trouble with the stairs. She's doing physical therapy twice a week."

"With that good-looking Jacob Kim, huh? I tell you, I wouldn't mind seeing him twice a week!" Miss Maryanne cackles. "It's nice that one of Doc's boys followed in her footsteps. And Emily's studying criminology, isn't she? That's a sort of science. Now, Mase, who knows what's going on with him these days." She shoots a disapproving look down toward the Tabby Cat Café. "Spends all his time frowning at that phone of his. He's going to give himself wrinkles. And did you see what he did with his hair? It's so *spiky*."

Bea smiles for real this time. "It's called a fauxhawk."

"Well, it doesn't do him any favors, if you ask me. And

neither does all that eyeliner. Gay or not, in my day, young men didn't wear makeup!"

"Mase is bisexual," Bea says, "and it's called guyliner. It's very trendy."

"Is it now? Well, speaking of handsome guys"—Miss Maryanne gives an exaggerated wink—"how's that young man of yours?"

Bea's smile goes sour. Gram's friends love to tease her about Erik. She didn't used to mind. It used to make her blush and giggle, but lately…lately she wishes they would mind their own damn business.

"Let me see your hand," Miss Maryanne says.

Confused, Bea holds up her right hand, aware of her ragged nails and chipped peach polish. Biting her nails is one of her worst habits.

But Miss Maryanne shakes her curly gray head. "No, no, the *other* one. Your *left* hand." Bea holds her left hand out obediently, and the woman cackles. "No ring yet, huh? What're you two waiting for?"

Bea's stomach lurches. "What? Um—we—" she mumbles, flustered. Why doesn't she have some kind of witty comeback? Kat would. Her younger sister is stupidly self-possessed. Kat would probably give Miss Maryanne a speech on feminism, maybe rant about how marriage is an antiquated notion based on property laws and dowries and how her worth cannot be measured in goats. It would be ridiculous and dramatic; the old lady would be confused but admire her spirit. *A real spitfire, that girl,* she'd say.

No one ever calls Bea a spitfire. She's *ambitious.* She's *smart.* She's *going places.*

Whether she wants to or not.

"Maryanne, give them time. They're so young!" Lydia Merrick, owner of the Tabby Cat Café, strolls up right in time to overhear. She pats Bea's shoulder. "Ignore her, sweetheart."

"You'd better go on in. You don't want to keep Erik waiting!" Miss Maryanne chides.

Bea is unreasonably irritated that Erik is already waiting. They aren't supposed to meet for another ten minutes, but he's always early. She used to like that he respected her enough not to waste her time. Now his punctuality annoys her. Like being on time isn't good enough. Even when she's early, he's earlier.

"You know she's going to Georgetown," Miss Lydia says as Bea heads inside. "She doesn't need to get married at eighteen, Maryanne. It's different now. She's going to do big things someday!"

Bea used to be proud of her ambition. It felt like her defining characteristic, how much she *wanted* things. How determined she was never to settle. Now her dreams feel anxious-making and impossible. All year, she's felt like she's drowning, barely keeping her head above water, barely making the next A or the next deadline. She's doing everything and doing it well, but somehow it feels like it's never enough. She feels like *she's* never enough. If she's so flustered by this—her internship and Erik and getting ready for Georgetown—how will she ever be a serious journalist? Do serious journalists have panic attacks?

She's so lost in her spiraling worry that she collides face-first with a broad chest. Iced coffee splashes onto her cheek.

Bea yelps as ice cubes slide down her chest. "Sorry!"

A callused hand reaches out to steady her. Warm fingers wrap around her shoulder, thumb brushing her collarbone.

She pushes up her glasses and looks at her victim. He's maybe a few years older than her, tall and tanned and scruffy, with dark-blond hair caught up in a man bun. Coffee drips down his black T-shirt.

She grabs some napkins from the counter. "I am so sorry." She starts to dab ineffectually at his shirt, then realizes that's kind of inappropriate and hands him half the napkins.

"It's all right. I think you got the worst of it." His voice has a Southern twang. His brown eyes dart to the scoop neck of her white shirt, where the coffee stain is spreading rapidly.

"It was totally my fault. I wasn't paying attention to where I was going. Can I get you another coffee?" She can't believe she ran right into him.

He shrugs and holds up the half-full plastic cup. "Nah, I've still got most of it."

"Are you sure?" Bea presses.

"Yeah. No problem." He grins at her. He is completely not her type—way too hipster. Besides the man bun and the scruff, he's got a half sleeve of tattoos. He looks as though he should be drinking bourbon and playing a banjo in some impossibly cool bar. But he is incredibly good-looking. *Totally lickable*, Chloe would say. Chloe Chan was their class salutatorian and yearbook editor and is going to the University of Pennsylvania in the fall. In the five years Bea's been dating Erik, Chloe's had a dozen boyfriends.

"It's okay, *really*," the guy says. His eyes dart to Bea's chest again and, while she knows he's only checking out the coffee stain, for a second, she wishes she had Kat's impressive cleavage instead of her own A-cup situation. "Have a good afternoon."

"Thanks. You too." She steps aside so he can leave. Then she pulls a stain stick out of her purse, applies it to her shirt, yanks on her mustard-yellow cardigan, and buttons it to hide the stain. Bea might not have been a Boy Scout, but she's always prepared.

She spots Erik at a table in the back, leaning against the exposed-brick wall, sipping his iced coffee, and flipping through a stack of books. He doesn't seem to have noticed her clumsy entrance. She squints, recognizes two guidebooks on Washington, DC, and feels like she might literally throw up.

But this is the plan, right? This has always been the plan.

Their grades and extracurriculars and letters of recommendation were impeccable. Bea was valedictorian. She aced three AP classes while working after school at Arden, editing the school paper, and copyediting the yearbook. Erik was third in their class, shining star of the debate and tennis teams. They have worked so hard, and now, in eight weeks, they'll head off to Georgetown. Together. Erik will be pre-law; Bea will study journalism.

Erik is highlighting something carefully, his forehead furrowed, his glasses slipping down his broad nose. There's an extra iced coffee on the table. Bea knows it will have three Splendas and a dash of cream in it. They've been dating since they were thirteen. Erik knows how she likes her coffee. Erik knows everything about her.

Except that she's not in love with him anymore.

CHAPTER THREE

KAT

"It's the twenty-first century," Penelope Lawton complains. "Why can't they email the cast list? Or text us? Why do they make us go through this torture in person? It's positively *archaic*."

Kat smiles, smug. "It's only torture if your name's not on the list."

A crowd is already gathered at the far end of the hall, between the men's and women's dressing rooms. A single fluttering piece of paper is tacked to the bulletin board.

"Easy for you to say," Pen grumbles. Jazzy piano music drifts from one of the practice rooms. "Your name is *always* on the list. I hate you."

Kat grins. But beneath the grin and her confident stride,

her stomach tips and tumbles. This show is important. This is community theater, not the fall play or the spring musical at Remington Hollow High. She's competing against seniors and girls from Bea's class, even some girls from Des's class who are home for the summer. And she *has* to be Jo. She has to be Jo, and Adam Warren has to be Laurie.

Kat has it all planned out. They'll banter and flirt all summer, onstage and off, and by opening night, when Jo refuses Laurie's declaration of love, Adam will be heartbroken. Only he won't be acting; he'll be legit heartbroken. By then he'll realize how much he misses Kat, he'll break up with bland blond Jillian, and things will go back to the way they're supposed to be. Except, once she has him back, once she has the upper hand, Kat will dump his ass.

It's written out in her head like a script. Like fate.

The crowd parts to make way for her.

"Congratulations!" a few girls squeal—at her or Pen or both, she's not sure, but Kat mutters her thanks, a smile stuck to her lips like poison as she scans the names printed on that all-important piece of paper.

JO MARCH: Kat Garrett.

She lets out a tiny breath of relief. She did it. She beat *everyone*; she was the very best.

"Oh," Pen says, her voice tinged with surprise. Kat keeps reading.

MEG MARCH: Penelope Lawton. Yes! Plays are always more fun when they're both cast.

BETH MARCH: Hannah Adler. Hannah was in Bea's class. She's fine. Nice enough. Plain. Nonthreatening.

AMY MARCH: Jillian Crawford.

Well. That won't be much of a stretch, acting-wise; Amy March is notoriously blond and bratty, just like Jillian.

But Kat's still the star. Jo is the lead role, not Amy.

Kat keeps reading:

JOHN BROOKE: Adam Warren.

THEODORE "LAURIE" LAWRENCE: Mason Kim.

Oh. Hell. No.

She whirls around, her blue eyes narrowed. Pen grabs her elbow and drags her down the hall, away from the chorus of congratulations, before she can erupt.

"What?!" Kat's voice rises. "What is Ms. Randall *thinking*? Adam would've been perfect as Laurie!"

Pen hesitates. "It wasn't his best audition. He was distracted."

By Jillian. That girl ruins *everything*. She and Adam read together, and she was so *nervous*, stumbling over her lines—giggle giggle!—that he kept screwing around to make her laugh. Ms. Randall had to tell him to knock it off and take this seriously—that maybe that kind of behavior was okay at school, but this wasn't a high school production, and she expected him to behave more profession-ally. Kat had been mortified for him. She never in a million years would have let him mess around like that if he'd auditioned with *her*.

"Jillian cost him that part. Maybe now he'll see—"

"He cost *himself* that part," Pen corrects.

Kat wants to argue, to blame it all on Jillian, but she knows that Pen's right. And she appreciates it when Pen stands up to her. Not many girls do. Kat blows out a big sigh and tucks one long leg behind her, up against the tiled wall. Her flamingo pose, Pen calls it. Kat's bendy from her years of ballet. Before she got hips and realized that she was never going to be the best at it, she loved dance. The year she was twelve, she stopped eating almost entirely in an attempt to erase the new curves her teacher had pointed out, humiliatingly, in front of everyone. Pen had worried and bargained and tried to shove food at her every chance she got. Eventually, she told Gram that Kat wasn't eating all day, and then Kat had to quit ballet and see a therapist. She didn't speak to Pen for six months, till they were both cast in *The 25th Annual Putnam County Spelling Bee*.

"Better that he marry me onstage than Jillian, right? You know *I'm* not going to flirt with him." Pen runs a hand over her bleached-blond hair, which is chin length on the left and newly buzzed on the right.

Kat nods. They have been best friends since kinder-garten, aside from those six months in seventh grade, and Pen has made it crystal clear that she thinks Adam is a lying, cheating snake. She is basically the *only* girl Kat trusts not to fall for his stupid storm-cloud eyes and his adorable dimples.

Kat's jealousy is legendary. She isn't proud of it. It's as if the whole year she and Adam were together, she was just waiting for him to cheat on her. Once a cheater, always a cheater, right? She should have known that. He and Kat had started flirting during *Into the Woods*, while he was still dating Bailey. When he and Jillian were cast opposite each other the following spring, Kat knew it was only a matter of time. When she caught them kissing backstage, she wasn't even surprised. Furious, absolutely. But it was almost a *relief*, knowing that her jealousy hadn't been unfounded.

So, yeah, Adam was fickle as hell.

Kat planned to take advantage of that.

"I'll talk you up," Pen offers. "I don't think he's worthy of you, but I'll do it."

Kat frowns. No one should need to talk her up. Adam should see her onstage, being fierce and passionate and freaking *unstoppable*, and remember that he loves her. *Her*, not bland, blond Jillian. She refuses to believe that she has lost him forever.

"Come on." Pen reaches in her Kate Spade bag. "Let's do this."

They go back to the cast list and take turns writing their initials next to their names—the ritual acceptance of the role. Even though things aren't going entirely according to her script, Kat can't help feeling a glow of satisfaction. Jo is unquestionably the lead. A lot of other girls auditioned for this part, and she beat them all. She was the very best.

Then Pen elbows her. "Ouch!" Kat yelps. Her glow fades as she turns and sees Adam strutting down the hall, hand in hand with Jillian. He has the same brown curls, light-brown skin, stormy gray eyes, adorable dimples, and all. It's not fair that he hasn't turned hideous.

Jillian's steps falter when she sees Kat and Pen. She's scared of them, but not as scared as Kat wants her to be. Not scared enough to keep her from kissing Kat's boyfriend and breaking Kat's stupid, traitorous heart.

Kat flips her long, flat-ironed hair over her shoulder. She's wearing high-waisted white shorts and Vi's black boatneck *The Future Is Female* T-shirt, which shows off her collarbones. She suddenly remembers Adam pressing his mouth there, kissing his way up to her ear. Her pale skin flushes.

She's glad now that she didn't have sex with him, even though he made it pretty clear that he wanted to. On her sixteenth birthday, back in April, his parents had gone out, and he'd made dinner—homemade pizza and chocolate mousse—and given her a necklace with a star on it. A star because she was going to be a star, he said, which was cheesy but sweet. Only all through dinner, he kept texting someone. He said it was his friend Carter, but he wouldn't let Kat see his phone, and he kept it with him all night so she couldn't snoop. He also said he wanted it to be a special night for them, and when he went to the bathroom, she found a new box of condoms in his nightstand. Kat was not about to have sex with someone who was texting another girl, though. Adam claimed she was being ridiculous. But a month later, she caught him kissing Jillian backstage. It was almost as vindicating as it was awful.

Would he have stayed with Kat if she'd had sex with him? Would it have been worth it?

"Congratulations," she says, syrupy sweet, before Adam and Jillian can reach the list. "You both got cast. Adam, you're John Brooke."

Adam frowns. He wanted Laurie. He *expected* Laurie, despite his crap audition. He always got the lead in school musicals.

"You're Amy." Kat gives Jillian a sharky smile. "Pen is Meg, and I'm Jo. We're all going to have *so much fun*."

"Kat," Adam says.

Kat doesn't like the way he says her name anymore. It's like he's said it a thousand times and he's tired of it now. Like she exhausts him.

"*Adam*," she says back mockingly. She hands him the pen. Acts like it doesn't affect her when their hands brush, like there's no chemistry anymore. "Too bad you didn't get Laurie. You were a little off your game at auditions. This isn't high school, you know. We all need to be our very best."

"Yeah, well. You heard what Ms. Randall said. She wants us to act professional." He looks between Kat and Pen and Jillian. "That means no mean-girl shit. No *drama.*"

It's got to be on purpose, the way he echoes the words from the day she caught him and Jillian kissing. *I can't do this anymore, Kat. I'm tired of fighting all the time. You're just— you're too much drama.*

The words hurt, and this reminder—right in front of Jillian and Pen and all the listening, jealous girls in the hall—stings almost as much.

The idea that she's lost Adam to Jillian, to this leggy girl with her blond ponytail and her tiny waist, is impossible. Jillian plays field hockey and sings in the school choir and has two doting parents and a black Labrador. She is perfectly, infuriatingly *ordinary.* She does not deserve—does not need—this play or this boy like Kat does.

Kat gives her an unnerving blue-eyed stare that sizes her up and lets her know she's been found wanting.

Adam thinks Kat is too much drama? Well, just wait. He has not seen what kind of schemes Kat Garrett is capable of when she really puts her mind to it.

CHAPTER FOUR
VI

Vi freezes, clutching a stuffed giraffe, when she hears Cecilia Pérez's voice.

"Hey, Des, do you have the new Nina LaCour book?" Cece asks.

"Oh, we sold out, sorry," Des says. "I should've told Vi."

"Vi?" Cece sounds puzzled.

"Where'd she go? She was here a minute ago," Des says, and Vi slouches lower in the little cupboard beneath the stairs, hoping her sister won't give her away. The reading nook for kids is decorated on the outside to look like a pirate ship, with a few small portholes cut into one side and a bigger porthole serving as the entrance and exit. It's awkward for grown-ups to crawl into. It's also awkward for Vi now, at fifteen, but it's her favorite place at Arden. Maybe her favorite place, period. She spends whole afternoons here during the summer, reading books and checking her Tumblr and writing fics on her phone.

"Vi's been recommending it to everybody, so we don't have any on hand. But we've ordered more. Would you like a text alert when it's back in stock?" Des asks. "It should be here in a few days."

"Um, sure." Cece starts to rattle off her phone number, but Des says they already have it. Cece's a frequent customer. It's one of Vi's top five favorite things about her, in addition to the way she has to stop and pet literally every dog she passes, her addiction to Skittles, how much she loves her Abuela Julia, and her incredibly long eyelashes.

Peeking out through the nearest porthole, Vi can see the backs of Cece's calves, sloping down to her ankles and her black gladiator sandals. She makes even torturous strappy sandals look amazing. She makes *everything* look amazing. Vi looks down at her own cutoff jean shorts and white *Empowered Women Empower Women* T-shirt. Her stick-straight auburn hair—not wild riotous curls like Des's and Kat's, not bright and eye-catching like Bea's—is falling out of its braid. She looks like a little kid, and Cece looks like a Latina supermodel. Like a younger, browner, taller version of Camila Mendes, Vi's biggest celebrity crush.

"Have you read any of her other books? She's one of Vi's favorite authors," Des says.

Vi is gay! she might as well shout.

Not that it's a secret. Vi's been wearing Pride shirts since she was thirteen.

But she's never had an actual girlfriend. Fact is, there are not a lot of out queer girls in Remington Hollow.

Cece scratches the back of one perfect calf with her other foot. "She's one of my favorite authors too."

"Have you read *Our Own Private Universe*? Or, um, *Georgia Peaches and Other Forbidden Fruit*?" Des asks, and Vi covers her eyes in embarrassment, even though no one can see her. Those are some of her other favorite contemporary young adult books; they're all about girls who fall in love with other girls. "What about *Tell Me Again How a Crush Should Feel*?"

"I've, um, I've read all of those, actually," Cece says quietly.

Vi strangles the stuffed giraffe in her arms. Wait a minute. What is happening?

Vi recommends these books all the time. To everyone. You don't have to be gay to read them. But she's never recommended them to Cece.

Why is Cece reading all of Vi's favorite books? It's not like they're giant bestsellers, even though Vi *wants* them to be.

She probably bought them right here, Vi thinks, affronted. *And my sisters didn't even tell me.*

Why didn't they tell her? This is *huge*. She drums her

nails—currently painted in rainbow colors to celebrate LGBTQIA Pride Month—against her knees and then takes a deep breath. Her sisters are not responsible for reporting their neighbors' reading habits. And the fact that they *didn't* tell her—maybe that means her crush on Cece is less obvious than she fears. Maybe her strategy of avoiding Cece is working. It's not easy, because Cece is a good customer, and the Pérezes' family restaurant, Tia Julia's, is right next door to the bookstore. Cece's Abuela Julia and Gram are good friends. Every Monday night, they get together with a bunch of the other town matriarchs and play Canasta and drink sangria.

When they were little, Vi and Cece were good friends too. Like, inseparable.

But that was a long time ago. Before the accident. Before Vi knew she liked girls. Before Cece got gorgeous and got a boyfriend.

Well…that's not *entirely* true. Cece was always beautiful, even as a toddler. People used to stop her mom on the street to coo over her. Even with avocado all over her face and hands, her dark curls tangled in knots, her knees scratched up, and covered in dog hair from the Pérezes' Great Danes, she was adorable. Vi's seen pictures. It's completely unfair.

"Well, what did you like about those books?" Des launches into reader advisory.

Vi starts to feel like she shouldn't be listening. Like

she's eavesdropping on a private conversation. Whatever Cece says next, she'll say it because she thinks she and Des are alone in the store. But to crawl awkwardly out of the porthole and admit she's been eavesdropping the whole time would be mortifying. Instead, Vi waits, full of equal parts anticipation and dread.

"Never mind," Cece says. "I'll just stick with this one."

There are soft footsteps, and then the bells above the front door chime. Vi is filled with a potent rush of relief and disappointment. She turns the giraffe over in her hands, her mind whirring. It can't be a coincidence that Cece's read all of those books, can it? There aren't *that* many YA books about girls falling in love with other girls. There are more than there were two years ago, when Vi was figuring out her sexuality, but still not *enough*.

Her sister's round, freckled face appears in the porthole, and Vi jumps. "Jesus, Des!"

"She's gone," Des says with a smile. "You can come out now."

"I wasn't hiding; I was reading." Vi drops the stuffed giraffe and snatches up her book, which is about two princesses who fall in love. She's only recently started branching out into YA fantasy, but she's digging this one.

Des rolls her brown eyes. "Uh-huh. Right."

Vi frowns as she crawls out of the pirate ship. So much for her crush being top secret. "Am I that obvious?"

She isn't sure she wants to hear the answer.

Des wraps an arm around her waist and squeezes. "Probably only to your big sister."

"Yeah, it's the 'probably' that concerns me." Vi sighs. She is both desperate for information about Cece, carefully filing away anything that Gram mentions from Cece's abuela or any gossip she hears at school, and terrified to betray her interest. She's not afraid that Cece would be mean. Cece would never; she's super nice. But Vi could not bear it if Cece felt sorry for her. She has had enough pity to last her a lifetime.

She knows what people in town say about her, even though it's been ten years since the accident. Gram's friends still treat her like a fragile, breakable thing. They ask her how she is in soft, careful voices, and as she walks away, they remind each other of what happened. How she was in the car the night her parents were both killed by a drunk driver. How she didn't talk for almost a year afterward.

"What do you think it means?" Vi blurts out, then glances over her shoulder to confirm there's no one else in the store. There isn't. It's a lazy, sunny Friday afternoon, and most tourists are out on their sailboats or still making their way over the Bay Bridge and up Route 213 to Remington Hollow.

"That Cece's reading about girls falling in love?" Des

straightens some board books about trucks. "I mean…I guess it could be a Pride reading challenge?"

"Right. I mean…maybe it doesn't mean anything. I don't want to assume…" Vi flushes.

Des raises one feathery eyebrow. "That she's gay? Or bi? Or pan?"

"She has a boyfriend," Vi points out. Ben. Tall. Handsome, she guesses; other girls seem to like boys with floppy dark hair. He's the school's best soccer forward.

"That doesn't mean she's straight," Des says.

Vi feels a tiny pinprick of hope.

"It doesn't matter," she says. Even if she *was* interested in girls, Cece wouldn't go from handsome, popular soccer star to strange, bookish little Vi Garrett. "Nothing's ever going to happen between Cece and me."

"Well, not if you keep running away every time you see her, no." Des tucks a wayward strand of hair behind Vi's ear.

Vi jerks away, annoyed. Maybe if her sisters weren't always babying her, Cece would see her. Really see her. Not as the weird girl next door with the tragic backstory, but as someone who's smart and interesting, who loves dogs and the same books she does.

"You should talk to her. You two have so much in common!" Des says. "Remember what Mom used to say? 'Don't hide your light under a bushel.' You have so much light in you, Viola Garrett."

Vi rolls her eyes. Des has to say that, because she's her big sister.

Vi doesn't feel like she's full of light. She feels weird and bored and lonely.

CHAPTER FIVE

DES

Late that afternoon, the bell above the door chimes, and Des looks up from her tattered copy of *Murder on the Orient Express.*

"Hey, stranger!" Emily Kim bounces in. "What's new?"

Em is Des's best friend. Or at least she used to be.

"Nothing," Des says, dog-earing her page. "What's up?"

"I was texting with Bri and Alyssa, and I have an *amazing* plan." Em flips her shiny black hair out of her face. Sometime this spring, she cut it into a long, asymmetrical bob. A *lob*, she calls it. It makes her look older. Less like the girl Des used to spend every Saturday night watching British mysteries and splitting a pint of Ben & Jerry's with.

Less like the girl who threw a murder-mystery dinner party for her seventeenth birthday and went to an escape room in DC for her eighteenth. More like the girl who spent her nineteenth getting trashed with her new friends at the University of Maryland.

"Is Alyssa the blond with the nose ring?" Des has trouble keeping Em's college friends straight.

"No, that's Lauren. Alyssa is the blond with the cute glasses. My lab partner. You'd know that if you ever came to visit," Em snarks, tapping her glossy pink nails on the counter. Since when does she paint her nails? "Anyway, Bri's having a party next weekend up in Pennsylvania at her parents' cabin. It's going to be epic. Lauren and Alyssa are coming, and so are Alex and Devonte…and Hunter." Em grins as she mentions the guy she's been crushing on all spring. "My parents said I could go, and I was thinking… Why don't you come with me?"

"Me?" Des asks, stalling for time. Em is so excited, she's practically vibrating. She definitely doesn't need the mint chip Frappuccino she's carrying.

"Yes, *you*. Bri said it's totally fine. Come on, Des! I was so bummed when you got sick and couldn't make it for my birthday. I can't wait for you to meet everybody! Then you'll finally be able to keep Lauren and Alyssa straight. And I know you'll love Bri. She's the *best*."

A little splinter of jealousy slices its way beneath Des's

skin. *She* used to be Em's best. "I can't. I have to work next weekend."

Em's shoulders slump, and she sets her Frappuccino on the counter with a little more force than necessary. "You have to work *every* weekend."

"I know. I'm sorry. I do story time Saturday mornings now."

Em rolls her eyes. "Let Kat do story time! She loves being the center of attention."

That's true. Em knows Des's sisters and all their annoying traits, just like Des knows that Em's brother Mase takes forever in the bathroom every morning and her brother Jacob leaves dirty socks all over his room.

From the day of their fifth-grade class field trip to the Baltimore Aquarium, when they sat next to each other on the bus, till Em left for college last August, she and Des were inseparable. And Des honestly—stupidly—thought that even though she wasn't going to college with Em, they would *always* be that close.

At first, it was okay; they texted and sent each other silly pics all the time. Em came home for fall break and Thanksgiving and for a month at Christmas. But this spring, things changed. *Em* changed. And Des doesn't know what to do. She thought—hoped—that when Em came home for the summer, things would go back to normal. But it's been almost a month, and this is only the second time Em's stopped by Arden.

"If Kat gets a part in *Little Women*, she'll have rehearsal Saturday," Des says.

"If. You don't know for sure," Em argues. "If she does, can't you figure it out with Bea? You seriously can't take *one* weekend off?"

Des hesitates, fiddling with the silver ring on her index finger. Kat's impossible; she'd never voluntarily work on a Saturday, even if she doesn't have rehearsal, but Des could probably trade with Bea. Georgetown isn't cheap, even with scholarships. Bea could use the extra hours.

Em sees her hesitation. "Come on. Gram would let you go; I know she would. Don't you want to get out of Remington Hollow? Have some fun for once? You're *nineteen*, not ninety."

"I have fun," Des retorts, stung. She twirls the ring faster, staring at the turquoise stone instead of Em's pout. The ring belonged to her mom; it was a birthday present from Dad the year Des was nine. She remembers him giving it to Mom at the dinner table, after they had all sung "Happy Birthday" and Mom blew out the candles. Mom kissed him, slid the ring on her finger, and held it up for all her girls to see. That was in June, two months before Des's parents were killed by a drunk driver.

Des doesn't drink alcohol. Not even a little. Em didn't used to. She said it was no big deal, that if it bothered Des—and it did—she wouldn't drink either.

That's another way she's changed this spring.

"What have you done in the last week that was *fun*?" Em asks.

Des bites her tongue. Maybe she doesn't play flip cup and get throw-up drunk. Maybe she doesn't go to the local all-night diner (because there is no all-night diner in Remington Hollow). Maybe she doesn't hang out until three a.m. playing video games with the boy she likes (because there is no boy she likes). But she has fun. In her own quiet, comfortable ways, she has fun… Doesn't she? Doubt worms its way through her as she remembers how hopelessly boring she felt this morning standing next to Paige.

"I led the mystery book club. We had a really great discussion on—"

"That's work," Em interrupts, tapping her nails impatiently against the counter. "What else?"

"I took a hand-lettering class at the arts center. I learned a new style I'm going to use for the sign for tomorrow's story time—here, let me show you." Des fumbles beneath a stack of books for her planner. "I made this weekly layout that I really like too. I used—"

"What do you even need a weekly layout for?" Em sneers. "You don't do anything but work!"

Des closes the planner without showing her—without explaining that she uses it to keep track of the books she reads, quotes she likes, upcoming programs at Arden, grocery lists, and dinner recipes, now that she does most of the cooking at home. Em used to have a planner too. They'd hang out on Sunday afternoons and make their weekly layouts, share stickers and pens and washi tape. Des wonders if Em still uses the bullet journal she gave her for Christmas. If it's full of reading assignments and exam dates and frat parties. Em hasn't posted a layout on her Instagram in months.

"I do too," Des says. But she honestly can't think of anything else that's *fun*. With her extra hours at the store, with everything she's been doing at home, she hasn't been illustrating any new quotes. Her high school friends are back in Remington Hollow for the summer, but she hasn't met up with any of them for coffee. She hasn't had time—or maybe she hasn't wanted to feel as small and stupid as Em is making her feel right now.

"Des." Em is rolling her dark eyes. "Would you seriously rather stay home next weekend and practice your handwriting? You can do that *anytime*."

Des shrinks. Her illustrated quotes are more than *practicing her handwriting*, and Em knows it. Or used to. "Why do you even want me to come if I'm so boring?"

Em sighs. "I want you to meet my new friends. It would mean a lot to me."

But she doesn't contradict Des. Doesn't say, *Shut up; you're not boring*. Or, *If you're boring, so am I*, like she used to when Kat teased them about staying in on Saturday nights to marathon Miss Marple instead of going to parties.

Des doesn't know what to say. She doesn't want to spend the weekend with strangers, with the Em who feels more and more like a stranger. She won't know the people and places Em and her new friends talk about; she won't understand their inside jokes. They'll all drink and talk about hooking up, and she'll feel lonely and confused, because she doesn't want what they want, what it feels like people her age *should* want.

"Wait a minute. You don't want to come," Em realizes. Maybe she's changed, but Des hasn't. Em can still read her like a book. "Oh my God. Des, did you actually have the flu on my birthday?"

Des stares at the counter in front of her. At the torn cover of *Murder on the Orient Express*.

"You lied to me." Em sounds so hurt. "You pretended to be sick so you didn't have to visit me. We talked about it for *months*, Des! I had the whole weekend all planned out!"

Including a frat party. The old Em wouldn't have wanted to go to a frat party, much less expected Des to go with her. The new Em insisted it would be super fun, that they *had* to go because Hunter was pledging. She said it would be okay if Des didn't want to drink; she could still dance, and maybe she would meet a cute pledge like Hunter.

It had been easier to text Em, fake having the flu, and

apologize profusely than to explain all the ways that Em's plan sounded like a nightmare.

But they never used to lie to each other.

The bell above the door chimes again, and Paige breezes in.

"Hey, Desdemona," she says, ignoring—or maybe oblivious to—the tension in the room.

Em gives Des a *WTF* look behind Paige's back and mouths, "Desdemona?"

Des ignores her. She can reinvent herself too. She puts on a big smile. "Hey, Paige. What's up?"

Paige sashays past Em, right up to the counter, and props her elbows on it. "I heard there's a party tomorrow night at the Penningtons' farm. Do you know where that is? Are you going?"

Em laughs, harsh, like gears grinding. "Des doesn't do parties."

"Is that right?" Paige gives Des a conspiratorial, purple-lipsticked smile. "The parties here are so boring, you don't even bother?"

"It's not the *parties* that are boring," Em mutters.

The blush starts on Des's chest and works its way up her freckled throat. She can't believe Em is acting like this in front of Paige. "I don't drink."

"Great, then you can be the designated driver." Paige grins.

She could. It hits her again: she could be *anybody* with Paige. She could have new friends and new hair and new ways of having fun too.

"Come on, Desdemona. I need a wingwoman, and I don't know anybody else in this hick town who's under forty," Paige pleads.

"Okay."

"*Okay?*" Em echoes, disbelieving. "You never go to Dylan's parties."

Des throws her hands up in the air. "You said that I need to have more fun!"

"*With me!*" Em shouts. Then, quieter, "I meant with me." She looks from Paige to Des. "Whatever," she snaps as she storms out, slamming the door behind her.

"That girl needs to chill," Paige says over the jangling of the bell. She gives Des a frank look. "I don't know what I walked in on here, Desdemona. Are you coming to this party with me, or were you just trying to piss her off?"

It's not the parties *that are boring.*

You don't do anything but work.

You're nineteen, *not ninety.*

"They aren't mutually exclusive," Des decides. "I'm definitely coming to the party."

CHAPTER SIX
BEA

"You'll have to add that to your list," Erik says.

"Right. My list." Bea's voice is flat. She isn't sure what she's supposed to be adding, because she wasn't paying attention while Erik was rhapsodizing about all the touristy Washington, DC, things they can do on the weekends. Like she's going to have copious free time between papers and reading assignments and her work-study job to check out the Tidal Basin and the Library of Congress with him.

"Hiking boots," Erik says. She isn't sure if he's repeating himself or prompting her to write that down too. She doesn't know why she would need hiking boots in the city, but Erik's been really into geocaching with his dad lately. He keeps telling Bea how relaxing it is to be out in nature.

"Hiking boots. Got it," she says.

Erik hesitates. "You've started making a list of things to pack for Georgetown, right?"

"Of course I have," she lies. Bea makes lists for everything. She *should* have started a list for her dorm room. Actually, she might need a few lists: items to pack, items to buy, and items to discuss with her roommate when she gets her assignment in August, so they don't end up with two mini fridges and four lamps and no microwave.

Why hasn't she started those lists?

It's still eight weeks away, Bea reminds herself. Eight weeks is a long time. Two whole months. Normal people wouldn't start making lists yet.

But Bea would. And Erik knows her so well. He's going to figure out that she's lying, that she hasn't made any lists yet—that she doesn't *want* to make any lists, that she hasn't looked at the guidebooks or the course catalog or dorm room Pinterest boards. He's going to know, and then he's going to ask her what's wrong, and she doesn't know how to answer that.

What the hell is wrong with me?

Bea looks around the crowded coffee shop. A family of tanned blond tourists in polo shirts and khaki shorts sits on the weathered leather couch: a mom and dad and two pigtailed girls fighting over who gets the last chocolate chip muffin. Her retired fifth-grade teacher, Mrs. Emerson, sits in the blue armchair, doing crossword puzzles and drinking a giant mug of tea. Madison Ross, a rising senior and the girls' tennis champ, holds court at the back table with her friends Amira and Kaitlyn. The music rises, and Justin Bieber croons over the speakers. Erik is watching her, his blue eyes full of concern.

He deserves better than Bea. Better than the way she's been avoiding him lately, better than her lies and half-truths. She has to tell him.

But tell him what? That the idea of going to Georgetown with him in eight weeks makes her physically ill? They've worked so hard for this. They decided Georgetown was their goal when they were *fifteen*. And it was always *their* goal—not Bea's, not Erik's—*theirs*, together.

I can't do this.

The fear sweeps over her, threatens to pull her under and drown her. Bea feels flushed and hot despite the roaring air conditioner. She tugs at the top button of her cardigan, then remembers the coffee stain on the white shirt beneath. It's too warm in here, too noisy. She feels sick. Like she can't get enough air to breathe.

"I forgot," she blurts out, heart racing. "I have to stop at Carl's and grab some vanilla. I'm making cupcakes for family dinner." She's being too specific. That's how people can tell when someone's lying; the liar gives more details than if she were telling the truth.

Bea did make dessert for family dinner. She's a stress baker, and lately, she is always stressed. Last night when she couldn't sleep, she made a big strawberry crumble with the rest of the strawberries Des got from the farmer's market.

Erik doesn't know that, though.

"Want me to come with you?" he asks.

"No!" She says it too quickly, too forcefully, and smiles to soften the rejection. "I mean…that's okay. You stay here and find more fun things for us to do in DC."

Saying it makes her feel even more sick and panicky.

"I'll make a list." He smiles back. Waits. His smile fades. "So…I'll see you tomorrow, I guess?"

"Yep. See you tomorrow." Bea toys with one of the buttons on her cardigan. Shit. He was expecting her to invite him to family dinner.

On Friday nights, after Arden Books closes at eight— because everything in Remington Hollow closes at eight—Des and Bea and Kat and Vi and Gram have dinner together. It's a tradition from before the accident, when Gram used to take them for sleepovers on Friday nights to give their parents a break. It's sacrosanct now. Only people who are practically family get invited: Des's best friend Em, Kat's best friend Penelope, and Erik. Bea doesn't ask him every week but often enough that he looks disappointed now.

"I'll text you later." He leans down to kiss her, but Bea turns her head, and his lips brush her cheek instead. Hurt flashes across his face.

She is hurting him. She *hates* that she is hurting him, but she can't seem to stop.

She can't get out of the Daily Grind fast enough. Miss Maryanne and Miss Lydia aren't sitting out front anymore, thank goodness. But instead of heading home or to Carl's Pharmacy, Bea makes a left turn and heads down to the marina, pulling off her cardigan as she goes. Her footsteps speed up, and her pulse slows down as she gets closer, as she hears the lapping of waves against the wooden pilings. She takes a deep breath—inhales the scent of briny river water and fish and salt and mud—and then lets it go.

It's a sunny Friday evening in mid-June, and lots of familiar boats are missing from their slips, but there's a houseboat she hasn't seen before. She makes her way down the adjacent dock to get a better look at it. The boat is a little floating blue bungalow, maybe thirty feet long. It looks newly painted, not too weathered yet, with white trim around the windows and roof. There's a porch on the front with two blue plastic Adirondack chairs. Bea peers curiously through the windows along the dock. Beneath the first window is a gray futon, and along the opposite wall, she spots a built-in wooden table with benches on either side. Beneath the next window is a double bed with a rumpled plaid duvet. She wonders what's on the other side of the bedroom wall—a tiny kitchen? A little bathroom with a marine toilet and shower?

Maybe it belongs to the family from the coffee shop. It seems awfully small for four people, but the futon might fold out. How amazing would it be to live on a houseboat? All the minimalism and efficiency of a tiny house—Bea is secretly obsessed with *Tiny House Hunters*—but with the added bonus of living on the water.

She plops down at the end of the dock, slipping off her black flats so that her bare feet dangle over the water. She leans her shoulder against the wooden piling—making sure that she's not inadvertently adding bird crap to the coffee stain—and sighs. Above her, gulls wheel and scream. The sun bakes the crown of her head. She wishes she could sit here forever. Or better yet, climb onboard that houseboat and drift away from everything. Erik. Georgetown. She pictures herself in the middle of the river and then the middle of the Chesapeake Bay, alone in the blue expanse of water and waves and sky, and she feels light as the meringue on a lemon meringue pie.

A staccato clicking interrupts her daydream. Bea startles and looks over her shoulder.

"Sorry. I didn't mean to scare you." It's the hipster from the coffee shop. The guy she literally ran into. He's wearing a fancy camera draped around his neck.

"I was *startled*," she corrects. "You didn't scare me."

He grins as he recognizes her. "Coffee girl. I thought that was you. Sorry, I usually ask before I take someone's picture, but that was a great shot."

"Of me?" Bea stands and steps back into her shoes.

"Yeah. You looked...pensive. Sad."

"I'm not sad." It's reflexive.

"All right." He shrugs. "Maybe more pensive. Thoughtful, you know? If I'd asked to take your picture, you'd have just smiled."

"*If* I said yes," she mutters. The guy grins again, a little cocky, like *of course* she would have said yes. Bea bets that most girls do say yes to him. "I'm not sad. And I know what pensive means. I'm going to Georgetown."

"Yeah?" He looks amused, and Bea flushes. Why does she always have to try to prove how smart she is? "Well, whatever you were thinking, I got some great pictures. The red hair and the white shirt against the blue water. And those freckles. Your freckles are great."

Bea puts a hand to her cheek. She's always liked her freckles.

Still. Her shoulders are tight again, when a minute ago, she felt so dreamy and relaxed. He ruined that. This is supposed to be *her* place. Her refuge right in the middle of town. "You should have asked first."

He squints at her. "Yeah. Sorry. I'll delete them if you want."

She was expecting more of an argument. Something about his easy apology drains the fight right out of her.

"You don't have to delete them. Maybe I am a little sad," she admits. "But I don't want to talk about it."

"All right." He peers down at her. He's really tall. Of course, she's really short. Five two. "You have a boat down here?"

Bea shakes her head. "I wish. I love the water. There's something about the sound of waves... It's so calming. Centering, you know?" Lately, sitting down here at the marina is the only thing that makes her less anxious.

"I feel the same way." He points at the blue houseboat. "That's why I bought the *Stella Anne*."

Bea's eyes go wide with surprise. "Wait. That's *your* boat?"

He grins and steps down onto its deck. "Yeah. I bought it dirt cheap last summer, and my buddy Jefferson and I gutted it. Took out pretty much everything but the engine. New paint job, new wood flooring, new kitchen, new furniture. Want to come aboard?"

Bea does want to, but she hesitates. "No offense, but I don't even know your name. You could be a serial killer."

He reaches out a hand. "Gabriel Stewart Beauford. Gabe." He's got a firm grip.

"Bea Garrett."

"Nice to meet you, Bea. I'm in town for the summer

helping fix up my grandmother's house. It's the purple Victorian over on Azalea Avenue."

Bea knows exactly which house he means. "Miss Amelia's old place?"

His handsome face lights up. "You knew Memaw?"

Bea laughs. Remington Hollow is so small. "Everybody knew Miss Amelia! She was my parents' second-grade teacher."

"That's her. Man, she was great. I didn't get to see her much the last couple of years, but she came down to Nashville every Christmas. She passed back in March, and my uncle's fixing the place up so he and my moms can sell it. He's a carpenter, but it needs a shit ton—excuse me—a whole lot of work, so I came up to help out."

Sweet old Miss Amelia's grandson *can't* be a serial killer, can he? Bea is tempted to check out the houseboat. Really, really tempted. But then she checks her rose-gold watch—a graduation present from Erik—and realizes that it really is time for her to get home.

"I have to go, actually. Family dinner." She looks with envious eyes at the *Stella Anne*.

Gabe gives her another easy grin. "Rain check? I hang out here pretty much every night after we finish up at the house. Come on by sometime."

Is he hitting on her? Bea is utterly unpracticed at flirting. She's been with Erik forever; everybody in Remington

Hollow knows she's with Erik. But Gabe seems sincere, not like he has an agenda. And he's so *chill*. He emanates chill. Like he has this innate calm that is totally foreign to Bea. Does it come from living on the water? Is it something he was born with or something he cultivated? She squints at him. Does he meditate? Does he smoke a lot of weed?

She is curious. About the boat, and about the boy on it.

"Okay." She gives him a smile that feels more genuine than anything she's said in weeks. "Rain check."

CHAPTER SEVEN

KAT

After they sign the cast list, Kat and Pen walk over to Gert's for celebratory ice cream. Pen offers to drive Kat home afterward, but Kat decides to walk. It's a gorgeous, sunny day, and Gert's Old Fashioned Ice Cream Shoppe is only a dozen blocks from home. If she's going to have ice cream *and* Bea's strawberry crumble, she wants to burn a few calories.

As Kat walks, she thinks about Adam, and her strides lengthen into a sort of angry march. How dare he accuse her of mean-girl shit—and in that frustrated, weary voice, like he's so *above* it all. Like the age difference between them is five years instead of one. Okay, *maybe* she and Pen played a few pranks on Jillian: Pen stole her phone and changed all her contacts to Harry Potter characters; Kat hid her clothes after gym (but Jillian eventually found them, so it wasn't *that* bad); and Pen made up a fake email to spam Jillian with poorly spelled messages for breast reductions. That last one *was* kind of childish. But they could have done way worse. They could have spray-painted *slut* on Jillian's cute red Mini Cooper or spread a rumor that she was pregnant; that would have been real mean-girl shit. But that's not how Kat rolls.

Still, maybe she's going about this all wrong. Now Adam feels protective of Jillian, like *she's* the victim, and he thinks Kat is even more of a drama queen than before. If she wants to flip the balance of power, she has to use his enormous ego against him. She has to convince him that she's moved on.

As Kat marches past the Tabby Cat Café, she spots Mason Kim behind the register, messing around on his phone. She wonders if anyone's texted him that he got the role of Laurie yet. Mase is well-liked, but he's been kind of a loner since his boyfriend left for college last fall. Kat peeks in the front window, angling around the HELP WANTED sign. Mase is always on his phone. Brandon, his boyfriend, decided to work at the Kings Dominion amusement park this summer instead of coming home.

Kat opens the door tentatively. She had her eighth, ninth, and tenth birthday parties at the café, but she hasn't been here for ages. Cat cafés might be all the rage in places like Los Angeles or Tokyo, but this one is geared toward little kids and old ladies and nobody in between. The furniture is mostly uncomfortable, flowered love seats and armchairs. Ugly cat figurines and decorative china plates clutter every table and shelf, half of them knocked askew by the cats. The litter boxes are upstairs, but the place reeks of potpourri in an overzealous attempt to cover the smell.

"Hey, Mase." Kat closes the door as he grabs a curious black-and-white cat before it can escape. The name tag on its collar reads *Suri*.

"Hey, Kat. What's up?" Mase says. They've been in a few shows together, but they aren't really friends. He's a year older, like Adam and Jillian.

"Did you hear? The cast list is up. I'm Jo." She smiles proudly. "Congratulations. You're my Laurie."

Mase nods. "Cool."

Cool? That's *all*? He got the male lead—why isn't he more excited? "Isn't that the part you wanted?" Maybe Mase has a major scheduling conflict and needs to take a smaller role, and then Adam will get to be Laurie after all. "You're not running off to Kings Dominion too, are you?"

"Nope." Mase clears his throat. "There are no trips to Virginia in my future."

"Are you sure?" Kat asks, petting Suri, who has escaped Mase's grasp and wandered over to her.

Mase's smile flattens. "Pretty sure, yeah. Brandon and I broke up."

"Oh," Kat says softly. "I'm sorry." They'd been together for two years. That is practically *forever* in the world of Remington Hollow High showmances. "The long-distance thing must have been hard."

"I didn't think it was that difficult." Mase's jaw twitches. "Till he cheated on me."

Kat purses her red lips sympathetically. "What an asshole."

"Yeah." But Mase looks brokenhearted, and his delivery lacks conviction.

"Adam cheated on me too," she offers.

"I heard," Mase says. *Everybody* heard. When she saw Adam and Jillian kissing backstage, she cussed them both out so thoroughly—and so loudly—that the vice principal gave her detention. "It's not the same thing. Brandon and I… He was my first love. And he slept with somebody else."

"That sucks," Kat admits. Poor Mase. He must be going totally stir-crazy working here all day with nobody to talk to besides Miss Lydia. He clearly needs someone to confide in. Someone to help him out of his heartbreak.

"I still love him," Mase confesses, his shoulders slumping.

"Yeah? What are you doing about it?" Kat props her elbows on the counter. Suri, annoyed at being neglected, tears off across the room.

"Doing about it?" Mase runs a hand through his spiky

black fauxhawk. "I don't know. Eating my feelings? Stalking him online? Texting that I miss him?"

Kat scrunches up her face. "What the hell? No. Mase, come on. That is a *terrible* strategy."

Luna, Miss Lydia's one-eyed gray cat, jumps onto the counter and butts her head against Mase's arm. "It's not really a strategy," Mase says.

"No kidding. You can't let him know you miss him! That gives him all the power."

"He *has* all the power. He's the one who broke up with me."

"But he doesn't have to know you're pining." Kat picks up a cat toy—a feather on a string—and twitches it back and forth. "Look. You have to make *him* miss *you*."

"How? I'm spending my summer working *here*." Mase gestures around the empty café. "I play with cats and dick around on my phone all day while I serve tea to little girls and old ladies."

Kat looks at the front window, where Cinnamon, the original tabby, is taking a nap in the sun. Where the pink Help Wanted sign is taped to the glass. "Miss Lydia's hiring?"

Mase nods. "She wants someone to help her spruce up the place."

"It could definitely use sprucing." The seed of a brilliant scheme plants itself in Kat's mind. Now that she's sixteen, she could have a summer job. A real one, instead of working at Arden. And she loves cats. She's always wanted one of her own, but Des is super allergic. "Wait a minute. How much sprucing? Like…a total makeover?"

Suri darts back across the room and stands on her hind legs to bat at the feather toy. "I don't know about that. Sales are down. Adoptions are down," Mase says. Miss Lydia works with the local rescue to feature cats available for adoption, as well as the ones that she's adopted herself.

"Bummer." Kat crouches—not easy in three-inch platform heels—and pets Suri. "Well, I know how to make things look cute for cheap. We aren't exactly rolling in cash. Would you put in a good word for me?"

"With Miss Lydia? I guess, but—" Luna nudges Mase till he pets her again. "Not to be self-absorbed, but how does this help me get Brandon back?"

"Between your good word, my natural charm"—Kat tosses her hair—"and what I'm assuming will be a real lack of applicants, I'm a shoo-in. And I have big ideas for this place." She looks around with a critical eye. "This could be cool. We could make it cool."

"We could?" Mase raises his well-sculpted eyebrows, clearly dubious.

Kat stands. "Yeah. I follow some cat cafés on Instagram. We'd have to get rid of the furniture first. Toss all those hideous figurines and china plates and cat pillows. Keep the pink wallpaper. Maybe paint this wall with chalkboard paint, and make signs for selfies." Kat strides around the room, pointing, with Suri trotting after her.

"Selfies?" Mase echoes. "Who'd want to take selfies here?"

Kat runs a finger over the textured pink wallpaper. "Everyone, once we're finished with it. We'll get futons with slipcovers so we can wash off the cat hair, and shaggy pink and black throw pillows. Think modern. Sleek, but super cute. Still a place that little girls want to come for birthday parties, but also a place that people our age would come and hang out and play with the cats. You get teenage girls, you get money. We're tastemakers. Don't you read *Teen Vogue*? Teen girls are totally leading the resistance." The more she talks, the more she *loves* this plan. "Brandon will see the place blowing up on social media, and he'll be intrigued."

Mase shakes his head. "Brandon doesn't care what's going on in Remington Hollow. He's moved on."

"That's part two of my plan. Maybe you should move on too." Kat grins. "Make him jealous."

Mase stares sadly at his retro wingtip shoes. "I don't think I'm ready to date anybody else, honestly."

"I know." Kat pats him on the shoulder. "But how about *fake* dating?"

Mase rolls his eyes. "Like, invent some other guy? Isn't that kind of pathetic?"

"Not a guy, and not made up." Kat twirls in a circle and does jazz hands. "Me!"

"You?" Mase stares at her, clearly thrown. "What?"

She sighs. "Mase. It's *so* obvious. You want to make Brandon jealous. I want to make Adam jealous. We'll be spending a lot of time together anyway between the play and me working here. It's *brilliant*."

"It's crazy." But she can tell he's considering it. He's eyeing her like he's evaluating whether they'd take good selfies. And they would. She's already thought this through. They both have great style. Mase is cute, in a punk sort of way, with his fauxhawk and guyliner and skinny jeans. He's got…what's the word Gram uses? *Moxie*. Kat digs moxie. It can't be easy being a bisexual Korean American drama nerd in a small town, dating another guy, and working at a cat café. When they were younger, back in middle school, Mase got bullied a lot. Then his brother, Jacob, kicked Troy Randall's ass and let it be known that he was coming for anybody who came for Mase, and nobody messed with Mase again.

"Come on. Your current strategy is clearly not working, right?" Kat insists.

Mase shrugs. "Truth. So, hypothetically speaking…how would this work? We post a cute Insta story?"

"No, that's not big enough. We have to stage it." A smile creeps across Kat's face. "You aren't averse to public displays of affection, are you?"

Mase shrugs. "Nah. It's like stage kissing." He stares at

her. "If I say yes, am I going to regret it? How do I know I can trust you?"

"What have you got to lose?" Kat fires back.

"If this gets out…my dignity? Self-respect?"

"It would be even worse for me. Everybody already thinks I'm a hot mess. I'm the stereotypical jealous ex-girlfriend," Kat admits. "But nobody will find out. I promise." She thinks for a minute. "What if we make our debut tomorrow night at Spencer and Dylan's party?" Spencer Pennington is totally obnoxious, but the parties she and her brother throw every summer are legendary.

"Your confidence is weirdly convincing." Mase nods. "All right. I'm in."

Kat grins. "This is going to be so much fun. Trust me."

Vi is setting a trap.

She has very slowly meandered the eight blocks from home back to Arden. In one hand, she holds the new Nina LaCour book. In the other, she holds a leash that leads to a sweet, fluffy white chow chow named Juno, who stops to sniff curiously at every flower, tree, bush, and telephone pole they pass. Vi is dog sitting while her next-door neighbors, the Mitchells, are on vacation.

Vi has decided to take Des's advice and stop hiding from Cece. She overheard that Cece wanted to read this book, the bookstore was sold out, and Vi had a copy on her bookshelf at home. It was easy enough to go home and grab it, pick up Juno for her evening walk, and then head in the direction of Tia Julia's, where Cece works most Friday nights.

Not that Vi has memorized Cece's schedule or anything. She's just noticed when Cece's there and when she's not, since Tia Julia's is right next door. Vi is very observant.

Especially when it comes to Cece Pérez.

And Juno is the perfect Cece bait.

Vi takes a deep breath, runs a hand over her carefully rebraided hair, and walks past Arden. Des has dragged the chalkboard sign advertising tomorrow's story time inside and is closing up. Vi has stalled as long as she possibly can. If she wants to get home in time for family dinner, she has to put her plan into action *now* and then return Juno to the Mitchells'. She tugs the dog along the brick sidewalk, past the couples sipping sangria and bright frozen margaritas in the front windows of Tia Julia's. Cece is stationed behind the outdoor hostess stand in the courtyard. Her dark hair is pulled up into a high, bouncy ponytail, and she's wearing a black dress that falls right above her knees. She is so, so ridiculously pretty.

Cece flies out to the sidewalk as soon as she sees the dog. "Juno! Who's a pretty girl?" She crouches to pet Juno, heedless of getting white dog hair all over her black dress. "Who's a good floof?"

Vi hides a smile. "Hi, Cece."

Cece looks up as if she's only now noticing that a person is attached to the dog. "Vi! Hey!"

The butterflies in Vi's stomach do cartwheels when Cece says her name. Like, *of course* Cece knows her name. They were best friends in preschool. They have been in the same grade, with more or less the same hundred people, since kindergarten. They don't have the same friends—Cece is popular and Vi is not—but last year, they were in the same algebra and government classes.

Still. *Cece said her name.*

"How do you know Juno?" Cece kneels on the brick sidewalk and pets the dog's big furry head. Juno wags her tail happily and licks Cece's cheek.

"Juno!" Vi chides. "I'm sorry."

"I don't mind." Cece laughs and rubs her hand over her cheek. Her nails are painted a bright bubblegum pink. She wears pink a lot, Vi has noticed.

"Juno lives next door. I'm dog sitting." Vi feels almost unbearably awkward in her own skin. She doesn't know what to do with her hand that's not holding the leash. It's just sort of hanging by her side, clutching the book that Cece hasn't noticed yet. What do other people do with their hands? She tucks the book against her chest.

"She's adorable. I'd rather babysit her than my brothers." Cece pouts, and Vi tries—and fails—not to stare at her pink-lipsticked mouth. "I love dogs."

"I know," Vi says, then grimaces. She doesn't want to sound like a total creeper. "I mean...me too."

"When Remus died last year, Mami said we couldn't get another dog. She said we're here all the time and it's not fair to them." Sirius and Remus were the Pérezes' Great Danes. "She said it's hard enough for her to manage the restaurant and the boys without worrying about giant dogs."

"Des is super allergic to dogs, so we can't have one either," Vi explains. "But I watch Juno whenever the Mitchells go out of town. This summer, I'm walking her at lunchtime. I've been walking the Chans' new puppy sometimes too."

"Athena? Oh my gosh, she's the cutest!" Cece squeals.

Vi loves that Cece knows all the neighborhood dogs' names.

"Yeah, she's such a puppy still. She has so much energy. She and Juno are kind of a handful together. Actually... if you ever wanted to walk them with me...I could use the help," Vi says. This is going so well! Is she being too obvious, though?

"That would be so fun." Cece stands up, bouncing a little on her toes. "If I don't have to work, I'd love to. Will you text me next time?"

"Sure. Yeah. Let me get your number." Vi hands Cece the leash while she fishes her phone out of her back pocket. She's getting Cece's number!

Cece rattles it off, and Vi adds it to her contacts. When she looks up again, Cece is staring at her chest instead of the dog. Vi looks down, self-conscious. Her *Empowered Women Empower Women* T-shirt does have a lower neck than she'd usually wear. Is her bra showing?

Wait, no. Cece is reading the back of the book in Vi's hand. The book Vi brought specifically to lend her. Right. *Get it together, Vi.* Cece passes the leash back to her, and their hands brush. Vi hopes she isn't blushing.

"Is that the new Nina LaCour book?" Cece asks. "I tried to buy it today, but Arden was out. Des said it's your fault 'cause you've been recommending it to everybody."

"It's so good. Here." Vi hands Cece the book, trying to sound casual, as though this hasn't all been carefully orchestrated. Cece immediately flips the book open and reads the flap copy. "Do you want to borrow it?"

Cece looks over her shoulder, like she's suddenly remembered she's supposed to be working, but there's no one waiting at the hostess stand. "Oh. Thank you, but…Des said she'd order it for me. I mean…aren't you reading it?" Cece flips to the first page and sighs. "She's such an amazing writer. *Everything Leads to You* is one of my all-time favorites."

"Mine too. And I love the book she cowrote with David Levithan, *You Know Me Well*. Have you read that?"

Cece nods. "I read in the foreword they were writing it when the Supreme Court ruled on marriage equality."

"I wasn't out yet then. I was still kind of figuring out that not everybody was *that* into Clexa, but…" Vi trails off, flushing. Cece isn't going to have any idea what she's talking about. Nobody in Remington Hollow ever knows what Vi's talking about. Not even her sisters.

"Clexa?" Cece echoes.

"That's, uh, the ship name for Clarke and Lexa. They were a couple on the TV show *The 100* in seasons two and three?" Vi has to stop herself from rambling. Clarke and Lexa's slow-burn romance—and the fan fiction that Vi devoured about it—led to her joining Tumblr and starting to write her own fanfic.

Cece smiles. "I'll have to check it out."

"It's on Netflix," Vi says, before she realizes Cece is probably only being polite.

"Cool. I'll have to sneak-watch it on my tablet." Cece stares at the brick sidewalk, her brown skin flushing a little. "Abuela Julia is Catholic, so…I mean…we're all Catholic, technically, but she's *really* Catholic. She thinks marriage should only be between a man and a woman. If she saw me watching something with two girls kissing, she would probably turn it off and tell me it was a sin."

"Oh." Vi's face falls.

"Yeah. I love her, but… Things were different when she was young, I guess."

Vi wants to point out that not everybody from their

grandmothers' generation is homophobic, but she doesn't want to make Cece feel bad, like she has to defend her abuela. Vi doesn't know what she'd do if Gram thought her crush on Cece was a sin. That being gay was a sin. That would be *awful*.

"It's okay if you want to borrow the book," she says finally. "I've already read it. But I don't want to get you in trouble."

"I can hide it. Mami doesn't really care; she just doesn't want to fight with Abuela," Cece says. "Are you sure? I won't cancel my order. I like having all my favorites so I can reread them."

Vi smiles. Something else they have in common. "Okay. No rush."

Cece shrugs. "I'm a fast reader. And I have the day off tomorrow. I don't have any plans till the Penningtons' party. Are you going? I could give it back to you there."

"I'll be there," Vi says, surprising herself. She's never gone to one of Spencer's parties. She doesn't even *like* parties. They're loud and crowded, and she has to make small talk, which is not one of her personal strengths. But if Cece's going, she wants to go too. If it sucks, at least she'll have a book to read.

"Awesome." Cece looks over her shoulder as a couple approaches the hostess stand. She leans down and pets Juno one more time. "I should get back, but...thank you so much for the book. See you tomorrow!"

Vi waves awkwardly. "See you tomorrow." She watches as Cece slides the book beneath a stack of menus.

Her plan worked. She not only got to talk to Cece, she got Cece's phone number, and now they have plans to see each other tomorrow at the farm party *and* to walk Juno and Athena. But Vi feels more concerned than victorious. She doesn't want to assume anything or pressure Cece to label herself if she's not ready for that. But it seems like maybe Cece is interested in girls and afraid that her family wouldn't support her.

If that's true, Vi wants Cece to know that she's a safe person to talk to. It seems like Cece could use a friend. And maybe—even if it doesn't go any further—Vi could be that person.

Vi would really like to be that person.

CHAPTER NINE
DES

"You can't wear that to the party! You look like a librarian," Kat complains, eyeing Des's ripped jeans, blue *Le Petit Prince* T-shirt, and navy Chucks.

Des shrugs and runs her hand through her messy red curls. "So? Librarians are cool."

"No. Not like a cool, sexy librarian." Kat looks at Des earnestly. "Don't you want to dress up a little? Maybe you'll meet somebody."

"Kat, I already know everybody who'll be at the party," Des says. Not that it matters. She doesn't have any interest in dating. She never has. She thinks it's just the way she's wired. Till last fall, she always had Em, and that best friendship felt like enough. "I don't have time for a relationship," she adds, because that seems more likely to placate Kat than *I don't* want *a relationship.*

Kat smirks. "Who said anything about a relationship?"

"Kat!" Des flushes. She doesn't have any interest in a random hookup either.

"Des!" Kat mimics. "You haven't dated anyone since you and Jake Mitchell held hands. You peaked romantically in the fifth grade."

"Harsh," Bea says, drifting into the bedroom she and Des share.

"But true." Kat fishes a tube of lipstick from her pocket and reapplies a perfect orange-red pout.

"Des doesn't need a relationship. She has work, and… everything she does around here." Bea flutters a freckled hand to encompass all of Des's responsibilities.

Des scowls. Is that how her sisters see her? As some sort of Cinderella? Maybe she wouldn't have to do so much if they helped out a little more. "And she has hobbies," Bea adds, gesturing to Des's half of the room, which looks like a craft store explosion.

Des twirls the turquoise ring on her index finger. Why is her art a *hobby*? No one dismisses Bea's writing or Kat's acting that way. Anger is hot in her chest as she remembers Em's comment about "practicing her handwriting." Maybe she isn't going to art school; maybe she isn't pursuing art professionally; maybe she hasn't been making much time for it lately. It's still important to her.

But can she blame her sisters for failing to realize that when she doesn't take it more seriously herself?

"Whatever." Kat flops down on Bea's twin bed. Bea's half of the room is immaculate: her bookshelf organized alphabetically, her notebooks stacked neatly on her desk, her sunny yellow duvet pulled up to her pillow. Even the photos on her wall are arranged at perfect right angles. "Tell Des she can't wear that to the party, Bea."

"It's on a *farm*," Des says irritably. "I'm dressed to go to a farm. At least I don't look like a giant toddler."

Kat shrinks into herself, and Des wishes she could stuff the word *giant* back down her throat. "I don't understand the romper trend," she adds hastily.

Kat pops up to look at herself in the mirror, tugging at the halter neck of her royal-blue romper. Des examines her sister while Kat's back is turned. Has she lost weight? Has she been eating enough? She's been sad, trying to hide it with a higher than usual amount of bitchiness, but it's hard to hide anything in a three-bedroom house filled with five people.

"Don't *look* at me like that," Kat snaps, catching her gaze in the mirror. "Do you want to know everything I ate today? You can text Pen. She'll tell you I had a strawberry ice cream cone yesterday to celebrate getting the part."

"No, I trust you. If you say you're okay…" Des trails off.

"I am," Kat insists.

Des turns her attention to Bea, who's taken off her glasses and is now carefully applying eyeliner in the mirror. There are dark circles under her brown eyes. "Hey, wait a minute! Bea's wearing jeans."

Kat tilts her head, evaluating Bea's dark skinny jeans and *Self-Rescuing Princess* tank top. "She and Erik have been dating forever. She doesn't have to try anymore."

Bea gives her a ferocious frown. "I don't dress for Erik. I dress for myself."

"I can tell," Kat says.

Des's phone beeps with a notification that Em has posted pictures. She's already at the party.

"I am a whole person all by myself," Bea continues. "I don't need a boyfriend to be complete. Neither does Des, and neither do you."

"Fine. Wear whatever you want." Kat stomps from the room. "But don't complain to me if people think you're lame."

"Don't say 'lame'! It's ableist!" Bea shouts after her.

Des frowns as she scrolls through Em's photos. Em's standing near a bonfire, a red Solo cup in one hand, posing and laughing with girls from their high school class. Girls she's gotten coffee with over the past few weeks. Des has seen those pictures on Instagram too and felt stung that she wasn't invited.

Maybe Em assumed she had to work?

Or maybe, she thinks bitterly, Em's embarrassed by her now. Tonight, Em's wearing a strapless pink sundress and dramatic pink, purple, and teal eye shadow. How did she learn to do eye shadow like that? Des feels left behind and somehow betrayed.

Vi leans in their doorway. "Bea? Will you braid my hair for the party?"

"Sure." Bea gestures to the floor in front of her green velvet armchair.

"Wait, what? Are you coming with us?" Des asks. Her littlest sister is only fifteen: too young, in Des's opinion, for farm parties. "Did Gram say it was okay?"

Vi nods. "I'm not a little kid anymore, Des." She smooths her teal skater dress, which is printed with cute purple and green dinosaurs. Vi has always had a quirky style that's all her own.

"That dress is super cute," Bea says.

Vi's face falls. "*Cute*? I don't want to look cute!"

"What's wrong with cute?" Des asks, baffled.

"Cece isn't cute. She's *gorgeous*." Vi sprawls on the floor.

So *that's* why Vi wants to go to the party: because Cece Pérez will be there. Vi's yearlong crush on Cece is enormous and adorable and, as far as Des can tell, entirely one-sided.

Bea sinks into the high-backed reading chair, brush in

hand. "Cece is beautiful, and so are you. There are a billion different kinds of pretty." She grabs a copy of *The Beauty Myth* from her bookshelf. "You should read this."

Vi eyes it warily. "Nonfiction isn't really my thing."

Des hides a smile. Bea's been bugging her to read *Bad Feminist* for months, but Bea's the only one of them who devours essays.

"Let's do braids around the crown of your head. You'll look like a fantasy princess." Some of the tension goes out of Vi's slim shoulders as Bea brushes her hair.

Des gets up and stares into her closet. She and Em used to judge other girls for taking dumb drunk selfies. They used to tease Kat for spending hours watching YouTube makeup tutorials. But somehow the rules changed when Des wasn't looking, and now Em cares about makeup and fashion and good angles for selfies. What will she think if Des shows up at the party like this, barefaced, in jeans and her *Le Petit Prince* T-shirt?

Des sighs. "Fine. What should I wear, Kat?"

Kat reappears almost instantly, holding a black cold-shoulder top. "This. With your nice jeans."

Des wonders if her sister's been lurking in the hall, just waiting for her to change her mind. She examines the shirt, which has a deep V-neck in addition to the cutout shoulders. It's not something she'd wear to the store, where she's constantly leaning over to shelve books.

But it is a party. "I'm not wearing heels. Or eyeliner. It gets in my contacts."

Kat produces a tube of mascara, some peachy lip gloss, and a pair of black flats. "Here. You can wear my shoes if you promise not to step in cow shit."

"There are going to be cows?" Vi perks up. "Do they have horses?"

"You are not spending all your time with the horses, you weirdo." Kat glances at Vi's tote bag. "Do you want to borrow a clutch? Wait—are you bringing a book?"

Vi shrugs. "I bring a book everywhere," she says as Des wriggles into her nice jeans.

Bea laughs. "You know, this is the first Pennington party we've all gone to."

"It's our last summer together," Vi says. "Who knows if you'll even come home next summer? You'll probably have some amazing internship at the *Washington Post* already."

"Don't be silly. Of course I'll come home for the summer," Bea says, but her jaw is tight, her smile forced. Des can tell Bea is super stressed out about something. She feels bad that she hasn't ferreted out what it is yet.

"I can't wait to get out of this stupid town!" Kat leans over Vi to apply brown eyeliner to her upper lash line. "Two more years, and then I'm going to New York. Or maybe Los Angeles. But probably New York."

"New York. Then we can be roommates." Vi holds her

hand out for the peach lip gloss. She confided in Des last week that she's thinking about going to NYU and then becoming a children's book editor.

Des's stomach sinks. They all want to leave Remington Hollow. Is that what the next four years will be—a series of goodbyes? Bea will head to DC in August, Kat will leave for New York in two years, and Vi will follow her in three. They'll come home for Christmas break and summer vacations at first, until they get internships and their own apartments. Until they get serious boyfriends and girlfriends. Until they're too busy and too big-city for Remington Hollow. What if they all start to think of it as a stupid hick town—and of her as their boring big sister who never went to college and never left home? Whose life hasn't changed since high school?

"Don't worry, Des," Kat says magnanimously. "We'll still come visit you and Gram."

"Gee, thanks." Des forces a laugh, but it stings that they assume she'll still be here, the same old Des, working at Arden and living with Gram.

That never used to bother her. It's what she assumed too. Now she wishes she were less predictable.

When they pull up outside Tia Julia's, Paige is already waiting on the sidewalk. Des made her sisters crowd into the back seat, which Kat has been complaining about nonstop for the five blocks from their house to Arden. She stops whining midsentence when Paige jumps into the car, and Des catches all three of her sisters gawking in the rearview mirror.

"Paige, these are my sisters Bea, Vi, and Kat. Guys, this is Paige," Des says.

"You're Des's friend?" Kat asks, as if there must be some mistake, as if this glam stranger has stumbled into their car by accident. Paige is dressed all in black, with her purple hair pulled into a high ponytail. She's wearing a septum ring and heavy, black eyeliner.

"Yep." Paige fastens her seat belt and pulls out a pack of cigarettes. "Do you mind if I smoke, Desdemona?"

"Yes," Vi answers for her, and Des cringes. "Des has asthma."

"No worries. We need some tunes, though." Paige plugs in her phone, and soon a party playlist is pounding through the car.

"You're squishing me, Bea," Kat complains. "Why didn't you get a ride with Erik?"

"He's camping with his dad," Bea says.

"Camping?" Kat says. "Gross."

"Who's Erik? Your man?" Paige asks. As they turn down the Penningtons' long gravel driveway, passing fields of corn and soybeans, Kat and Vi gush about Bea's boyfriend.

"He's a big nerd, but he's sweet. And patient. Like, super patient." Kat rolls her eyes. "He'd have to be to put up with Bea."

"They're going to get married," Vi adds. "He's kind of like our brother already. When he comes over, he takes out the trash and changes lightbulbs and stuff."

"We don't need a boy to change our lightbulbs," Bea snaps. "What kind of feminist are you?"

Des's brow furrows while her sisters bicker. Bea is definitely more prickly than usual. Is she mad that Erik went away for the weekend? Maybe she feels anxious about going to the party without him; the two of them are usually inseparable.

Des's stomach ties itself into knots as Bea directs her to a field where two rows of cars and trucks—mostly trucks— are already parked. God, why did she agree to come? This is stupid. Why is she trying to be someone she's not? To prove something to Em?

Her sisters and Paige spill out of the car, laughing. Kat strides across the field toward the flickering orange light of a bonfire, towing Vi along behind her. Bea follows, fiddling with her phone.

Des climbs out last, reluctantly, already regretting her choice. Paige is leaning against the hood, waiting for her. "You seem a little tense, Desdemona."

"Yeah. Emily—my friend, the one you met yesterday at

the store?" Des gives an awkward shrug. "She was right. I don't usually come to these parties."

Paige cocks her head like a bright parrot. "Are you two fighting or something?"

"Yeah. I don't know why I said I'd come. I mean, I do know…I wanted to do something…unexpected. To prove that I'm not—" Des falters. Paige can't be more than a year or two older, but she seems utterly self-assured. Like she genuinely doesn't care what other people think. How is that possible? Can she teach Des her secrets?

"Not what?" Paige prompts. Then: "You know what, never mind. It's none of my business. But if you want my advice, you don't have anything to prove to anybody. You're rad, Desdemona."

"I am?" Des asks, surprised and flattered.

"Sure. I mean, whatever, you shouldn't care what *I* think either. But you've got that sexy red hair and tits I would kill for. You just need a little confidence." Paige is fumbling with her cigarettes. "Look, not to sound like a bad after-school special, but do you want to smoke some weed with me? It can really help with anxiety." She offers the joint to Des.

"Oh, um. No thanks," Des says.

"Right. Asthma." Paige lights the joint and draws in a deep breath. She doesn't pressure her. Isn't disappointed. It hits Des again with a slap of euphoria: Paige doesn't expect anything from her.

"You know…what the hell," Des says slowly, holding out a hand. She wants to be less predictable, right? More adventurous? Well, no one is expecting her to show up at this party, much less show up high with a purple-haired punk girl. "Sure. It would be nice to chill out for once."

CHAPTER TEN

BEA

As soon as Bea reaches the bonfire, Chloe Chan rushes up and envelops her in a hug. "Bea!" Chloe shrieks. She smells like beer and marshmallows, and she almost impales Bea with the stick in her left hand.

"Hey, Chloe." Bea shoves the sharp, gooey stick away from her Princess Leia shirt.

"How are you? Want a s'more? I'll roast a marshmallow for you!" Chloe offers. There's a little chocolate smeared at the edge of her mouth. Chloe's a messy drunk. Bea has always derived some petty satisfaction from that.

Honestly, she's always been a little jealous of Chloe. As if being salutatorian and editor of the yearbook wasn't enough, Chloe was also captain of the girls' tennis team and president of the Future Business Leaders of America. And she still found time to party. She's the cute, enthusiastic golden retriever to Bea's yapping, high-strung terrier.

"No, thanks," Bea says. She doesn't like marshmallows. It's a texture thing.

"We're friends now, right? You beat me. You got valedictorian. But now we've graduated, so none of that matters anymore," Chloe slurs, linking her arm through Bea's.

Is that how it's supposed to work? After years of competing with Chloe for the best grades, the highest GPA, and positions on the yearbook staff, they're...done? Chloe's off to the University of Pennsylvania, and Bea's off to Georgetown, and their old rivalry doesn't matter anymore?

When she gets to Georgetown, will there be a brand-new Chloe to contend with?

The thought is so exhausting that Bea wants to cry.

She won. She was valedictorian. She got the best grade in AP English. The newspaper advisor said she was the best editor they'd had in years, that she was practically guaranteed a spot on the *Hoya* staff at Georgetown.

But Bea's brain keeps reminding her that it's not enough. *She's* not enough. Maybe all the people who say she's talented are lying, or maybe she fooled them somehow, through luck or hard work, but someday, they will figure out the truth.

She shivers despite the June heat, despite Chloe's sweaty

skin pressed against hers. It's like her worst nightmares have slithered out from beneath her bed to chew on her. *Not good enough, not good enough, not good enough,* they chant, while Chloe chatters on like nothing's wrong.

"Where's Erik?" Chloe asks. His name brings Bea back to the present.

"Camping with his dad." The party is too loud. There are dozens of people from her class here, all of them laughing and having fun and eager to spend time together before everyone heads their separate ways come August. Why can't she have fun too? Why can't she stop *thinking* so much?

"Oh," Chloe says. "It's weird to see you at a party without him."

Bea frowns. Surely she's come to one of the Penningtons' parties without Erik. Hasn't she? She wracks her brain, trying to remember, and can't. Who would she have come with? She has friends from newspaper and yearbook, but after school, she was always too busy with Erik and Arden and studying. It never bothered her that she didn't have a best friend, like Des has Em and Kat has Penelope. *Erik* was her best friend. It never bothered her when people said their names like one: Bea-and-Erik.

Lately, it infuriates her. She wants to be Bea, only Bea, but she isn't sure she remembers how. They've been dating for five years. Who is she without Erik? What would it be like to be single? Or to kiss someone else?

Gabe Stewart Beauford's sunburned nose and easy grin pop into her head. He couldn't be more different from Erik. Erik is nerd-cute, combed blond hair and square black glasses, polo shirts and Nantucket Reds. She can't imagine any scenario in which Erik would take a summer off to restore an old house and live on a boat. That isn't nearly goal-oriented enough for him; it wouldn't be impressive on a transcript. But there's something about Gabe, about how fantastically *chill* he is, that intrigues Bea.

"Bea?" Chloe waves a hand in front of her face.

"Sorry. I'm going to get a beer." Bea doesn't actually want a beer; she thinks beer is gross; she just wants to escape Chloe. She digs through a cooler and snags a Diet Coke. It's sweet and fizzy on her tongue. But the party is still too close, too loud. She's not in the mood for making small talk, for being asked another dozen times where Erik is and pretending to care.

She does care, though. She wonders if he and his dad got the new camp stove to work, if they caught any fish, if they're getting eaten alive by mosquitoes. If Erik's reading by lantern light in his sleeping bag right now.

Bea loves him, even if she isn't *in* love with him anymore.

She makes her way through the stubbly field down to the river and walks along the water till she reaches the rickety old fishing dock. She sits at the end and lets her legs dangle out over the dark water. The reassuring lap of it against the wooden pilings calms her. She takes a deep breath, and then she's crying.

She stuffs a hand over her mouth and tries to stifle the sound, but trying to cry silently makes her throat ache. Her shoulders shake with the force of her sadness. She can't stop. She hasn't cried like this since she turned nine, her first birthday without her parents. Jesus, she misses them. She could really use advice from her mom right now.

Mom, I'm not in love with Erik anymore. I need to break up with him, but I don't know how. I kept thinking after AP exams, and then it was after finishing the yearbook, then the last issue of the paper, then finals, then graduation… I'm such a coward. I don't want to be with him, but I don't know who I am without him. I don't know if I even want to go to Georgetown anymore. I'm so tired all the time, but I can't sleep. What should I do?

Bea tries to conjure up her mom's face, her voice, her smell, but she's left with only a hazy smile and soft red curls and the scent of fresh bread. Mom loved to bake bread. She said kneading it was relaxing.

Bea can't remember the exact sound of her voice anymore, the tenor or rhythm of it. The realization makes her cry harder.

Behind her, footsteps slap against the weathered wooden dock.

Bea hastily scrubs at her eyes. She doesn't want anyone to see her like this. Imperfect. Out of control.

"Hey, I thought that was you." It's Gabe. "How come you're down here by yourself? Everything all right?"

"What are you doing here?" Her voice is all froggy. "How do you know Dylan?"

"I don't. Savannah Lockwood invited me," Gabe explains.

"Savannah Lockwood?" Bea echoes, disgusted.

Gabe peers down at her. "Seriously, are you all right?"

"Why? You want to take a picture? I hear I'm pretty when I'm sad," she snaps, scrambling to her feet. Gabe takes a step back, hands up, and she softens. "I'm sorry, I—"

"No, I deserved that," he says ruefully. "For what it's worth, I bet you're pretty all the time."

Bea shakes her head. She's not begging for compliments, but she knows she's not a pretty crier. She's sure that her eyes and nose are all red and her mascara has probably left wet black trails down her freckled cheeks. She can't remember if she used the waterproof kind or not.

"I don't really want to be here," she admits. "I'm not in the mood for a party. But my sisters all wanted to come."

"How many sisters do you have?" Gabe asks.

"Three." She smiles a little as she remembers them bickering earlier. She'll miss them if she goes to Georgetown. *When.* "Des drove, so I'm stuck till they're all ready to leave."

He fishes a set of keys out of his back pocket. "You want a ride?"

"I don't want to interrupt your date." It hits Bea that she's jealous. Of *Savannah.*

Gabe grins, like he knows what she's thinking. Jesus. How insufferable. "It's not a date."

Bea hesitates. "Have you been drinking?"

"Nope. Just got here," he says. "I'm fine to drive. Promise."

"Okay." Bea bites her lip. She doesn't want to be here, but she doesn't necessarily want to go home. "Is that invitation still open? To see your boat?"

"Yeah. Sure." He starts off toward the rows of parked cars. "You need to tell anybody you're leaving?"

"I'll text my sister." Bea sends a quick text letting Des know she isn't feeling well and is getting a ride back. She doesn't specify with whom or that she's not going straight home. In the unlikely event that Gabe does turn out to be a serial killer, there will be lots of other people down at the marina and over at Captain Dan's Seafood Shack to hear her scream.

Gabe opens the passenger door of a gray pickup. "Thank you," Bea says.

Country music plays low on the radio, and the windows are rolled all the way down. The wind rushes through the cab and through Bea's hair, and the fields are full of fireflies, and she starts to feel better. She catches Gabe looking over at her occasionally, and she can tell he wants to ask why she was crying, but he doesn't. He drives with one hand on the wheel and the other on his thigh, tapping along with whatever's on the radio.

Gabe parks in the marina lot and then leads the way down the maze of docks to the *Stella Anne*. He steps onto the deck, taking Bea's hand to help her down. His hand is big and warm and callused, and he doesn't let go right away. Bea's heart begins to beat faster.

"Come on in." He lets go of her hand to push open the sliding glass door and flip on a lamp.

Bea looks around curiously. The walls are wood paneled, and the décor is definitely IKEA minimalism meets college guy. A couple of decks of red-and-white cards, a few dirty mugs and water glasses, and a yellowed Stephen King novel are scattered across the table. Beyond the table is a very small kitchen. There's a two-burner gas stove, a mini fridge, a sink, and a couple of built-in cabinets.

"This is *so cool!*" she says. "It's like a tiny floating dream house."

Gabe grins. "Thanks. Jefferson and I spent all last summer fixing it up." He points to the small, walled-off room behind the kitchen. "That's the privy. Marine toilet and shower." The boat rocks gently in its mooring, but he moves gracefully through the small space and throws open the door opposite the kitchen. "And that's the bedroom. Sorry it's a mess."

Bea peers in quickly. There's the double bed she

glimpsed through the window, with the rumpled plaid duvet and tangled white sheets. There's a narrow white wardrobe in the corner, but the wooden floor is a jumble of jeans and boxers and T-shirts. She blushes and turns away, trying not to imagine Gabe standing there shucking off his clothes.

"It's so peaceful out here," she says. All she can hear are the murmured voices of people on a nearby boat and the lapping of the river beneath them. A far-off motor growls as a powerboat approaches.

"I'd live here all the time if I could. You want anything to drink? Water? Whiskey? Tea?" Gabe moves past her into the kitchen. The floor rocks beneath them on a wave from the incoming boat, and Bea stumbles. He reaches out and steadies her.

Bea looks up at him. Beneath the scruff, his lips are full and rosy and a little chapped. His hands are warm through the soft gray cotton of her Princess Leia shirt. He smells like spearmint gum and something else, maybe some kind of cologne. It's a little spicy and not unpleasant.

I've never kissed anyone with a beard before, she thinks.

Then: *I've never kissed anyone but Erik before.*

She strides away on the pretext of looking out the front door. "Tea would be great," she calls over her shoulder.

Jesus, what is she doing? She wanted to kiss him. She's never wanted to kiss anybody but Erik, except maybe Chris

Evans, who is very unlikely to ever cross her path. What is *wrong* with her?

"You want to play cards?" Gabe asks.

Bea glances at the well-worn cards on the table. "I'm not playing strip poker with you."

Is she flirting? She's totally flirting. Shit.

Gabe laughs. He has a nice laugh, low and rumbly. "That's too bad. I don't think you'd have a very good poker face," he jokes, but all Bea can think is that she must, because Erik doesn't know. Erik doesn't know that she isn't in love with him anymore or that she wanted to kiss somebody else.

"Actually, I was thinking Canasta," Gabe continues. "I found all those cards over at Memaw's place."

"You...want to play Canasta," Bea says slowly. Is he kidding?

"Sure, why not? You know how?" He pulls a kettle from the overhead cabinet.

"Yes, but...you want to play Canasta and drink tea?" She isn't sure what she was expecting, but...okay, she expected him to make a pass at her. She isn't sure if she's relieved or disappointed that he hasn't. It would have been easier to flounce off and never look back if he had.

"Well, *I'm* gonna have a glass of whiskey. But I'm happy to make you some tea." Gabe pulls a box of herbal tea and a bottle of honey from a cupboard. He fills the kettle and lights the stove. "Momma and I are coffee drinkers, but Ma loves this stuff. Honey lemon chamomile. Says it helps her sleep." He turns and smiles at Bea while she's processing that he has two moms. "You want to shuffle and deal? Thirteen cards each."

"Um. Sure." She sits down at the table and grabs the cards.

Gabe grins, filling a small glass with whiskey and ice. "I should warn you, I'm a Canasta shark. Memaw taught Lyric—that's my little sister—and me how to play one summer we were at the Gulf. Rained the whole week. Lyric and I play all the time now."

"How old is she?" Bea asks.

"Ten." Gabe pulls out his phone and shows her a photo of a grinning girl with brown skin and black braids.

"She's really cute," Bea says.

"She knows it," he says.

Bea can't stop sneaking looks at him as she shuffles and deals. A sort of warm contentment is making its way through her, even without the tea, lighting her up inside.

CHAPTER ELEVEN

KAT

Pretending to fall for Mason Kim is surprisingly *fun*.

Maybe it's because they're both actors. Or maybe it's because Mase is actually kind of hilarious. He and his friend Maxwell have snagged two long, sharp sticks intended for roasting s'mores and are using them to fence. Mase is winning, jabbing and feinting and backing Maxwell toward the small crowd gathered in an empty field near the bonfire.

"Not bad, Mase!" Kat calls grudgingly. She likes having a reputation as hard to impress.

"I took a stage combat class last summer," Mase says without looking away from his opponent.

Maxwell trips over his own feet and turns it into an

elaborate pratfall. Mase pokes him in the chest with the gooey marshmallow end of the stick.

"A hit! A very palpable hit!" Maxwell hollers, then pretends to die a dramatic death with a lot of gasping and groaning.

Kat and Pen and the rest of the crowd applaud. Nearer the bonfire, Spencer Pennington and her friends roll their eyes, and Kat suspects they're complaining about how the theater kids always have to make a scene. As usual, any attempt at cowing her only inspires Kat to make *more* of a scene.

"My turn," she says, scooping up the stick next to Maxwell's prone body.

Maxwell sits up. "Revenge my foul and most unnatural murder!" he moans, à la the ghost of Hamlet's father, and then flops back down.

Mase ignores him. "You want to fence with me?"

Kat grins. "I want to kick your butt." She hasn't taken stage combat, but her Theater I class did the Reduced Shakespeare Company's *The Complete Works of William Shakespeare (Abridged)* last spring. It required a lot of sword-play. And she has all those years of ballet to her advantage; she's graceful and super flexible, not to mention sneaky.

Mase gestures like Mercutio in Baz Luhrmann's *Romeo + Juliet*. "Bring it."

"*En garde!*" Kat calls. They circle each other warily.

More theater kids have gathered to watch, including Adam and Jillian. *Perfect.*

Kat lunges forward, but Mase parries. She backs away, and he advances. They circle each other like gladiators in the ring, striking and retreating. Then he attacks with a flurry of blows, knocking her stick askew. Kat barely keeps hold of it and grand jetés away.

"This isn't a dance party, Garrett," Mase growls.

"I'm sorry; are my methods too unconventional for you?" she teases. "When I win, you have to go get me a Diet Coke."

Mase parries her thrust and drives her toward the bonfire. "What do I get if I win?"

"What do you want?" Kat asks flirtatiously.

They cross swords and get in each other's faces. "How about a kiss?" Mase asks, low—but not so low everyone around them can't hear. He projects well.

"*Ooooooooh,*" the crowd says.

"Get it, Mase!" Maxwell hollers.

Kat looks into Mase's dark eyes. He has incredibly long, thick eyelashes. "Okay." She twirls away, hiding a smile. This is *excellent* romantic banter. She couldn't have scripted it better herself. Everyone will find it adorable, even if it does require her to lose the bout. She hates losing—but if it's in the service of the plan, it's ultimately a win, right?

They exchange a few more blows and parries. Maxwell

is leading a cheer for Mase; Pen is shouting encouragement to Kat. Mase expertly backs Kat toward the bonfire. Then he feints, and she falls for it, and he knocks her sword into the grass. It turns out she didn't actually have to *pretend* to lose.

"Do you acknowledge defeat?" he asks.

"Never!" Pen yells.

Kat gives Pen major side-eye. "Temporarily."

Mase steps closer. "May I?" They are almost exactly the same height.

"You may," she says graciously, closing her eyes. He wraps an arm around her waist, and she expects to be dipped into an elaborate stage kiss. Instead, his mouth moves over hers, soft and warm and sweet. He tastes like marshmallows and chocolate. His hand hovers at the small of her back for a moment, and then he lets go, but he doesn't step away.

"Yeah, Mase!" Maxwell cheers.

Mase silences him with a glare. "Hi," he says, blinking at her.

Kat smiles, a little dazed. It was fake, but it was also a really nice kiss. Better than nice. Adam could take some lessons. Like, not all kisses have to involve tongue, for starters.

"Hi," she says back.

"I'll still get you a Diet Coke," Mase offers.

She threads her fingers through his. "Maybe later."

Maxwell's truck is parked nearby. They climb onto the

gate and sit, legs swinging, hands clasped, while Maxwell and Pen and a bunch of their friends take turns making s'mores with the swords.

After a while, Mase leans toward Kat. "I think it's working," he whispers in her ear, tilting his head toward the bonfire. Adam is standing nearby with Jillian, arms crossed over his broad chest, looking pissed off about something. Is it because Kat's holding hands with Mase? She feels a flash of satisfaction. She also feels a little shivery at Mase's warm breath against her ear.

"I'm going to get you that Diet Coke," Mase says.

"In a minute," Kat says, and she kisses him. Maybe she should have asked first, but he doesn't seem to mind; he returns the kiss with interest. One hand lingers on her waist; the other tenderly cups her cheek. For a minute, Kat forgets this is all a ruse, a performance for a watching audience, and she lets herself sink into it.

When they break apart, they smile at each other. Maxwell hollers again. Mase jumps down, takes Kat's hand, and kisses it gallantly. "I shall return with your caffeine posthaste, milady."

"Dork," she laughs.

The moment he's gone, a group of girls swarms her.

"You and Mase?" Kendall asks.

"You two are *so cute* together!" Makayla gushes.

"Super cute. I got the best picture. Look!" Gemma

adds, holding out her phone. She's posted an Insta story of Kat and Mase kissing, with the words *new couple?* written above it.

Kat covers her face with both hands like she's embarrassed, but beneath her palms and her waterfall of red hair, she's smirking. This is all going *perfectly*. Even kids who aren't at the Penningtons' party will see.

"Out of the way, best friend coming through!" Pen elbows Gemma aside. She hops up on the tailgate and grabs Kat's arm. "Are you *drunk?*"

"What? No!" Kat makes a face. At the end of last summer, she convinced Gram that she was responsible enough to go to a farm party with Bea and Erik and that *of course* she wouldn't drink. But she and Pen proceeded to split several cheap strawberry wine coolers. They both got giggly, then spinny and sick, and then they threw up sour pink puddles in a cornfield. It was disgusting. Kat still owes Bea big-time for getting them home and in bed with water and Advil and not ratting them out to Gram. She has vowed never to drink again.

"Then why are you kissing Mase?" Pen says. "You don't even like Mase."

"I do too like him," Kat argues.

Pen raises one arched eyebrow. It is really annoying that she can do that and Kat can't. "Yesterday you were *irate* that he got the part instead of Adam."

"But then I stopped by the Tabby Cat Café to tell him the list was up, and we started talking, and…he's not so bad." Kat lets a sly smile spread across her lips. "He's a good kisser. Is my lipstick all smudged?"

"Your lipstick is *fine*. It's your judgment I'm worried about. This is total rebound behavior," Pen opines.

She's looking out for Kat, like always, and Kat wishes she could tell her the truth. But she and Mase promised each other that they wouldn't tell *anyone*. Kat had argued that they could totally trust Pen, but Mase was clear: if she told a single person, the deal was off. No exceptions. And she understands his concern. If word got out that they were only hooking up to make their exes jealous, they would both look pathetic.

"I thought you wanted me to get over Adam," Kat points out.

Pen glances over at Adam. "I mean, Mase is definitely an improvement, but…didn't he and Brandon just break up?"

"So?" Kat hears the snotty tone in her voice, but Pen isn't cowed by it.

"So, you're going to be in rehearsal together for the next month, and it's going to be super awkward for *everybody* if you wake up tomorrow morning and regret this," Pen says.

"Or it could be awesome." Kat smooths her royal-blue romper and then goes for the kill shot, looking at Pen with big sad eyes. "I thought you'd be happy for me."

"I am." Pen runs a hand over her buzz cut. "Of course I am, if this is what you really want. I just—"

"Hey." Mase jumps up on the other side of Kat and hands her a Diet Coke. "Am I interrupting?"

"Yes," Pen says.

"No." Kat leans against him. He smells nice. Like chocolate.

Pen sighs. "I'm going to make another s'more. Do you want one?"

"No, thanks. I already had two," Kat says. Because she knows that saying *no* will make Pen squinch up her brown eyes and look at her all concerned, the same way Des was looking at her earlier, like she was trying to calculate everything Kat's eaten in the last week.

Kat's been healthy for three years, but she still feels the pull of the disorder, still has to make herself eat on bad days. And she knows Pen and Des, especially, still worry. The weekend after she caught Adam and Jillian kissing, she stayed in her room and cried and refused to come out for meals. But she noticed how Des snuck extra avocado into her sandwiches and poured big puddles of chipotle ranch dressing next to her carrots. She knows Des was afraid it was the start of a relapse. And maybe Kat caught herself wondering whether Adam liked Jillian better because she has a tiny waist and a thigh gap. But logically, Kat knew not eating wasn't going to get Adam back. He would probably tell her to stop being so *dramatic* and have a damn cookie.

He is kind of an asshole like that.

As soon as Pen's out of earshot, Mase leans in to whisper with Kat. "I ran into Zachary and Josh, and they asked what was up with us." Zachary Harris is Brandon's best friend; Josh is Zachary's boyfriend.

"What did you tell them?" Kat whispers back.

"That we'll see what happens, but you're super cute and super fun."

"I am, aren't I?" Kat takes his hand again. His nails are painted a black. "What did they say?"

"I think they were kind of weirded out that you're a girl, honestly," Mase explains. "When I was dating Brandon, a lot of people assumed I was gay. But when I'm dating a girl, it's like my bi card gets revoked and people assume I'm actually straight."

"There's a card?" Kat teases, but it makes her wonder how Mase is feeling about their ruse. Not because she's a girl, necessarily, but because she's not Brandon. Two years is a long time to be with one person. It must be weird to kiss someone else. To hold her hand.

To be honest, she hasn't devoted a whole lot of thought to how this plan affects *him*.

"Zachary was texting someone when I walked away. I bet it was Brandon." Mase sounds less happy about it than Kat thought he would.

She glances over at the bonfire and sees Adam with

his tongue stuck down Jillian's throat. One of his arms is wrapped around her, his hand on her skinny ass; his other hand is holding a red cup Kat would bet is full of cheap beer. Ugh. She used to make him chew gum when he was drinking before he kissed her.

Obviously, his jealousy didn't last long. Maybe he wasn't jealous at all. Maybe he doesn't care whether she's over him.

Maybe he never really cared about her at all.

Kat lets go of Mase's hand. "Do you still want to do this?" she asks, suddenly unsure. Is lying to everybody, including her best friend, worth it? Is Adam worth *any* of this?

"Yeah. Definitely," Mase says. But she doesn't know him well enough to tell what he's thinking. He doesn't take her hand again, and he doesn't sound so sure anymore either.

CHAPTER TWELVE

VI

Parties are stupid.

This is the first real party Vi has ever been to, but she feels pretty confident in her assessment. Dozens of people—most of them from Kat and Bea and Des's classes—are clustered around the bonfire; dozens more are tailgating nearby. Country music blasts from the jacked-up speakers of a black pickup parked next to the fire. A keg sits on the ground behind it; coolers of sodas and s'mores fixings rest on the gate. People mill around, laughing and dancing and drinking. Even though they're on a farm in the middle of nowhere, it's loud and smoky and feels too crowded. There's no sign of Cece yet, and only a handful of Vi's classmates are here. Kat ditched

Vi shortly after they arrived to hang out with the theater kids.

Even though Vi's hovering at the back of the crowd, someone still manages to bump into her. Ugh. *Personal space, people.*

"Sorry," a guy says. Vi turns to find Chas Carter leering at her. "Hey, aren't you Bea's sister?"

She nods. Chas was in Bea's class. A baseball player. He's blatantly checking out her long, freckly legs in her short dinosaur-print dress, and Vi can feel herself making a grossed-out expression.

"Want a beer?" he asks.

"No thanks." She starts to move away, but he puts a hand on her arm.

"Want to hang out? We could take a walk."

Vi steps back, annoyed. "No thanks."

"You sure?" he presses. "You don't look like you're having any fun."

"Chas, get the hell away from her," Emily snaps, suddenly at Vi's side. Em is Des's best friend—or maybe former best friend. Vi isn't sure what's going on with them. "She's fifteen, you creep."

"All right, all right." Chas disappears back into the crowd.

"Vi, what are you doing? Where are your sisters? Aren't you too young for farm parties?"

"Kat came last summer, and I'm not even drinking," Vi points out.

Em is wearing spectacular pink and purple and teal eye shadow that makes her look like a high-fashion model or an alien. A pretty alien. But still. "Seriously, where are your sisters? They should be watching out for you."

"I can take care of myself," Vi says, but she turns in a slow circle, scanning the crowd for redheads. *Well*, that's *interesting*. "Kat's over there. Kissing your brother."

"My—Mase?" Em stands on her tiptoes and peers over the crowd. "Oh wow. What's up with that?"

"I have no idea. I thought Kat was still pining over Adam. There's Des. Heading down to the river with Paige and Dylan." Vi scowls. "I told Paige not to smoke cigarettes around Des. She has asthma!"

"That's not a cigarette, sweetie," Em says. "What's the deal with Paige, anyhow? Is she Des's new best friend or what?"

"She's Miss Lydia's granddaughter," Vi explains. "She's an art student from Baltimore, and she's in town for the summer waitressing at Tia Julia's. That's all I know. Maybe you should ask Des."

Em takes a long sip from her red cup. "Des and I aren't speaking."

"Well, I'm not getting in the middle of it," Vi says. "Thanks for looking out for me, but I'm fine. I'm going to go get a Coke."

"Just Coke!" Em calls after her.

Vi rolls her eyes. She has no intention of drinking. She winds her way through the crowd and grabs a Coke from the cooler. She still doesn't spot Cece anywhere. It's been almost an hour. How long will Des want to stay? Since when does Des even like parties? And where did Bea go?

Vi texts Des that she's going to look for the horses. She did put some baby carrots in her bag, despite Kat's objections.

The old farmhouse is a white blur in the distance, with a big red barn and a tall grain silo on the far side. Vi heads in that direction. The farther she goes, the quieter it gets, till it's just crickets chirping and the wind rustling the cornstalks and her flats crunching against the gravel drive-way. She uses the flashlight on her phone to light her way. Above her, the moon is a waning crescent, and stars glitter in the dark sky.

Vi can hear the horses whickering to each other before she sees them. As she gets closer to the paddock, she sees two brown horses with spotted white hindquarters and another smaller one that looks like the horse version of a Dalmatian.

She hangs over the wooden fence. "Hi," she calls. "Hey, horses. Hi."

Footsteps crunch on the gravel behind her, and Vi spins around, her heart hammering, clutching her phone. *Please let it not be creepy Chas. Please let him not have followed me.*

"It's just me," a girl's soft voice calls. "Sorry if I scared you."

Vi's heart races for entirely different reasons. "Cece! Hi!"

"I saw you walking away right as we got here. I thought you might be coming to see these guys." Cece points to the two brown horses. "That's Storm, and that's Gambit. The black-and-white one is Rogue. Dylan named them when he was really into *The X-Men*."

Vi turns off her flashlight and pulls out the Ziploc bag of carrots. "Are we allowed to feed them?"

Cece pulls an identical bag from the pocket of her pink minidress, and they both laugh. Vi thinks her sometimes-Grinchy heart grows three sizes. She and Cece have so much in common; they are clearly destined to be together!

"I came to the party last week with Ben, but from our class was here. It was kind of boring. So I came and talked to the horses before Dylan put them in for the night. Spencer said it's okay to give them carrots," Cece explains, leaning over the wooden fence, clicking her tongue. "Hey, Rogue." The horse's ears perk up. "Aw, you know your name, don't you? You want a carrot? Come here, girl."

Cece came to the party with Ben, but she was bored? *Interesting.* Vi tries not to read too much into that. She glances over at Cece, but it's so dark, she can't read her expression.

"He seems nice," she says. "Ben, I mean."

Rogue trots over, her dark tail twitching back and forth.

Cece stretches out her hand. Rogue takes the baby carrot and chomps it in her giant teeth.

"Gambit! Storm! You gonna let Rogue get all the carrots?" The other horses look up from grazing and plod over. Cece looks at Vi. "You want to feed them? They're really gentle."

Vi steps up to the fence and stretches out her hand. "Hey, Gambit." The horse's mouth tickles her palm, but he doesn't nip her. Tentatively, Vi pets his soft brown nose. Rogue and Storm nudge each other, competing for carrots from Cece.

"Ben is great. He's my best friend," Cece says.

"You guys have been dating for a while, right?" Vi asks.

"Hey, girl. You remember me?" Cece coos as she feeds Storm. She's quiet for a minute. "Actually, we're not dating anymore. We broke up a couple weeks ago. We're still best friends, though."

"Oh." Vi wants to ask why they broke up, if Cece's still in love with him, if Cece was *ever* in love with him, but that is completely none of her business.

"Yeah. He lives right down the street, and our parents are friends, so we grew up together. Then, you know, for a while it's weird to be friends with boys because they have cooties." Cece laughs. "Last year, he was having trouble in English, so I tutored him, and we became friends again. We started eating lunch together and walking home together when he didn't have soccer, and people assumed we were *together* together. And then it was like, why not? It's what everybody expects. Our parents were really excited about it."

That doesn't exactly sound like a passionate romance to Vi. "Were *you* excited?" she asks, then grimaces. "I'm sorry. That's none of my business!"

"It's okay." Cece doesn't look at Vi. "That's a good question, actually. I was. I thought I was. For a while, anyhow." She pets Rogue's dappled nose. "I should have been, right? He's the cute boy down the block. He's super nice, he treated me well, and my parents loved him. It was like something out of a romance novel."

Except the boy-next-door story isn't the kind of romance Cece reads.

"I love him, but we're better off as friends," Cece continues, her voice a little firmer. Her curtain of wavy dark hair falls across her face, so Vi can't see her profile anymore. "Breaking up was a mutual decision."

Vi wonders if that's really true. How could anyone in the whole world be around Cece and *not* feel sparks? She's gorgeous, she's kind, she loves animals and books and—

Vi wants to reach out and tuck Cece's hair behind the soft brown seashell of her ear. She wants to be able to see her face, to read something true in her dark eyes and in the way her pink mouth shapes her words. They are standing so close, their elbows are almost touching. The horses are crunching carrots and nudging their noses against the girls, and the crickets are singing love songs in the trees. It smells like horse and murky river water and Cece's cherry lip gloss. It feels as close to a perfect moment as Vi might ever get.

"I haven't told my parents we broke up yet. Please don't say anything to anybody, okay?" Cece lets out a sad little chuckle. "That must seem silly to you."

"No, it doesn't. Why would you say that?" Vi asks.

"You're so confident." Cece turns to face her, leaning her shoulder against the wooden fence, and Vi has to work to keep herself from gasping. Confident? She feels like the most awkward girl in the world *at least* seventy-five percent of the time. "You sit by yourself at lunch and read, and you wear feminist T-shirts and Pride T-shirts and that dress—I love that dress, by the way—and you speak up in class even if you disagree with the teacher. You don't care what anybody thinks of you."

I care what you *think.*

Vi doesn't say that. "I do care," she explains. "But I've always been the weird kid. The one who didn't talk for almost a whole year back in kindergarten. The one who saw her parents die. After that—I mean, yeah, on some level, who cares if somebody calls me a geek or a loser or… or a dyke?"

Cece's hand balls into a fist against the fence. "Who called you that?"

Vi doesn't have to ask which slur Cece means. "Liam. He asked me out in seventh grade, and I said no. Nobody knew that I was gay—*I* didn't even know for sure—he said it 'cause he was embarrassed I wouldn't go out with him. But it felt like he slapped me right across the face."

Cece winces. "Vi—"

"It's okay," Vi interrupts, because she doesn't want Cece to look at her like that. Like she's scared that if she *is* bi or pan or whatever, she might face the same kind of slurs someday. "I mean, it's not okay as in acceptable. Liam's a dick. But most people are pretty cool. I've got my sisters, I've got Gram, and they're all super supportive."

"You're lucky. My parents," Cece begins, and then she hesitates. Maybe she's wondering if it's okay to criticize her parents to a girl whose mom and dad are dead. Vi nods encouragingly, and Cece continues. "I love my parents, but...they're very conservative in some ways. Not politically, but when it comes to gender norms, they're very old-fashioned still. Mami is *brilliant*, you know? She's incredible at math. She's been doing the accounting for Tia Julia's for years, and now that Abuela Julia's getting older, Mami basically runs the restaurant. But I'm her only daughter, and she treats me so different from my brothers. She was *appalled* when I started tutoring Ben. She thinks boys don't like girls who are smarter than them."

"That's ridiculous!" Vi says. "Why do you think she feels that way?"

That was one of Vi's therapist's favorite questions.

"She had kind of a hard life before she met my dad." Cece goes back to petting Rogue. "Her parents were first-generation immigrants, and they had to work really hard for everything. Her dad left her mom and got remarried and had a whole other family. Money was tight. Abuela Maria worked super long hours, so my mom practically raised her little brothers. I think she feels like she married up, you know? A family that was more established here, that had their own business instead of cleaning houses for other people. I mean, it's not like she married my dad for money or anything. They're in love. But I've never heard him compliment her on how smart she is. It's always how pretty she looks. And he's the same way with me."

"But you get straight As!" Vi says, outraged. Cece's always on the honor roll.

"Yeah." Cece gives her a gorgeous, dimpled grin. "I do."

They've both run out of carrots. They pet the horses in silence for another minute or two, and then, one by one, the horses wander away.

Cece turns to face Vi. "You're a good listener."

"You're interesting." Vi drops her eyes to the fence, tracing the top rail with one fingertip. "I mean...no problem."

Cece laughs. "I guess I don't think of myself as very interesting."

"I don't think of myself as confident," Vi confesses. "Mostly I feel awkward, like I was raised by wolves and don't know how to interact properly with other humans. I guess I'm a feral bookstore child." Cece's looking at her—really *looking* at her—and she can't seem to stop talking. "I'm more comfortable with books than with people."

"Me too. I just fake it really well." Cece is still looking at her, and Vi knows she is blushing. "I feel like maybe too much of my life is faking things lately."

Vi wants to tell Cece that she can change that, but she knows it's easier said than done. Instead, she reaches out and touches Cece's arm. Cece's skin is soft and warm against her fingertips. Then Vi lets her hand fall to her side. "I'm here any time you want to talk."

"Thank you. That means a lot." They look at each other for a minute, and Vi has to force herself not to hold her breath. Her heart is racing. Then Cece's phone buzzes, and she pulls it out of her pocket. "It's Ben. I should probably go back to the party. You want to walk back with me?"

Vi looks over at the horses and up at the stars. "No," she says. She needs some time to think about everything that's happened. "I think I'll stay here a little bit longer."

CHAPTER THIRTEEN
DES

On Tuesday afternoon, Gram stops by Arden after physical therapy.

"Hi, honey. How are things going?" Gram's using a cane now instead of her walker, but her mouth always looks a little pinched after physical therapy, despite her toothy smile and signature red lipstick.

"Slow." Des sighs. There have hardly been any customers since she opened the store at ten. Outside, their neighbors scurry past with umbrellas, eager to escape the rain. "How was physical therapy?"

"All right." Gram makes her way behind the counter, takes off her rain-speckled glasses, and wipes them on her long gray tunic. "Honey, there's something I want to talk to you about."

Des's stomach twists. "Is everything okay?" This is how Gram started the conversation last month about her power of attorney and end-of-life care. They also discussed her will, the money she's set aside for each of the girls, and her funeral wishes. It was *awful*. Des hopes they won't have to revisit it for another twenty years at least.

"I hope so. Don't look at me like that; I'm fine." Gram runs a hand over her straight, shoulder-length gray hair. "You know we had our girls' night last night."

Des nods. Gram's "girls" are the sixty- and seventy-year-old town matriarchs, grandmothers, and savvy businesswomen who run some of Remington Hollow's most successful shops and restaurants. They get together every Monday night when Tia Julia's is closed to drink sangria and play cards and gossip.

"I don't like to tell tales out of school," Gram starts. Which is a bit of a stretch. Des is nosy, and she knows exactly who she gets it from. "I don't know if I should say anything at all."

"Now you've got me curious, so you have to." Des suspects that is exactly what Gram intended.

Gram's blue eyes brighten behind her glasses, and she settles back into the sturdy, flowered armchair beside the counter. "Lydia said her granddaughter went out to the Penningtons' with you on Saturday night," she begins.

Uh-oh.

"She did." Des scoots past Gram, out from behind the counter and over to the racks of board books. She's been worried that this conversation was coming. That Gram would find out she smoked weed with Paige and give her a lecture. Kat and Vi aren't stupid. They must have wondered why Des let Kat drive home. Or why her hair reeked of smoke. Or why she and Paige were so giggly in the back seat. Des is not the giggly type.

Would one of her sisters actually *tattle*, though? Without talking to her first? She scans her memory for recent offenses, but she can't think of any reason they'd want to get her in trouble.

Des frowns. Why is she freaking out about this? She is technically, legally, an adult. Gram trusts her to run the bookstore, to hold her power of attorney, to take care of Kat and Vi if something terrible happens. Why is Des still scared of getting in trouble, like she's still in high school?

"I think I'm going to reorganize the board books. They're a mess," she announces. Toddlers are always pulling them out and throwing them on the floor, and their harried parents don't put the books back in the right section.

"*You* want to reorganize?" Gram laughs. "You're good at a lot of things, Des, but organization isn't one of them. What are you avoiding?"

"Nothing!" Des yanks books off the rack. She has a bad habit of losing interest halfway through organizational projects and convincing Bea or Vi to finish them. But she needs something to do with her hands right now. "What were you saying about Paige?"

Gram hesitates. "Lydia is worried. I don't know what Paige has told you about why she's in town this summer…"

"Not much," Des admits. Only that it wasn't her decision. But Paige is twenty-one, which is pretty old to be shipped off to spend the summer with her grandma. The more Des thinks about it, the stranger it seems that—as a senior in college—Paige is waitressing at Tia Julia's and not doing an internship at some fancy art gallery in Baltimore. Does she need the money?

"Her poor mother is at her wits' end with that girl," Gram explains.

"Why?" Des settles cross-legged on the alphabet rug. She doesn't like the way Gram says *that girl*, as though Paige is bad or broken. "We haven't spent much time together, but I like Paige."

Gram gives her a sharp look. "I want you to be careful around her, Des. Maybe she seems glamorous to you. Free-spirited. Bohemian. But she isn't the kind of girl I want you emulating."

"What kind of girl? What is that supposed to mean?" Des asks, irritated, as she stacks the books by subject: one pile about trucks, one pile about animals, one pile about bedtime, ones for learning colors and numbers and ABCs.

"It means she's made some bad choices," Gram says bluntly. "Drugs. Stealing from her mother. I know you and Em have grown apart . Maybe you're looking to make a new friend. I'm not doubting your judgment, honey, but…" She trails off.

"Okaaay," Des says, but it feels like Gram is doing exactly that. Like she's one step away from saying she doesn't want Des to hang out with Paige anymore. Which would be *ridiculous.* So Paige smokes weed sometimes. Gram went to all kinds of protest marches back in the sixties. She's probably smoked weed herself. And stealing isn't okay, but whatever problems Paige and her mother have, Gram's only heard one side of the story. "I'm a little old for you to pick out my friends, aren't I?"

Gram purses her red lips. "You are. Is that your way of telling me to mind my own beeswax?"

"It's my way of telling you that you don't have to worry," Des says. She's never really lied to Gram before. Never had to. But she can choose her own friends, and she doesn't plan to stop hanging out with Paige.

"That's what I thought. You're never any trouble," Gram says.

Somehow, that irks Des. She's nineteen. Isn't she supposed to be a little bit of trouble? Isn't she supposed to have a wild, rebellious stage where she gets a tattoo or stays out all night or sleeps with a boy who breaks her heart? Isn't she supposed to do *something* her seventy-year-old grandmother would disapprove of? She doesn't have any interest in sleeping with anybody, and she's usually in bed with a book by eleven o'clock. But maybe…maybe it's time for a physical change. Something to signify that she's not the same girl she was a year ago. Like how Em cut her waist-length hair into a *lob*.

Des twirls an auburn curl around her finger. She saw the way people looked at Paige on Saturday night. They saw her purple hair and her septum ring and her tattoos, and they made certain assumptions. They looked at her like she was somebody they didn't want to mess with.

Nobody ever looks at Des like that.

Des is never any trouble.

She doesn't want to worry Gram. But maybe Em had a point. Maybe she could stand to be a little more *nineteen* sometimes. To step out of her small, safe comfort zone and her rigid routine. As she starts to reshelve the books, Des feels an unfamiliar restlessness sweep over her. She wants to *do* something. Something different. *Be* someone different.

What would it be like to change her hair? It's been long and red and curly since she was little. She remembers Mom braiding it for her first day of first grade. If she dyed it, everyone would notice. Being a redhead is just part of being a Garrett girl, like having freckles and working in the bookstore.

Maybe it would be nice to do something that set her apart for once.

She thinks of how *surprised* Em looked on Saturday night, when she saw her laughing and dancing with Paige.

Des had liked that. Being surprising.

Em would never expect her to dye her hair.

"I'm going to take my break," she says suddenly.

"Now?" Gram looks at the stacks of board books strewn across the bright alphabet carpet. Des isn't even halfway through reshelving them. "The books are all over the floor, honey."

"I'll be right back," Des promises.

Gram looks like she wants to object, but she doesn't. Des has been working ten-hour days, without complaint, for the last month. It's a struggle for Gram to go up the steep staircase to the second-floor stockroom and office; she climbs the stairs at home slowly and arduously with her cane and with Des hovering anxiously behind her.

"Five minutes, okay?" Des flies out the front door, down the sidewalk, and into Tia Julia's before she can change her mind. She spots Paige behind the bar cutting limes.

"Hey, Desdemona!" Paige says.

"I want to dye my hair blue. Can you help?"

Paige grins. "Hell yes, I can."

"Planning a murder?"

Des looks up, startled, to find her high school classmate

Savannah Lockwood peering down at her with enormous cornflower-blue eyes. "Excuse me?" Des says.

"I'm joking." Savannah nods at the elbow-length rubber gloves and the bottle of bleach in Des's arms.

"Oh. I'm dyeing my hair," Des explains. Of course there's a line at Carl's Pharmacy tonight, and of course the town bigmouth, Savannah Lockwood, has to be here. Des should have driven over to the CVS.

"Ooh, what color?" Savannah leans into Des's personal space. "My readers will want to know."

Des takes a step back. "You honestly think your readers will care that I'm dyeing my hair blue?"

"A Garrett girl without red hair? That's positively shocking, by Remington Hollow standards," Savannah drawls. "What prompted the change? Can I quote you?"

"No," Des says.

Savannah huffs. "There are no secrets in Remington Hollow, you know. Not for long."

"That's creepy," Des says, leaning back against the rack of magazines. "Seriously, isn't nepotism still a thing in journalism? Couldn't your dad give you a real assignment?"

Savannah flips her shiny dark curls over her shoulder. "The blog is helping to establish the *Gazette*'s online presence for a millennial audience. I wouldn't expect you to understand, working *retail*."

Des smiles. "I actually know a lot about journalism from

Bea. I'm sure you've heard about the new feature she scored, writing about women-owned businesses in Remington Hollow? Interviewing a different proprietor every week? Your dad has been so impressed with her work. We're all *super* proud."

Savannah's eyes narrow. She *hates* Bea. As a senior, Savannah assumed she would be named editor of the school paper—not because she showed any real talent for it, but because her father is editor of the *Remington Hollow Gazette* and she thought it was somehow her due. She was furious when Bea, a junior, got the position instead. Last summer, Savannah interned at the *Gazette* and—to hear Bea tell it—mostly fetched coffee and flirted with the sports reporter. This summer, she's pressured her dad into letting her write an *About Town* blog, which is a thinly veiled gossip column.

"Yes, Daddy's so impressed with Bea. Editor of the school paper. Copyeditor for the yearbook. Valedictorian. Georgetown. That handsome boyfriend too." Savannah taps one pointy mint-green nail against her dimpled chin. "It must be hard for the rest of you, having such a *perfect* sister."

Des blinks. She isn't sure where Savannah's going with this, but Des certainly isn't going to give her anything quotable. "Like I said, we're very proud."

"But how can any of you compete? I mean, look at *you*. I don't blame you for deciding not to even try. Not everyone's cut out for college," Savannah says, so condescending that Des has to resist the urge to slap the smile off her face.

"Well, you know, with my *dead parents* and all, I felt some obligation to stay home and help Gram with my sisters and the bookstore," Des says through her gritted teeth. It's rare that she plays that card, but Savannah deserves it. "Also, I happen to love working at Arden. A bookstore is such a vital part of a community, don't you think? It's important to me—to all of us—that we're fulfilling my mom's legacy."

"I'm sure it is. You poor things," Savannah coos.

Des's fists clench around the rubber gloves. Planning a murder is starting to sound awfully appealing.

The door opens, and a tall, scruffy guy with dark-blond hair caught up in a bun walks over to the old-fashioned soda fountain. Des has never seen him before, but Savannah's face lights up.

"Excuse me, my *date* is here," she says, hurrying in his direction right as the line finally moves forward.

Des sets her gloves and bleach on the counter. *Poor guy,* she thinks. *He has no idea what he's gotten himself into.*

CHAPTER FOURTEEN

BEA

When Bea stumbles bleary-eyed into the bathroom on Wednesday morning, the first thing she notices is blue. Watery blue spots polka-dot the white-tiled floor. The towel crumpled in the corner is stained blue. Bea yanks the shower curtain back and finds blue streaks all over the tub. It looks like somebody murdered a damn Smurf in there.

It is too early to deal with this. She brushes her teeth and then marches downstairs to the kitchen. "Des? I think maybe Kat dyed her hair. Have you—?"

She stops short in the doorway. Her older sister is sitting at the kitchen counter, eating her bowl of Cheerios, drinking a mug of tea, with her planner and Tombow pens in front of her and NPR on the radio, exactly as expected at eight-thirty on a weekday. Totally, completely *unexpected*? Des's hair is bright blue.

"Jesus Christ," Bea gasps. "What did you do to your hair?"

Des pulls back some of her curls, revealing more blue beneath. "Do you like it?"

"I—" Bea swallows. "I don't know yet."

"I like it." Des smiles shyly. "I really like it."

"Good. It's probably going to take a while to wash out." Bea grabs the last browning banana on the counter and starts to peel it, still staring at her sister.

Des chuckles. "You thought it was Kat!"

"I definitely didn't think it was *you*." Dyeing her hair on a whim isn't like Des, but the blue suits her.

Des shrugs. "Paige helped me dye it last night."

Of course. Des has a total new-friend crush on the purple-haired waitress over at Tia Julia's. Half of her sentences lately have started with *Paige says*. Frankly, Bea finds Paige more than a little pretentious, but she's hoping Paige will give Des a sense of direction. Not that being a bookseller isn't amazing. Bea loves books, especially nonfiction (and, secretly, the occasional hot Regency romance). But Des has real artistic talent. After she drew an illustrated Tom Stoppard quote for Bea's graduation gift, Bea told her she should start her own shop on Etsy or Society6. Des totally blew off the suggestion. Maybe if *Paige* tells her, she'll consider it.

"You were out late," Bea says. That's new too; usually Des is in bed with a book by eleven. "Even I was asleep, and I haven't been sleeping much."

She regrets the words as soon as they're out of her mouth. She doesn't want to draw attention to her late-night stress baking, although the banana bread on the counter is a bit of a giveaway. Maybe she'll take it to work. Is trying to bribe one's boss with baked goods against the rules? *It can't be any more against the rules than nepotism,* she thinks, glaring at the very idea of Savannah Lockwood and her stupid blog. Gossip is *not* real journalism.

"Is everything okay?" Des asks.

No. For a minute, Bea thinks about confiding in her sister. *I almost kissed another boy on Saturday night. And when I said I wasn't feeling well, what I meant was that the idea of going to Georgetown with Erik makes me want to throw up.*

"Bea?" Des prompts, her brown eyes worried.

Bea focuses intently on her banana. Des is already doing so much. *Too* much. Bea knows she should be helping out more at home and at Arden instead of spending hours down at the marina, staring into the river. But being around her family is hard. It feels like she's lying to them every second she doesn't confess her growing doubts about the future.

What if she did confess? If she said the words *I'm not sure I want to go to Georgetown anymore* out loud? They would freak out. Gram has sacrificed so much for her. She paid for

Bea to go to journalism camp four summers in a row, and that was not cheap. She's delving into her savings so Bea doesn't have to take out too many loans for tuition. She has read every single one of Bea's papers and articles. And Des—Des has taken Bea's shifts at Arden and her chores at home, uncomplaining, so that Bea could focus on school. Des would have every right to be furious that she's sacrificed all of that for *nothing*.

Bea feels like the worst, most selfish girl in the world.

"I'm fine, but the bathroom is a mess. Are you supposed to wash your hair this soon? You should Google that," Bea says. "It looks like a Smurf homicide in there."

Des's shoulders go stiff. "Sorry. I'll clean it up later."

"I've got to get ready for work," Bea says, and she rushes back upstairs.

At the newspaper, Bea delivers the banana bread to her editor, who compliments her on her baking *and* on the article she wrote last week about Mrs. Ellinghaus, the owner of Remington Hollow's flower shop, In Bloom. They review Bea's assignments for the next week: in addition to her usual proofreading, she'll be interviewing Mrs. Lynde about her yarn shop, Unraveled; writing a book review of a new memoir; and doing a movie review of the latest Marvel blockbuster. She and Erik are supposed to see it tonight.

Her iced coffee lurches in her stomach. Erik will want to hold her hand during the movie. He always wants to hold her hand. She used to love that, but now it seems so clingy. She's hardly seen him since he got back from camping with his dad, but the thought of their date tonight makes her feel panicky and cornered. She used to miss him when he went away for the weekend; they'd text and send each other silly pictures and talk on the phone before bed. This time, she was relieved he didn't have cell service. She made excuses not to meet up when he got home Monday night. They had a quick coffee date yesterday after the group meeting for this year's Tea Party raft, but then she lied about having to run back to the office.

Erik is going to catch on soon that something's wrong. Gabe was right; she has a terrible poker face.

Why is she thinking about Gabe? She has to stop thinking about Gabe.

She sets her coffee on her desk and pulls out her to-do list.

"Hey, Bea! Did you hear the news?" a familiar voice chirps.

Bea looks up to find Savannah leaning against the cubicle wall. She's wearing a black miniskirt, pink blouse, and black crocodile heels. Her lipstick perfectly matches her blouse, and fake lashes emphasize her already enormous eyes. Bea is suddenly very conscious of her still-wet hair and the wrinkled yellow cardigan she snatched out of her laundry basket.

"What news?" she asks.

"Alison is having a girl! She found out the gender this morning at her ob-gyn appointment!" Savannah squees. Alison is the *Gazette* copyeditor.

"She found out the sex," Bea corrects. She debates and dismisses giving Savannah a lecture on the difference between biological sex and gender identity.

"It's one of my blind items, but I think people will figure it out pretty fast," Savannah says. "Also, a certain member of a notoriously redheaded family was spotted buying bleach and gloves to dye her hair yesterday. I heard she was going *blue*! Can you confirm?"

Bea pastes a smile on her face. This is not the kind of journalism Savannah should be proud of, but fine. Whatever. "Yep. Des dyed her hair blue!" She takes a long sip from her iced coffee, hoping Savannah will go away. She doesn't understand why Savannah pretends to be all chummy. It's so fake. Bea knows it's fake. Savannah has hated her for at least two years, since Bea was appointed editor of the school paper. Savannah tried to convince Bea to *give* it to her, since she was going to be a senior. Needless to say, Bea did not.

"That's a long list."

Bea covers her to-do list with one hand. Savannah was totally reading it over her shoulder. What a snoop.

"So you're going out with Erik tonight?" Savannah asks. "I was wondering if maybe there was trouble in paradise."

"No. What? No. Why would you say that?"

Savannah props her hip against the corner of Bea's desk. Bea already regrets that she asked. What does Savannah know?

There's nothing to know, she reminds herself. Not unless Savannah's a mind reader.

"I met the cutest guy the other day at the Daily Grind. Turns out he's old Miss Amelia's grandson, Gabe." Her cornflower-blue eyes are trained on Bea, hawklike, and Bea tries to keep her face carefully blank. Where is Savannah going with this? "I vaguely remember him coming to visit when we were kids, but he has grown up really well. Like, really, *really* well. I thought we hit it off, so I invited him to the farm party last weekend. I thought he stood me up. But when I ran into him yesterday, he said he left early. Because he was giving a *friend* a ride."

For a minute, Bea panics. *Savannah knows. She's going to tell everybody.*

She forces herself to breathe evenly. She cannot have an anxiety attack right now. All she and Gabe did was play Canasta and drink tea. Okay, he drank whiskey. But there's nothing scandalous in that.

Except that she never mentioned it to Erik.

Savannah is still staring with her big, curious, anime eyes.

"That would be me," Bea says cheerily. "Sorry. I wasn't felling well, and Gabe offered me a ride home. He didn't say he was on a date."

In fact, he specifically said he *wasn't* on one. She bites back a smile.

Savannah drums her nails on the desk. The sound grates on Bea's nerves. "Where was Erik?"

"Camping with his dad. Last time I checked, I'm still allowed to talk to other guys." It doesn't make sense to get all worked up about this; Savannah is pushing her buttons. But she seems to have this creepy, unerring sense of exactly *which* button to push.

"Sure. As long as you're just *talking*. I call dibs on Gabe." Savannah gives her a sharky smile. How many teeth does she *have*? "Hands off, okay?"

"He's a *person*. You can't call dibs. It's not like riding shotgun." Bea knows she should let it go. But the second Savannah says *hands off*, all she can think of is Gabe's hands *on* her. Holding her steady as the boat rocked beneath them.

She wanted him to kiss her.

Does that make her a terrible person?

"But you and Gabe are just friends. You've already got a boyfriend," Savannah reminds her.

She's like a damn bloodhound. Bea forces a laugh. "Obviously."

"Obviously," Savannah echoes, but she sounds skeptical. "Have fun tonight. Maybe I'll see if Gabe wants to catch a movie too." She gives Bea a sly smile and saunters off.

Bea props her chin on her hand and stares into space. She and Gabe talked a lot while they played Canasta, not all of it trash talk. She told him about her sisters and Gram. He told her his mom and dad got divorced when he was five and he wasn't in touch with his dad anymore. How his moms adopted Lyric from foster care as a baby. How excited he was to be the best man when his moms were allowed to get legally married in Tennessee.

Bea should have told him she had a boyfriend.

Except, when she was with him, she didn't *want* to have a boyfriend. It was such a nice evening. The nicest. She felt more serene than she'd felt in ages. The only thing she worried about was whether Gabe had those last three kings in his hand.

She frowns down at her to-do list. She and Erik need to talk. Whatever is going on with Gabe is making that super clear. Erik has to know something's wrong. Maybe he doesn't want to see it. But she's been so distant. They haven't had sex in months. She's made up dozens of different excuses to cut their dates short or cancel and avoid him altogether.

She tries to picture herself saying the words. In her imagination, they are sitting in his car outside her house.

We need to talk, she'll say. *I'm so sorry. You haven't done anything wrong. You are amazing. I will always love you, but I'm not in love with you anymore, and we need to break up.* She has written it out twenty times in her notebook, trying to find the perfect words, words that won't hurt as much. She has memorized it. But when they're together, she can't seem to bring herself to say any of it.

She keeps coming up with excuses. Not at the coffee shop—it's too public. Not at her house—there's never any privacy. Not at his house—she can't face his mom and dad and his little sisters afterward. She's known his sisters since they were in *kindergarten*. His parents struggled to have another kid after Erik, and then they did IVF and had the twins when he was eight. Erik adores them. He's a good big brother.

He's been a good boyfriend too. He is clever and ambitious and kind. He was her first love. Her first everything. He's been endlessly supportive, no matter how competitive and bitchy she gets about Chloe or Savannah or anyone else. He never complained when she wanted to study instead of make out or when she canceled a date to work late on the newspaper. He planned and plotted right alongside her. She honestly can't remember whose idea it was to go to Georgetown. It was *theirs*.

How can she go without him?

She isn't sure she can. She isn't sure she wants to.

But she has to tell him the truth. She owes him that much.

Tonight, she decides. After the movie. She'll tell him tonight.

CHAPTER FIFTEEN
KAT

Wednesday night is the first rehearsal for *Little Women.*

Kat is super nervous, which is *absurd*. She doesn't get stage fright. She *never* gets stage fright. Not for her ballet recitals as a kid. Not during four years of fall plays and spring musicals or last year's Theater I class productions. And this is just a read-through of the script! She knows she can rock this part. She's not worried about her acting. No, she is suddenly, stupidly self-conscious about *merely existing* in front of Adam and Jillian.

Last night, she had a nightmare about being onstage, playing Jo, while the two of them critiqued her from the audience. It was awful. She woke up feeling panicky and insecure, and the feeling has stayed with her all day. She knows they won't mock her *during* rehearsal—Ms. Randall would put a stop to that—but what if they make fun of her later? It's not like it's beyond the realm of possibility. Adam's done it before.

Sophomore year, after weeks of Adam flirting with Kat during *Into the Woods* rehearsals, his girlfriend Bailey broke up with him. And then he made fun of her incessantly, whenever the director wasn't paying attention. When Bailey didn't hit one of her high notes, when she tripped during a dance, when she ruined her costume brushing up against wet paint on a forest backdrop—Adam pointed it out. He said he was just kidding and she needed to lighten up. But it made Bailey so nervous that she made even more mistakes. Once, after a curtain call, Kat saw her crying alone backstage.

And Kat never spoke up. Never once told Adam to knock it off. His petty behavior actually made her feel good, confirmed that she was the one he wanted to be with. She was excited that a gorgeous, talented upperclassman— the one playing Prince Charming himself—had chosen *her*. So she enabled him and laughed it off when he was an asshole.

She never thought she would be in Bailey's position.

Now that she is, Kat knows she cannot trust Adam to be kind. What if he embarrasses her? Undermines her in front of the whole cast *and* Ms. Randall? Kat wants this to be the first of many community theater productions she stars in. Impressing Ms. Randall is key.

"Kat!" Bea hammers on the bathroom door. It is ridiculous that they only have one bathroom to share among five women.

Kat throws the door open. "What?" she demands, eyeliner pencil in hand.

"Do your makeup in your room. I need to pee," Bea says.

Kat steps into the hall. "The lighting's better in the bathroom."

"You look gorgeous. Just let me pee. Please." Bea pushes past her and shuts the door.

Kat finishes her makeup and then wanders downstairs to the living room. Erik is watching CNN while he waits for Bea. "Hey, Kat."

"Hey, Erik." She looks in the mirror over the couch and tugs on one errant red curl. Should she have flat-ironed her hair? Would that make her look more professional?

Erik mutes the TV. "I heard you have a new job."

"I do." Monday morning, Kat went to the Tabby Cat Café and filled out an application. Then this morning, Miss Lydia called and offered her the job. Kat had to check with Gram before she accepted, but of course Des was at Arden when she went to ask Gram. And Des was now pissed that Kat wanted to work somewhere else.

"She only wants to work at the café so she can keep an

eye on Mase," Des said brattily. The blue hair seemed to have given her some new, entirely unwelcome sass.

Gram raised her feathery eyebrows. "Mason Kim?"

"They were making out at the farm party," Des tattled.

Kat leaned over the counter and swatted her sister on the shoulder. "We were not making out! We kissed. That's all. Mase is really funny and sweet and—"

"Opposites attract, I guess," Des muttered.

"Des," Gram chided. She was sitting in her armchair, her knee propped up on the footstool, her laptop on her thighs. "So *that's* why you want to work for Lydia?"

"No. Well. Maybe," Kat confessed. "I also want to help more cats get adopted. Mase said the adoption numbers are down because people haven't been coming to the café as much. I really think I can help Miss Lydia. You don't want the cats to be *killed*, do you? It's not like *we* can adopt one." Kat glared at Des. "Since *someone* has allergies."

"All right, all right, you two," Gram said, tucking her shoulder-length gray hair behind her ear.

"Please?" Kat knelt at Gram's feet, her hands clasped together. "Pretty, pretty please?"

Gram chuckled. "Are you sure this is what you want? Lydia doesn't suffer fools, Kat. She'll expect you to show up on time and work hard. No quitting if she asks you to clean out the litter box or something you think is beneath you. No calling in sick if you and Mason get into a fight."

"Of course!" Kat felt injured by Gram's implication that she was a diva.

Gram pushed her glasses up her nose. "All right. It's fine with me."

"Thank you! You're the best!" Kat threw herself at Gram for a hug. "And Mase is great. You'll really like him. He's easy to like."

It was true. It was easy to say nice things about Mase.

"I heard you have a new boyfriend, huh? Mase better treat you right," Erik says now, echoing her thoughts.

Kat smiles at his stern look. He and Bea have been dating since Kat was eleven years old; he's seen her with braces and awkward, gangly limbs. When she wasn't eating, he brought her nonfat strawberry fro-yo to try to tempt her. He always remembers her birthday and gets her a goofy card with cats on it, like she's *still* eleven. When Adam broke up with her, Erik threatened to kick his ass. It made Kat laugh, because she had never heard Erik swear before and she was pretty positive he would never actually fight anyone. She appreciated the symbolic patriarchal gesture, though.

"No worries. Mase is super sweet," she reassures Erik.

"He'd better be," Erik says darkly, straightening the collar of his navy-blue polo.

"You're such a good big brother. I'm going to miss having you around. I'll miss Bea too, I guess. But I've got more sisters. You're my only brother. Well, *almost*."

Erik smiles over her shoulder. "We'll be back for fall break. Right, Bea?"

Kat turns to find Bea standing behind her in the doorway. She's changed from her pencil skirt and cardigan into a T-shirt and jeans, but she still looks stressed. In fact, she looks sort of *stricken*. "Right. Yes," she says quietly. When Erik takes her hand, Kat notices the tiniest hesitation before Bea links her fingers through his.

Are they fighting? They never fight. Kat can't imagine it. They're both so smart and ambitious and—well—boring, honestly. They used to be all gooey-sweet, holding hands and kissing, but now they seem so *comfortable* together. Like everything they do is a routine worn soft by time. Maybe that's what happens when you've been dating forever like they have.

At least Bea doesn't have to worry about Erik cheating on her. He would never. Bea is totally the person in charge in their relationship.

Kat hides a smile. Earlier this spring, she asked Bea what sex was like. She was pretty sure Bea and Erik had sex: they had been together for five years, and she'd seen birth control pills on Bea's nightstand. She didn't know who else to ask, since Pen was a virgin too. Bea told her sex was fun and awkward and great. She said a girl should know her own body, figure out what she liked and didn't like, and not be afraid to speak up about it. Kat definitely didn't want to imagine her sister having sex, but she was amused by the idea of Bea ordering Erik around in bed. It was very Bea to want to be in charge, always.

Bea also told Kat not to have sex with Adam unless she could trust him.

There's a knock on the door, and Kat rushes to open it. Mase. He's wearing skinny jeans and a T-shirt for a band she's never heard of. His eyeliner is on point, and his fauxhawk is appropriately spiky. "Hey, gorgeous," he greets her cheerfully. Then he sees Bea and Erik and his body language changes. "Uh, hi, Bea. Erik."

"Hi, Mase," Bea and Erik say in unison.

"Kat's curfew is midnight," Erik announces.

"No worries. Rehearsal is over at eleven," Kat says. Then she wonders if she should have said something else. Pretended they were going to make out in the car or something. *Are they going to make out in the car? How far does this fake-dating thing go? What if they don't seem authentic?*

"Drive carefully," Bea says.

"Of course." Mase is solemn. He knows what happened to their parents. Everybody knows what happened to their parents.

"Okay, bye. Have fun at the movie!" Kat takes Mase's hand and pulls him out the door. "Sorry about that. After Adam, they obviously don't trust my judgment in guys."

"Adam's an asshole," Mase says as they climb into the

VW Bug he shares with Em. "I mean…no offense, but why do you even want him back?"

"Don't worry. I'm going to make him work for it. He'll have to treat me like a queen," Kat says, side-stepping the question. She feels weird telling Mase that she wants Adam to fall in love with her so *she* can dump *him*. "Why do you want Brandon back? He cheated on you too."

"Truth. But…" Mase pulls on his seatbelt and waits for her to pull on hers before he starts the engine. "We were really happy before that. I mean, we fought a little at Christmas break because I wanted him to come home more often, and I think he felt kind of suffocated. Maybe I was too clingy or whatever. It was just…I could feel him pulling away."

His honesty startles Kat into responding in kind. She isn't very good at being emotionally vulnerable with people who aren't Pen, but Mase is easy to talk to. "I felt that way with Adam all the time," she admits. "It's awful."

"So why do you want to feel that way again?" Mase presses.

"When we get back together, it'll be different," Kat says. "Obviously, he'll appreciate me more."

Mase looks at her with a funny expression, and Kat can't tell what he's thinking. "I hope so," he says finally. "You deserve that."

They're quiet for the rest of the drive, till Mase parallel

parks on High Street, a block away from the Remington Theater. "You ready for this?" he asks after they climb out of the Bug.

"I guess so. Do I look okay?" Kat twirls in a circle. She's wearing a red maxi skirt with a white tank top that is backless except for two wide horizontal straps.

"You look amazing," Mase says.

"Yeah? Thank you. It's not too much for rehearsal?"

"Nope. You look good. Really good." Mase tugs at the collar of his T-shirt, and Kat grins. Is he blushing? Does he think she's pretty? Like, not in an intellectual, we-take-good-selfies way, but like he's actually attracted to her?

"Okay. Let's do this." She holds out her hand, Mase takes it, and they walk down the street, into the theater, and down the quiet, echoing hall.

Adam and Jillian aren't in the rehearsal room yet. Pen has saved Kat a seat, but only one. *Awkward.* Pen raises her eyebrow when Kat and Mase saunter in hand-in-hand. The stage manager is handing out scripts and contact sheets. Coffee and tea and freshly baked chocolate chip cookies are on a long table near the door.

Kat sets her script and her contact sheet and her clutch down between Mase and Hannah Adler, mouths an apology at Pen, and then goes to make herself a cup of tea. The air-conditioning is on full blast, and it's freezing. Maybe the backless shirt was not the smartest idea. Adam has strutted in, and he and Jillian sit on the other side of Hannah. Jillian's wearing her field hockey jacket.

Kat grabs a mint tea packet and dunks the tea bag into a cup of hot water, trying to ignore them.

"Hey, Kat," Adam says behind her.

She startles, spills the hot water on her hand, and swears. "Um, hi." She sets the tea down and grabs a handful of napkins.

He pours himself coffee and then hands her a packet of Splenda. Her eyes rush up to meet his. He remembers what kind of sweetener she uses. What does that mean?

It means they dated for almost a year and he's minimally polite. *Get it together, Kat.*

"I saw you at the party the other night," he says. "With Mase."

"Yeah," Kat says, guarded. "I saw you too. With Jillian."

"Are you guys dating now?" Adam asks.

Kat tosses her hair over her shoulder and turns slightly away from him, purposely revealing the long, pale curve of her back. "Not that it's any of your business, but yes."

"Huh. I didn't think he was your type."

Kat purses her lips. So that's his tactic? He's going to be snarky about Mase? "He's nice and he treats me well. I think that's my new type."

"Just kinda surprised. I didn't think you'd want to share your makeup," Adam mutters.

What an asshole. Kat smiles. "I don't mind. Guyliner's totally on-trend. I don't think *you* could pull it off, but it works for Mase. It definitely works." Adam rolls his eyes as Kat throws the tea bag in the trash. "Jealousy is unbecoming, Adam."

"What?" he sputters. "I'm not—"

Kat has already walked away. She takes her seat between Hannah and Mase, then leans over to plant a kiss on his cheek. Her lipstick leaves a red lip print, and she giggles.

"Kat. How many times do I have to tell you?" Mase says, loud. "Stop. I'm going to have lipstick all over my body at this rate. Everywhere. *If you know what I mean.*"

She swats at him, laughing. "Shut up!"

He leans in to whisper in her ear. "Aren't we trying to make him jealous? He's totally watching you."

Kat smirks. "Yes, but we've only been dating for three days. I'm not a slut."

"*Four* days. You wound me," Mase whispers. "Maybe you were overcome by my many charms. You couldn't help yourself. You swooned when presented with the prodigious talent of my tongue." He waggles his eyebrows at her.

Oh God, now she's wondering what Mase does with his tongue. Their kisses have been nice but close-mouthed so far. Or did he mean—wait, did he mean *other things* with his tongue? Like, below-the-belt things? Adam had wanted her to go down on him, and she'd done it a couple times, but he'd never offered to reciprocate. Kat flushes.

"Aw, I forget your youth and innocence," Mase teases.

"Shut up!" Kat says.

"Oh my God, Kat, you look like a tomato," Pen says.

Now everyone's looking. Curse her redhead genes and loud-mouthed friend.

Kat kicks Mase beneath the table. Then kicks him again, harder, just for good measure.

"Ouch," the man playing Mase's grandfather says.

"Sorry! I thought that was the table," Kat lies, mortified.

"What did the table do to you, young lady?" the older man jokes.

Kat buries her face in her hands. "Nothing! I have done this to myself," she mutters.

CHAPTER SIXTEEN
VI

"Cece's book came in," Des tells Vi on Thursday afternoon. "Do you want to call her?"

Vi shakes her head emphatically, her red braid flying out behind her. She hates talking on the phone.

From behind the counter, Des raises her eyebrows and gives her a look that clearly says, *You are being silly.*

"I could maybe text her," Vi concedes, kneeling on the colorful alphabet carpet. She's in the middle of reorganizing the board books for real. Des started the project on Tuesday, then lost interest in the middle of it and threw all the books back on the shelves in random order. Vi is cleaning up her sister's mess and thinking about Cece. She's been thinking about her a lot since the farm party, but she hasn't had a good excuse to text her till now. Mrs. Chan doesn't need Vi to walk Athena this week, so their dog-walking date (not that it's a real date, obviously) has been postponed. Just when she's finally stopped avoiding Cece, she hasn't actually run into her since Saturday night.

Is Cece avoiding *her* now?

Vi stares at the lock screen of her phone—a picture of Betty and Veronica from *Riverdale*—as she wills up the courage to text Cece. She types and backspaces and then retypes: **Hi Cece. Your book came in at Arden. You can come pick it up anytime. —Vi**

As soon as she presses send, she doubts herself and reexamines her word choice. Was that too formal? She slips her phone into the back pocket of her jeans, then immediately fishes it back out and stares at it as though it's a bomb.

She shouldn't expect Cece to text right back. She might be at work, or babysitting her brothers, or reading a really good book.

Oh. The ellipsis shows that Cece is typing. Vi holds her breath.

Her phone buzzes. **Awesome! Thanks! I'll come over now.**

Vi's stomach starts to twist itself into nervous knots. They confided in each other at the party. Maybe it was only because there was nobody around to overhear except the horses. Maybe it was because it was so dark, they could hardly see each other's faces. Whatever the reason, they let themselves be honest and vulnerable. What if Cece regrets that? What if she's cool and distant now? That would hurt. It would hurt a lot.

A storm's been brewing all afternoon, and it finally breaks. Rain pounds against the front windows. Thunder cracks, loud, above the classical music playing over the speakers. Vi eyes her sister warily. She isn't used to the blue hair yet. She isn't sure she likes it. Des changing her hair—the red hair that all four Garrett sisters share, in varying hues and textures and lengths—seems like a portent of some kind. Like more change is on the way. Vi doesn't like change. Bea is already leaving at the end of the summer; isn't that bad enough?

When Cece walks in, the yellow hood of her sweatshirt pulled up over her dark hair, rubber duck rain boots on her feet, and raindrops glittering on her eyelashes, Vi is certain her crush is written all over her face. How could it not be? How could one girl, dripping wet from dashing through a thunderstorm to pick up a book she's already read, be so completely perfect? Vi looks at Des, helpless. She remembers the way Cece confided in her on Saturday about her family, about Ben, and it feels like a distant, impossible dream. Of all the girls in their class, why would Cece choose to befriend *her*?

"Hey, Cece," Des says. "Here to pick up your book?"

Cece nods, lowering her hood, but she heads right for

the children's section, where Vi is still kneeling on the rug, stacking books by subject. "Hey, Vi. What are you doing?"

As Vi explains, Cece settles cross-legged next to her. "Can I help? I love organizing things."

Is Cece avoiding the storm? Or does she actually want to hang out? Vi tries to temper her excitement. "Sure."

As they sort the books into piles and then reshelve them by subject (books about animals, families, manners, trucks, bedtime, colors, numbers, ABCs, etc.), they talk about the Nina LaCour book, which Cece says she loved. Vi tells Cece how she went with Des to the NoVa TEEN Book Festival in northern Virginia two springs ago, where Nina LaCour was the keynote speaker, and how beautiful and inclusive her speech was. How it made Vi cry. How she brought a stack of Nina's books with her and got them all signed. How Nina wasn't even the only LGBTQ author there.

Somehow, as they've talked, they've reshelved all the books.

"Do you want to get Frappuccinos? My treat," Vi says. "As a thank you for helping."

"You don't have to do that." Cece gives her a dimpled grin. "But I'll never turn down a Frappuccino."

"Yeah? Des, I'm going to take a break, okay?" Vi gives her sister a quelling look. If Des objects, Vi will murder her.

"Take your time. I think I can handle things here." Des gestures to the empty store. "I owe you for fixing my mess."

They dash around the corner to the Daily Grind. By the time they push open the door, Vi's green Chucks are soaked, and her hair is dripping wet. As they wait behind a pair of elderly women taking a really long time to decide which herbal tea they want, Vi unwinds her messy wet braid.

She looks up to find Cece watching her. "Your hair is so pretty."

Her hair? Her hair is stick-straight and hangs limp in the summer humidity. Cece's hair is all thick dark curls. Vi wonders what it would be like to tangle her fingers through it, and then she flushes. "Thanks. What kind of Frappuccino do you want?"

"Mocha chip. Always. What about you?"

"Black cherry." Vi doesn't say that anything cherry reminds her of Cece's lip gloss.

"Let's play the question game," Cece says, and Vi's mind races. Does Cece think she's a terrible conversationalist, or is this Cece's way of getting to know her better? "I'll start. What's your favorite color?"

"Violet. Violet for Viola. Cliché, I know. What's yours?"

"Pink." Cece holds out her shimmery fuchsia nails and grins. "When I was ten, I convinced Mami to let me paint one of my bedroom walls hot pink. The other three are bubblegum."

"I remember. From when we were kids." Cece had a big, wooden dollhouse, and they acted out stories with their dolls. They made their Barbies kiss. Is it weird that Vi remembers that? Do straight girls do that too?

"I still like it, even though I hate the stereotypes that go with it. People assume that if I wear pink and do my nails, I must be super girly and not very smart. You wouldn't believe some of the comments I get at the restaurant." Cece rolls her eyes. "So many gross old guys telling me how pretty I am and asking if I have a boyfriend. Or they see that I'm brown and I speak Spanish, so they ask where I'm from. Sometimes they compliment me for speaking English so well."

"People seriously do that?" Vi asks, horrified.

Cece nods, pursing her lips. "All the time. A couple of months ago, Papi was bussing some tables at the restaurant, and he spoke Spanish to one of the waiters. Some dumb ass told him to speak English because he was in America now and asked if he was illegal. It's 'undocumented,' first of all, and second, Papi was born right here in Remington Hollow. Obviously, the guy didn't know our family owns the restaurant."

"I hope your dad spit in his drink." Vi feels clueless for never considering the microaggressions that Cece and her family must encounter on the regular. Unless she chooses to wear one of her Pride shirts, her neighbors can't tell she's gay just by looking at her, whereas Cece is one of only three Latinx kids in their grade.

"Papi kicked him out. But he made sure he left that night with some of the kitchen staff in case the guy and his friends were waiting around to cause trouble. I heard him tell Mami about it, and she said he should have just let it go." Cece makes a face. "Anyhow. Sorry to be a downer. Let's change the subject."

"You're not a downer!" Vi protests. "Let's see…what's your favorite TV show?"

"*Jane the Virgin*. Is yours *The 100*?"

Vi can't believe Cece remembers that detail from their conversation a week ago. She remembers pretty much everything Cece has ever said, but that's different. "No. I still watch it, but my favorite is *Riverdale*. I kind of have a crush on Veronica."

She has a type. Dark-haired, feminine, badass but big-hearted. Like Cece.

"I've seen commercials for it," Cece says as the elderly women in front of them finally pay for their blueberry iced teas and strawberry scones.

Vi and Cece order Frappuccinos, and Vi pays for both. Almost like it's a date. It's not a date, obviously. It's a thank you. But she can't help wondering what a date with Cece would be like.

As they settle at a small café table in the back, Cece grins at Vi. "Okay…what's your favorite book of all time?"

"Of all time? That's a *terrible* question," Vi teases. "How can I possibly choose? But I read a really awesome fantasy book yesterday, *Reign of the Fallen*. It's about a badass bisexual necromancer who has to save her kingdom from monsters called Shades, which are kind of like zombies. The world building is so good. And it's going to be a duology! I can't wait for book two."

Cece looks interested. "Do you have it at Arden?"

"We do, but you can borrow mine…if you tell me what *your* favorite book of all time is." Vi sips her Frappuccino.

Cece laughs her high, fizzy laugh. "I can't choose either! I'm such a hypocrite. Um…my recent favorite is *Wild Beauty*. I love that it's intersectional, you know? There aren't enough books about queer Latina girls."

"Truth." Vi wonders if Cece is especially interested in that representation, not in an academic way, but because she wants to see *herself* in more books. "Ooh, I've got an even more evil question. Who's your favorite dog?"

Cece's eyes widen. "That *is* evil. There are so many adorable floofs!" She drums her pink fingernails against her chin. "Okay, no, I do have a favorite: Algernon."

"Aw, Algernon! He's so sweet!" Vi says. Algernon is Mrs. Ellinghaus's three-legged white terrier. He has the run of her flower shop, In Bloom, and he's super friendly. "I have to go with Juno. At least until I get my own dog. I love Des, but she has to move out *eventually*, right?"

"What kind of dog would you want? Would you rather have a big dog or a little dog?"

"Both!" Vi laughs. "I want to rescue all the dogs who

need homes. When I have my own house, I'm going to have three or four."

"Me too." Cece grins at her, and Vi can't help thinking about an episode of *Riverdale*—okay, she happens to know it was the second episode, actually—when Betty and Veronica got milkshakes at Pop's and vowed never to let a boy come between them. It was totally adorable. After she saw it the first time, she wrote a fic where Betty and Veronica had their first kiss and then held hands across the table as they drank their milkshakes.

Vi looks at Cece's hands, at her slightly chipped polish. She wonders what it would be like to hold hands with her here, at the Daily Grind, where anyone could see.

"I like this game. It's nice to have somebody to talk to," Cece says.

"You have a zillion friends," Vi points out. At lunch or walking to and from class, Cece is always surrounded. Everyone wants to partner with her on group projects because she's smart and responsible and kind.

"I have a lot of friends, but since Shaniyah moved away, I haven't had a best girl friend," Cece confesses. Shaniyah Washington and Cece were inseparable from kindergarten through seventh grade. They both played soccer, and both of their families own restaurants in town; Shaniyah's grandmother, Miss Evie, runs Mama's BBQ. "No one I trust to share my deep dark secrets with, you know?"

"You have deep dark secrets?" Vi teases.

Is she flirting? Oh God, she thinks she is.

"Don't we all?" Cece retorts, smiling. "Don't you?"

"Well." Vi sits back in her chair, bracing herself for Cece to laugh and think she's a total nerd. "I write fan fiction."

Cece leans forward. "About *Riverdale*?"

Vi nods. "About Beronica. That's the ship name for Betty and Veronica. I post it on Tumblr and AO3. I think my favorite part is getting feedback from other Beronica shippers. They have the best requests."

"Like, they request that you write certain stories?" Cece asks.

"Yeah. It's a big fandom. People write fics about lots of different characters and couples. Some of them follow the official canon, and some of them—like Beronica—don't." Vi can't believe she's explaining this to Cece. She doesn't talk about this with *anybody*.

"But...how is it secret, if people read it?"

"Nobody knows it's me. It's all anonymous." Vi's careful to sign out of her accounts in case her sisters borrow her tablet. And her phone is password protected. She hides her notebooks too, because Kat is a total snoop.

"What about your sisters?" Cece asks, and Vi shakes her head. "How come?"

"I don't know." She shifts on her stool. "It's super fun to take characters I love and write stories for them. But

Bea's the real writer. She was the editor of the school paper, and now she's interning at the *Gazette*. She's going to Georgetown for journalism. Telling them I write fanfic sounds kind of...I don't know...silly, in comparison."

"No, it's not," Cece says, and Vi falls a little more in love with her. "Do *you* think it's silly?"

"No." Vi is blushing again. "I love it."

Cece shrugs. "I bet your stories are great. And there's no rule that only one of you can be a writer, is there?"

"I guess not." Her sisters think she keeps a journal. She let them think that. If they found out she was actually rewriting scenes so that her favorite TV characters kiss... What if they laughed at her? She would die.

"Okay, your turn," she says. "Tell me a deep, dark secret."

"Oh. Um." Cece fiddles with her straw, and Vi's breath comes faster. Is this why Cece started the question game, looking for permission to share a secret? To confide in Vi about something more than her favorite TV show and her favorite color?

"My abuela had a brother who was gay," Cece says finally. "Her parents disowned him back in the sixties. She hasn't seen him for almost sixty years...since they were only a little older than us."

"That's really sad," Vi says. This is not what she was expecting.

Cece nods. "She doesn't even know if he's alive. I

wonder sometimes, if I were gay—or if my brothers were," she adds hastily, "if my abuela would disown us too."

Oh. Vi's heart squishes at the fear written across Cece's face. She doesn't think this is actually about Cece's brothers at all. "No. I mean, she might be Catholic, but—"

"She's *really* Catholic. Like, she has an altar to la Virgen in her bedroom." Cece's brown eyes widen. "And Mami says that even if we don't agree with her, while we're living under her roof, we have to respect her beliefs. So, if I'm reading a book with two girls on the cover, I read it in my room. And when I go out, I bring it with me or hide it in my bra drawer, because I know my brothers won't snoop in there."

Vi bites her tongue to keep from saying something ugly about Cece's abuela. It is unfair that Cece feels ashamed about what she reads and maybe about who she is. Her parents should stick up for her, even if that means moving out of the elder Mrs. Pérez's house.

Coming out was pretty easy for Vi. Gram was kind of a hippie back in the sixties; she went to all kinds of civil rights and anti-war protests. She took Vi and her sisters to the Women's March last year. She put a sign in the front window at Arden about how everyone is welcome there. Vi doesn't want to criticize Cece's family or minimize her fears. She knows there are still people who kick their gay kids out of the house or send them to conversion therapy.

But she can't imagine the Pérezes would really be that cruel. Gram wouldn't be friends with Julia Pérez if she was so close-minded, would she?

"Your abuela is so proud of you," Vi says, choosing her words carefully. "She's always bragging on you to Gram: how good your grades are and what a good cook you are and what a big help you are with your brothers. I think she would accept you…or, um, your brothers. I have to believe that even if she doesn't think marriage equality is okay, in theory, she would feel differently if it were her own granddaughter…or grandson. But…if she didn't, or if she needed a little time to get used to the idea, you—or they—could always stay with us."

Cece nods, her lower lip trembling. She stares down at the table, avoiding Vi's gaze. "Thank you. And I mean… it's hypothetical anyway. Let's do an easier question. What's your favorite subject?"

You, Vi thinks. *You are endlessly fascinating to me.*

"Language Arts," she says.

CHAPTER SEVENTEEN

DES

Monday night, as Des is about to change into her pajamas, Paige texts her to get ready; they'll pick her up in five minutes. Des assumes that "they" are Paige and Dylan.

On Saturday night, at Des's second farm party, she and Paige hung out with Dylan down by the river, smoking and talking. Paige showed them pictures of her artwork—these cool, impossibly small, incredibly complex wire sculptures she'd been working on. Then, as they were leaving, Dylan grabbed Paige's hand and pulled her close and kissed her. This afternoon, Paige'd met him for coffee at the Daily Grind, and he'd shared a sketchbook with ideas for a comic. *He's not half bad for a kid*, Paige had texted Des, ignoring that Des and Dylan are the same age.

Now Paige leans out the window of a dented blue car. "Desdemona! Are you ready for an adventure?"

"No?" Des says, hesitating on her front porch. Honestly, she doesn't like adventures. She has tested Hufflepuff in every Hogwarts sorting quiz she's ever taken. She doesn't like surprises either. Em tried to throw her a surprise sixteenth birthday party, but she got so stressed about the mysterious surprise and whether she would react appropriately that Em gave in and told her about it three days before her actual birthday.

Paige opens the door and scoots over to make room. "Get in the car."

Des slides in. Dylan's friend Ty is driving.

"You know Ty, right?" Paige says, as though she's the one who's been living in Remington Hollow her whole life. Of course Des knows Ty. They were in the same grade, and they had a U.S. history class together junior year and some other classes before that. Earth science in eighth grade. Wood shop in seventh. "And, Ty, you know Desdemona?"

"Desdemo—? Yeah," Ty says, glancing at her in the rearview mirror.

"Doesn't she look amazing?" Paige strokes Des's blue curls. "I *love* the blue."

"She looks different," Ty says.

Des can't tell whether he thinks that's a good or bad thing. She isn't sure she cares.

"Next week, I think we should get tattoos," Paige says.

"Like…permanent tattoos?" Des asks.

Paige cackles. "Yes. Come on. Tell me there's not some quote from a book you're dying to get engraved on your skin forever, you nerd!"

Des hides a smile. There is, but she's never been brave enough.

"I knew it!" Paige says triumphantly. "You need me around, Desdemona."

"I think maybe I kind of do," Des admits.

They park on a quiet, tree-lined street behind the Episcopal church and the library, which—like almost everything else in Remington Hollow—closed three hours ago. Paige pulls out a glass pipe, packs the bowl, and then lights it. She smokes and passes it to Dylan. After his turn, Dylan passes it to Ty, who hesitates and looks at Des.

Des looks up and down the shadowy, tree-lined street. This seems like a bad idea but—

"Okay," she says quietly, accepting the bowl.

They pass it around the car until they're all giddy. When Paige pronounces it kicked, Dylan throws his door open. "All right, let's do this."

"Do what?" Des asks. No one answers her. They're cutting through the church's back garden, not through the parking lot or down the sidewalk. "Seriously, guys. What are we doing?"

Dylan points. "We're going up there."

Des tilts her head back and looks at the clock tower, five stories above them. She gets a little dizzy and stumbles.

Ty puts a hand on her arm. "You okay?"

Des pulls away. "I'm good."

"You're so good." Paige wraps an arm around her and pulls her away from the boys. "I told Dylan to bring Ty for you. What do you think?"

Des looks at Ty, who's leaning against the red brick wall of the church. She looks at his blue polo shirt, his khaki shorts, his ugly boat shoes, his shaggy brown hair. She has never understood why he and Dylan are friends. Dylan works on his parents' farm but, she thinks, reluctantly; he only ever seems interested in comic books and skateboarding. Ty is a preppy rich kid who played tennis and goes to college for free because his dad is a professor.

Maybe it's as simple as Dylan and Ty both like getting stoned. Still, she isn't sure what Paige thinks *she* and Ty would have in common.

"What do you think?" Paige asks again. "Is he cute?"

Des shrugs. He is cute, but she doesn't have any desire to grab his belt loop and pull him close and kiss him, like

Paige just did to Dylan, or thread her fingers through his. She isn't attracted to him like that.

Paige laughs. "I mean, he's not as cute as Dylan, but…"

Obviously, Paige finds Dylan, with his shoulder-length corn-silk hair and skinny jeans and that vintage Grateful Dead T-shirt, irresistible. And he is pretty, with delicate, almost elfin features and green eyes. Like the slacker version of Orlando Bloom in The Lord of the Rings movies. But Des doesn't want to kiss him either. She doesn't want to kiss anybody.

Paige squints at her. "Desdemona, have you ever had a boyfriend?"

Des shakes her head. She isn't embarrassed about it.

"Are you a virgin?" Paige asks. Des nods. "Oh my God. Okay. Well. You can do better than this kid. We'll find somebody better."

"You don't have to do that," Des says. "I mean—I don't want you to do that."

Paige looks at her for a minute, and then she nods. "Okay. You're the boss."

Dylan and Ty are at the back door of the church. "Wait, are you serious?" Des demands, charging toward them. "Oh my God, we're going to get arrested!"

"We are not going to get arrested," Paige says.

"We are. We're going to get arrested for breaking and entering, and our grandmas are going to have to come bail us out of jail." For some reason, that is suddenly hilarious. Des doesn't even know where the town jail is. *Is* there a town jail? There are town cops, right? And county sheriffs. And state troopers. And…park rangers? Are there any park rangers in Remington Hollow?

"We're not going to get arrested." Dylan holds up a little brass key. "We're not breaking in. My brother gave me the key. He and his friends used to smoke in the cupola all the time. It's no big deal."

Des cocks her head. "It's a church. It's Father Daniel's church. We can't smoke weed in his church without his permission. We're gonna go to hell."

"Hell is other people," Paige says. "Someone famous said that, right?"

"Sartre," Des supplies. "It's from his play *No Exit*."

Paige hugs her. "Aw, you're such a little nerd."

"Kat read that play last summer and wouldn't shut up about it," Des explains. But it's nice to be the smart one for a change. Usually, that's Bea.

Thinking about her sisters makes Des feel weird and guilty. She is not being a good big sister. She is not setting a good example. Smoking weed and then breaking into the clock tower—entering the clock tower without permission—is not behavior she would want them to emulate.

Dylan unlocks the back door. Inside, the hallway is dark and shadowy. Paige uses her phone's flashlight to scan the room. The alarm beeps, but Dylan presses four numbers into the keypad, and it goes silent. Ty moves to flip on the lights, but Dylan catches his arm. "No lights, dude. The rectory is right next door."

"We're so going to get caught," Des says. "How did Aaron get that key? Did he steal it?"

"I could tell you, but then I'd have to kill you," Dylan jokes.

Paige elbows him. "Just tell her before she freaks out, okay."

"One of Aaron's friend's older brothers volunteered here and duplicated the key. It and the alarm code got handed down to Aaron and his friends and then to me. I'm not naming any names." Dylan leads them up the stairs, past the church offices, and into the choir loft.

Des's family doesn't go to church. Gram used to go to Catholic Mass on Christmas and Easter. But after the accident, Des thinks she sort of lost faith in God.

Des has been in this church before, though. The Kim family attends services here every Sunday. She was Em's plus-one last spring when her brother Jacob got married, and she was here three summers ago for Em's dad's funeral. One summer in middle school, she even came here for church camp. It was mostly arts and crafts and some songs about Jesus, but she wanted to go because she wanted to go everywhere with Em.

Dylan is heading through the door at the back of the choir loft. It leads to a stairwell that winds up through the clock tower into the cupola. Dylan goes first, then Paige, then Ty, then Des. As they climb, the bells start to chime eleven. It's loud. Loud enough that it vibrates through Des's whole body. She's glad when they reach the top.

The cupola, with its white arches and domed roof, is the tallest point in town. There aren't exactly any skyscrapers in Remington Hollow. Up here, Des can see the whole town spread out before her: the marina, with the sailboats bobbing in the dark water; blocks full of colorful Victorian houses and green lawns to the east; the shops and restaurants that make up the little business district to the west. She gazes out over the town, and she feels curiously disappointed.

From up here, Remington Hollow looks so small.

CHAPTER EIGHTEEN
BEA

"Okay, I'll email the minutes from tonight's meeting with everyone's to-do lists. Don't forget to get your money for supplies to Sierra. Thanks for coming, everyone!" Bea says.

The raft team—Bea; Erik; Chloe; Erik's tennis doubles partner, Drew Bishop; Drew's girlfriend, Faith Ellinghaus, who was the layout editor for the yearbook; and class treasurer Sierra Alvarez—is finishing up its meeting. It's a gorgeous evening, sunny and mid-eighties, and Chloe insisted on moving from the Daily Grind to Bishop Park.

"I've got to get home for dinner." Erik stands and stretches and cracks his neck.

Bea winces. She hates that sound. But as she peers at

him, worry pierces her heart. There are dark circles under his blue eyes, and a slump to his shoulders. He looks almost as exhausted as she feels. She touches his forearm. "You look tired."

Erik shrugs, grabbing his messenger bag. "Early morning." He's interning this summer for his uncle's law firm. "Text you later?"

"Okay." She watches as he hurries away, falling into step beside Sierra. Part of her wants to hurry after him and beg him to talk to her. To find out whether he's been feeling as out of sorts and anxious as she has. Whether he knows she's unhappy, and whether he's been unhappy too.

The other part of her is relieved it was so easy to extricate herself. It's only seven thirty, and the evening is all hers. It stretches out before her, full of promise, and she finds herself looking down the river toward the marina.

"Hey," Chloe says, sidling up to her. Drew and Faith have packed up and wandered off while Bea was daydreaming. "Is everything okay?"

"What? Yes," Bea says automatically. "Why?"

"You seem a little distracted," Chloe explains, pulling her long black hair into a bun. "The meeting ran late. Your meetings never run late."

Bea's shoulders stiffen. She *was* distracted. She feels guilty because she still hasn't talked to Erik. She was going to—she absolutely was—last Wednesday, after the movie, but then she overheard Kat telling Erik how much she'll miss him when he and Bea go to Georgetown. *I'll miss Bea too, I guess. But I've got more sisters. You're my only brother. Well, almost,* she'd teased. And Bea's heart had broken a little.

For five years, Erik has been part of her family, acting like a big brother to Kat and Vi. He taught Kat how to play tennis and sees all her shows. He threatened to kick the ass of anyone who hassled Vi after she came out. He brought Gram flowers after her surgery.

Bea's family *adores* Erik. She couldn't help thinking that maybe they like him better than they like her. Bea knows she isn't always very likable. She can be prickly. Self-centered. Selfish. If she broke up with him, would Kat and Vi be mad at her? Would they take his side?

"Is there somewhere you need to be?" Bea asks Chloe, her voice icy.

"I wasn't criticizing you," Chloe says. "I just meant… you seem a little off. I thought maybe…do you want to grab coffee?"

"With you?" Bea asks, surprised. They've known each other since kindergarten—been competing against one another for nearly as long—but they've never grabbed coffee. Not without some kind of group project or class assignment to work on. What is Chloe up to?

"Yeah, with me. I thought maybe we could hang out."

Chloe smiles, and Bea feels bad that her first instinct was to be suspicious. She remembers Chloe hugging her at the farm party: *We're friends now, right? You beat me. You got valedictorian. But now we've graduated, so none of that matters anymore.*

"You look like you could use a friend," Chloe says.

Is she that obvious? That pathetic? "I'm fine."

Chloe sighs and flops back down on her Burberry plaid blanket. "All right, maybe *I* could use a friend. We don't have to have coffee. We can sit here and watch the boats."

"Oh. Okay." This is very new territory. Tentatively, Bea sits cross-legged on the blanket. "Um…how's your internship going? You're doing an internship this summer, right?"

"Yeah. With Dr. Holt at Remington Vet. She's great."

Bea recognizes the strained tone in Chloe's voice, the way Chloe avoids her eyes. Something *isn't* great.

"Is it weird not working at the inn?" she asks. Chloe's parents run the most popular bed and breakfast in Remington Hollow. Her mom is the manager; her dad is the chef. Chloe's worked there every summer, after school, and on weekends, except during tennis season. Like Bea, Chloe has always had a plan. She's going to the University of Pennsylvania (the fifth-best undergraduate school of business in the country) to study business, and then she'll come back to Remington Hollow and help her parents take the inn to the next level. Maybe even start a franchise in other cute touristy towns on the Eastern Shore.

"It's definitely weird." Chloe sighs, stretching her legs out in front of her. "But you should see Amber—Dr. Holt—she's amazing. She cares so much about every single animal who comes in, and she has a sliding scale for people who can't afford pet care. She volunteers at the rescue clinic. She's incredibly kind. When we had to put Percy to sleep—that was our old golden retriever—she sent us a sympathy card and a bouquet of flowers."

"That's really nice." Bea remembers Chloe coming to class red-eyed after Percy died.

"Yeah. When we took Athena for her first puppy checkup, I asked Dr. Holt about interning for her this summer. My dad was pissed. He and Mom were expecting me to work at the inn, like always. He wanted me to back out of my internship with Amber—and usually Dad is super firm about not going back on my word. He thinks I just want to slack off and play with puppies this summer. I mean, I *do* want to play with puppies, but it's not slacking off. It's hard work. And I love it."

Bea looks at the mix of exhilaration and anxiety on Chloe's face. It feels familiar. "That's cool," she says. "Are you…maybe rethinking your plan?"

Chloe nods without looking at her. "Penn is one of the best veterinary schools in the country too. Super competitive."

Bea laughs. "Wait, how long have you been thinking about this? Do your parents know?"

"A while," Chloe admits, meeting her eyes. "Amber is super inspiring, but I did all my community service at the animal rescue, and I really loved that too." Bea remembers. She was a little jealous of Chloe; she did her one hundred hours scanning and archiving ancient issues of the *Gazette*. "I haven't told my parents yet. It meant so much to them that I wanted to go into the family business, you know? We've been planning that for ages. I decided I was going to help turn the inn into a franchise back when I was twelve, when we went on a trip to St. Michaels. But I was *twelve*. I'm not the same person now. I don't want the same things. Does that make sense?"

"It definitely makes sense to me." Bea's mind is whirring. "I think it's brave to pursue a career you love, especially when it's not what your parents expect."

"Well, I haven't done the hardest part: telling them. But thank you." Chloe smiles. "What about you? Still excited about Georgetown?"

"I've been—um. I've been kind of wondering whether Georgetown is still the right move for me, actually." Bea feels an incredible relief from saying it. She turns to Chloe, expecting her to—she doesn't know—drop dead from shock or something.

Chloe nods, tucking a stray hair back into her bun. "I've wondered."

"You have? *How?*" Bea whisper-shrieks.

"I've known you since kindergarten, Bea. Sometime this spring, you started to get this...*look* when someone asked you about Georgetown. Like you were stuck in a mouse-trap. Super panicky. I knew the feeling." Chloe gives a sympathetic grimace. "Did you apply anywhere else?"

"Nope. Just Georgetown, early action."

Chloe winces. "Does Erik know?"

Bea shakes her head. She is grateful that Chloe doesn't assume *of course* Erik knows. That Chloe isn't judging her.

"Are you guys okay?" Chloe asks.

Bea shakes her head again. She can't bring herself to say the words.

"Wow. I—that must be really hard," Chloe says.

Bea blinks back tears. Chloe is being so *nice* to her. After all the snarky things Bea has thought—and said!— about her over the years, she doesn't feel like she deserves this kindness.

She takes a deep breath.

"I think I want to break up," she whispers, tracing the squares of the Burberry plaid blanket. "Am I a terrible person?"

"No! No. Bea. Hey. Look at me." Bea lifts her chin. Chloe grabs her hand. "You are not a terrible person. You're just not the same person you were when you were thirteen, or fifteen, or seventeen. You don't want the same things. And that's *okay*."

Tears trickle down Bea's cheeks. She lets them. She is sitting in the park, holding hands with Chloe Chan and crying, and for once, she doesn't care who sees her. She is profoundly relieved. "Thank you."

Chloe smiles. "Oh my God, why haven't we ever actually talked to each other before?"

Bea sniffles. "I don't know. Can we—will you be my friend?" As soon as she says it, she feels stupid. If Chloe laughs at her, she will die of embarrassment.

Instead, Chloe beams and squeezes her hand. "Hell yeah, I will. Let's be friends instead of frenemies, Bea Garrett."

∽

Bea and Chloe stay at the park till the shadows lengthen and turn to twilight. Then Chloe has to head home and walk the puppy before dinner.

Bea doesn't want to go home. She's tired of pretending, but she's not ready to tell Gram and her sisters the truth. The difference between her and Chloe is that Bea doesn't know what she wants to do, if not Georgetown. She doesn't have a plan at all.

How has she—a consummate list-maker, the ultimate goal-oriented girl—found herself with *no plan at all*? It's totally anxiety inducing. Thinking about it makes her stomach tie itself into a knot.

Instead of heading home, Bea finds herself walking toward the marina. Toward the *Stella Anne*.

She stands on the dock for a long time, weighing the decision. The lamp is on. Gabe is settling down at the table with a box of Sabbatini's pizza. Bea feels the pull of all of the things she should want, all the things she thought she wanted at thirteen and fifteen and seventeen. And she feels the pull of something new and scary and thrilling, something that could be a mistake—or could be a new beginning.

She steps gingerly onto the deck of the houseboat. Knocks on the open sliding glass door.

"Permission to come aboard?" she calls.

Gabe comes to the door. "Permission granted." He's shirtless, barefoot, clad only in a pair of paint-splattered jeans. His dark-blond hair is pulled up into a bun. The sight of him—of his broad, tanned chest and the sharp cut of his hips—makes Bea's mouth go dry. Makes her stomach flutter and swoop. She feels almost unbearably nervous, like a string stretched too tight.

"Hey." His smile is ginormous.

He's happy to see me, she realizes with relief. She was worried he liked Savannah, or had a girlfriend back in Nashville, or maybe just wasn't attracted to her. But the way he's looking at her…

"Hey," she says back, and she's smiling so wide, she thinks her face might break.

"Come on in. You here for a Canasta rematch?"

She hasn't seen him since he destroyed her at cards last week. But she's been thinking about him all the time. About this.

"Yes." She walks inside. "No. Yes, but—but first—"

She's so nervous. Jesus. Has she ever in her whole life been so nervous?

She has never kissed anyone else.

Once she does this, she can't go back. Can't undo it. It's an ending as well as a beginning.

"First?" Gabe prompts.

Bea launches herself at him. She is not graceful about it. She is awkward and eager. She rises up on her toes and throws her arms around his neck and pulls his head down toward hers. He makes a surprised noise at the back of his throat, and then their mouths crash into each other. Their first kiss is hard and curious and hungry. Bea can't stop touching him. She runs her hands over the muscles of his shoulders, over the jut of his hipbones, over the smooth warm skin of his back. Gabe's hands skim down her sides to settle on her hips, and she shudders and presses a kiss against the salty curve of his shoulder. Bites him gently. She's always been assertive, the one who initiates things, but not like this. Never like this, wild and a little desperate.

Gabe sucks in a breath, and then he's picking her up. He sits her down on the table, shoving the pizza box aside.

A glass crashes to the floor, and he mumbles *shit*, but it doesn't shatter, and he doesn't stop kissing her. They kiss until Bea feels like she might combust, like she's ready to fly apart into pieces. Then she breaks away.

"Wait," she pants. She's lost time. Has it been minutes or hours?

This can't go further. Not tonight. And definitely not sitting on the table in front of the window, where anyone walking by could see them.

She's breathing hard. So is he, she notes with satisfaction. She takes a deep breath and leans her forehead against his chest, listening to the rapid beat of his heart.

"That," he says, "was unexpected."

She looks up at him. "Good unexpected or bad unexpected?"

He grins. "Definitely good unexpected."

She slides off the table. "Excellent." She smiles. "Now I'm ready for that rematch."

CHAPTER NINETEEN
KAT

"Watch out!" Mase yells as a black cat streaks toward the open door of the Tabby Cat Café.

"No! *Bad* Shadow!" Kat shrieks, kicking the door closed behind her. She drops several IKEA bags on the floor, narrowly missing the cat. "I thought they were all penned upstairs!"

"Obviously, we missed one. Did you count wrong?" Mase puts his bags down and picks up Shadow. "What are you doing, huh, troublemaker? Making a run for your freedom? It's nicer in here. You get all the head scratches and Fancy Feast you want."

"I did not count wrong!" Kat wonders if she counted Sassy twice, though. Shadow and Sassy look a *lot* alike. She strides across the mostly empty café, examining the chalkboard wall they painted yesterday. "I think this is ready to prime."

"Did we buy primer? I don't think primer was on the list." This morning, Mase drove them across the Bay Bridge to the IKEA in College Park, where they picked up all the pillows and baskets and lamps that Miss Lydia had signed off on. The new futons and end tables will be delivered later, but Kat got to use the company credit card. It was very exciting. No one has ever trusted her with a business credit card before.

"You don't use regular primer. You cure it with chalk," she explains. "If you hurry, we can get this done before rehearsal."

"Ugh, you're so bossy," Mase teases, sliding his sunglasses on top of his head.

"Only because you're such a slacker." She grins. Miss Lydia agreed to close the cafe this week so they could paint and clean and redecorate to their hearts' content. She'd put them in charge of the redesign, although she had to approve every purchase over fifty dollars. But she loved Kat's ideas.

Kat claps her hands twice. "Come on! We still have a lot to do! Everything has to be perfect by Tea Party weekend for the grand reopening."

"Known as the Fourth of July in other, normal places," Mase stage-whispers to Shadow.

"I love Tea Party weekend," Kat confesses. "We had

so much fun last year on the raft. Till it sank. Even after it sank, really." She only remembers after the words are out that Mase *and Brandon* were on the drama club raft too.

"Maybe it was a harbinger of the garbage year to come," Mase says.

At least he's joking about it now.

"Put the cat upstairs, slacker," she commands.

"But he's my favorite!" Mase complains, petting Shadow.

"I thought *I* was your favorite." She gives him an exaggerated wink. "Come on. I'll let you play *Hamilton* again if you put Shadow upstairs with his friends!"

Mase is still obsessed with the *Hamilton* original cast recording. She can't tell how much of it's because of Lin-Manuel Miranda's genuine musical brilliance and how much is Mase's enormous crush on Daveed Diggs. Then again, who *doesn't* have an enormous crush on Daveed Diggs?

"Fine." Mase fake stomps toward the stairs.

"Take some of those bags with you, please," Kat calls.

"Bossy!" Mase tosses over his shoulder.

"You love it!" She rifles through some bags. In order to prime the chalkboard, they have to cover it entirely with chalk, rub the chalk in with a clean rag, and then erase it. She doesn't want to screw this up.

Kat thought that having to be at work every morning at ten a.m. would be a drag; she usually sleeps until noon during the summer. She thought packing up Miss Lydia's figurines and china plates and emptying the cats' litter boxes and painting the walls would be a pain. And it is, in the literal sense that her shoulder hurts after all the painting they did yesterday. But mostly it's been super fun. Miss Lydia has been popping in twice a day to check their progress, but she trusts them to execute their vision. So mostly it's Kat and Mase working, singing show tunes, and running their lines for *Little Women*, with breaks for lunch and playing with cats.

Kat cannot imagine a better summer job.

Her phone chimes, and she fishes it out of the back pocket of her cutoff jean shorts. It's a text from Pen.

What are you doing? Want to come over?

Kat rolls her eyes. They have had this conversation every single afternoon this week. Pen doesn't have a summer job besides occasionally babysitting her little cousins, which means she's lounging around her pool every afternoon, eating Popsicles and reading Regency romance novels. It's how Kat spent most of last summer too, except for the three afternoons a week she worked at Arden with Gram. Pen ate all the purple Popsicles because Kat hates grape-flavored anything, and Kat ate all the strawberry ones, and they read the most salacious parts of the novels out loud, red-faced and giggling.

I can't. I'm working, she texts back.

With Mase? 🙄
You spend all your time with Mase now.
I do not! I'm WORKING.
Working on your sexytimes!
Am not.
We are priming a chalkboard wall.
Want to come help?
No.
I'll leave you alone with Mase and his twitching member 🐛

Kat laughs. The books they read last summer involved a *lot* of euphemisms for the hero's penis.

We've been dating for 2 weeks! I am nowhere near
seeing his member!
IDK.
You're all over each other at rehearsals.

Kat sighs. They kind of are. She wishes she could tell Pen it's all an act, but things have been going so well, she can't risk it. Everyone keeps saying how cute she and Mase are: the adults in the cast, when Mase makes her a cup of tea during breaks or loans her his cardigan with the leather patches on the elbows (which she has now permanently borrowed); her family, after Mase came over to watch a movie and brought her a pint of strawberry gelato from the creamery; Miss Lydia, after she caught them kissing outside the café one afternoon; even strangers on the street. And when they've had rehearsal together, Adam has been downright *surly*. It's delicious. Kat can only conclude that he's miserable because she's happy.

The thing is, she has been really happy.

She's been having so much fun with Mase. She's rocking it at rehearsal *and* at work. Ms. Randall has been very complimentary about Kat's portrayal of Jo. Miss Lydia loved her design suggestions and has given her a ton of responsibility. No one has ever trusted Kat with a project like this before. Everyone, even Gram, thinks she's the flighty Garrett girl.

Sure you don't want to come help us prime the chalkboard wall? she texts Pen.

Ugh. No.
Then I'll see you at rehearsal!
Fine. ☼ ⌇ ☹

Kat sighs. She has been kind of neglecting Pen. It's been surprisingly challenging to find time for her best friend between work and rehearsals and Mase.

Mase clatters downstairs. "Okay. Let's do this."

Kat hands him a piece of chalk. "You start on that side, and I'll start over here, and we'll meet in the middle. Just do what I do." She drags a stepladder over to her side, climbs up, and starts scrubbing the chalk against the top of the wall. Her shoulder aches, and she stretches it. "Ugh."

"What's up?" Mase asks, dragging a step stool across the floor.

"Do you have Advil? My shoulder hurts."

Mase waggles his dark eyebrows at her. "Want a massage? I've got magic hands."

"You don't want to prime the wall," she says.

"I am not especially looking forward to it," he admits, shoving the step stool in her direction. "Sit. Come on. Don't be a martyr. Brandon was a swimmer, and he was always messing up his shoulder. I know what I'm doing."

He talks about Brandon differently now. Like maybe it doesn't hurt so much to mention him or the things they used to do together.

Kat sits on the step stool, and Mase stands behind her. "Move your hair."

She pulls her hair into a high bun. "All right, show me what you've got."

He does. Kat doesn't know exactly what he's doing with his thumbs and forearms and maybe his elbow, but it's definitely untangling some knots along her shoulder and neck, and it feels amazing. "Oh my God," she breathes.

"I know, right? I told you so," he gloats.

"You're such a jerk. Why haven't you been doing this, like, every day? I'm going to make you do this every day now."

"What do I get in return?" His thumbs are moving in small, firm circles around her neck.

Kat tosses a flirty smile over her shoulder. "What do you want?"

He leans down and kisses her. It's a soft, sweet kiss, but it surprises her, because there's no one watching. No audience. Aren't they only supposed to be kissing where people can see them?

It's not the first time that's happened this week. They've *both* initiated it. Last night when Mase dropped her off after rehearsal, they sat in his car talking and joking around for half an hour, and then Kat leaned over and kissed him. The street was quiet and dark, and she hadn't done it in case one of her sisters was peeking out the window. She'd kissed him because she wanted to.

He hadn't exactly complained either. He'd kissed her back, tugging gently on her bottom lip. It had been a really nice kiss.

"Okay, boss," he says now. "Let's prime this wall."

"Nooooo," Kat complains.

He tweaks her bun. "Come on, slacker."

Then his phone sounds a weird chime, and he freezes.

"What?" Kat asks.

Mase is already across the room, snatching his phone off the counter, punching in his password. "That's Brandon! That's his ringtone. He hasn't texted me since—since the last time I texted him. When he told me he needed some space."

Which was the day Kat waltzed into the Tabby Cat Café and suggested they start fake-dating.

Her stomach tenses. She's nervous for him; that's all. She stands up. "What does it say?"

Mase stares at his phone and then at her. "He's coming home for Tea Party. He wants to know if we can talk." Mase grins. "I think our plan is working! Oh my God, Kat, you're freaking *brilliant*!"

Kat's stomach sinks.

Isn't this what she wanted, though? What they *both* wanted?

Wasn't this the whole point?

CHAPTER TWENTY
VI

The next day, at lunchtime, Vi walks down Queen Street with Athena and Juno. She's meeting Cece in Bishop Park for their first dog-walking date. It's not really a date, of course—Cece hasn't even said that she likes girls!—but Vi keeps calling it a date in her head. Which is making her nervous. Which is absurd.

Just ahead of her, Bea pushes through the door of the Daily Grind with Chloe Chan. They settle into the wrought iron chairs with a pair of iced coffees. Vi stares in astonishment as she approaches them. She has never heard Bea say anything nice about Chloe. Not once. They've always been fiercely competitive. Or at least Bea has. Vi's never been sure if the competition was quite as fierce on Chloe's side.

Athena sees Chloe and yanks Vi down the street toward her owner, barking ecstatically.

"Hey! Oh my gosh. Hi, Athena!" Chloe squeals, kneeling on the sidewalk to pet the little golden retriever. Athena puts her enormous paws on Chloe's shoulders and almost knocks her over.

"Hey, Vi," Bea says.

It's nice to be greeted *before* the dogs for once…although, to be fair, Vi knows her neighbors' pets' names better than she knows her neighbors'. For a good six months, the Hannigans were "the couple with that fat ginger cat named Crookshanks."

"Hi. Are you guys working on your raft?" Vi asks.

Bea leans over to pet Juno. "No. We're having coffee. We can have coffee without working on something."

"You can?" Vi asks. Bea is the queen of multitasking. She usually acts as though if she stops to just breathe for a minute, the world might fall apart.

"It's weird, right? We're friends now," Chloe says, climbing back into her chair.

"Oh. Okay." Vi honestly thought Bea hated Chloe. "Where's Erik?"

"It's just Chloe and me. Having coffee. I'm allowed to have coffee on my lunch break without Erik," Bea snaps.

"You're saying 'coffee' a lot," Vi points out. "Are you okay?"

Chloe laughs, and then Bea is laughing too, both hands covering her freckled face. "No. Not really. I don't want to talk about it."

Vi frowns. Bea has seemed more stressed than usual lately. She's been staying up super late, baking. Usually, she only does that before big exams. Vi wonders if her sister is getting nervous about going to Georgetown. She doesn't want to embarrass Bea by asking in front of Chloe, though. "Um, okay. See you later."

"Thanks for walking Athena," Chloe calls. "See you later, boo!"

Vi is ninety-five percent sure "boo" is directed at Athena, not her. She loops Athena's leash around her wrist and heads down the street. She only gets as far as the Tabby Cat Café before she runs into another of her sisters. Kat is hauling a giant bag of trash out to the curb. She dumps it next to the already-full trashcan and heaves a theatrical sigh. Naturally, both dogs hurry over to sniff the garbage and see if there's anything they could eat.

"Kat?" Vi says.

"Vi! Hey, are you busy?" Kat scratches her nose, leaving a streak of white paint across it.

Vi waves her free hand at the two dogs. "Kind of, yeah."

"Oh. I have three more trash bags to bring out, and they're *heavy*," Kat complains. There's white paint on her knee too. And on her elbow.

"Where's Mase?" Vi asks.

"Mase. Called. Out. Sick." Kat's voice is brittle, and she overenunciates every word.

Vi takes a big step back. "You probably have whatever he has. Don't breathe on me."

Kat narrows her blue eyes. "He's not actually sick, Vi. He's hiding from me."

"Oh." There seems to be a lot going on with her sisters today. "Is—um, is everything okay?"

"No. I don't know. I hate boys," Kat says. "Is being a lesbian easier?"

"I don't think so," Vi says. She doesn't exactly have any point of comparison.

"Wait, is today your dog-walking date with Cece?" Kat looks at her, suddenly interested.

"It's not a date!" Vi blushes. She confided in Des this morning at breakfast that she was excited about her plans with Cece, and maybe she referred to it as a date. Kat had been lurking in the hall, eavesdropping, and overheard her poor choice of words. "Please don't call it a date. Also, do you know you're covered in paint?"

"I know." Kat sighs.

Vi is surprised that her sister hasn't already scrubbed it off then. Kat is usually immaculate in public. Vi peers at her: Kat's long, bright-red curls are straggling out of their bun; she's wearing jean shorts and an old *Star Wars* T-shirt with the neck cut out; she's covered in paint; and she's not wearing lipstick. Something is definitely wrong.

"I'm repainting the trim because it was all gross and gray. I figured while I'm waiting for it to dry so I can give it a second coat, I should haul out the trash. It's full of all those ugly old cat figurines and china plates. But Mase isn't here, and I really need his help."

Vi frowns. She likes Mase. He's one of the handful of openly out kids at school; he's in the Gay Straight Alliance with her. When he came over to watch a movie with Kat the other night, she found out that he's also a *Riverdale* fan. He is about a hundred times nicer than Kat's last boyfriend. Still, something is clearly amiss. Kat looks like she's going to cry—not fake, crocodile tears to get something she wants, but legit cry.

"Cece and I are going to walk the dogs in the park, and then I have to take them home," Vi says. "But...I could come help you paint the trim after that, if you want."

"Seriously? You're the best!" Kat steps forward as though she's going to hug her, and Vi hastily steps back.

"Don't touch me; you're gross. I'll help you, but I get to choose the painting music," she stipulates. "No Broadway stuff. I'm thinking Halsey."

Kat nods. "Fair. Totally fair. Thank you, Vi."

Vi watches her sister trudge back inside. Then she leads the dogs past the SunTrust and Carl's Pharmacy and the post office with its flags hanging limp in the still summer air. The working historical replica of the USS *Abigail* is anchored down at the dock, with a crowd of tourists waiting to board. There will be tours every afternoon for the next week, till the Tea Party reenactment next Saturday.

Athena spots a little black spaniel across the street and starts barking and yanking Vi forward. The Chans are still working on leash training so that she doesn't pull so much, but for now, she's wearing a special puppy harness instead of a collar. Vi turns onto Water Street. Tall, narrow brick colonials stand like sentinels right up against the sidewalk, with gorgeous back porches overlooking the river. Vi always wonders what it'd be like to live in one of those houses. She imagines spending whole afternoons reading and watching sailboats go by. She imagines holding hands with Cece and watching the fireworks, just the two of them.

Cece has stopped by the store twice this week before her shifts at Tia Julia's. On Tuesday, she and Vi sat inside the pirate ship beneath the stairs, their knees almost touching, and talked about their favorite books for two whole hours. Yesterday, Cece texted Vi to tell her she had seen Algernon, and then they texted back and forth about *Reign of the Fallen*, which Cece had borrowed and loved. Now, every time her phone buzzes, Vi's heart leaps.

As she waits for Cece at the entrance to Bishop Park, it

feels like her heart is still leaping. Like it's in a permanent state of hope.

Are they becoming friends—awesome in itself, of course—or is it possible that maybe, just maybe, Vi's feelings aren't totally unrequited? She might write swoony Beronica fics, but IRL Vi's never had a girlfriend. Back in eighth grade, she and her online friend Cara, a.k.a. CaraLovesClexa, flirted and chatted and sent each other snaps on Snapchat all the time. But Cara lived all the way in Portland, Oregon, and after a while, they drifted apart. Vi's never kissed anyone. At school, she's always been a loner. She's not ostracized or anything, but most of the time, she'd honestly rather be alone with a good book.

It turns out, it's kind of amazing to have someone to text back and forth with. Someone who stops by the store to see *her*, not Des. Someone who thinks she's cool and funny and confident, not weird. Vi still feels self-conscious with Cece, better at listening than talking, but she's learning to open up. She's afraid to hope for more and get disappointed—or, worse, risk losing this fledgling friendship.

"Vi!" Cece is jogging toward her. Athena jumps up, planting her oversized paws on Cece's thighs. Cece is wearing short pink shorts that show off her long brown legs. She's only an inch or two taller than Vi, but it seems like her legs go on forever. She's like a stork, or—something prettier than a stork. "Hey! How are my favorite girls?"

Vi would like to think that *she* is one of Cece's favorite girls, but she's pretty sure Cece means the dogs. "Hey," she says. "Want to take Juno? I'm trying to leash train this monster."

"Of course. Aw. Furry little monsterface, you're so adorable. Yes, you are," Cece coos, petting Athena's floppy ears. She reaches for Juno's leash, but Vi's banned books bracelet gets tangled up with it. "Hold still," Cece says, her fingers gentle against Vi's wrist. Vi blushes and hopes Cece can't feel her pulse racing.

They follow the jogging path down to the river and around the perimeter of the park. The midday sun is killer, and there's no breeze coming off the water today. After two laps, sweat is trickling down Vi's neck and along her spine, and her hair is escaping its braid in little wisps around her face.

A kid on a skateboard whizzes past, and Athena barks and lunges toward him. "Athena, no!" Vi says, trying to redirect her with a treat. It is more successful than it was yesterday, but her job is going to get harder as the town gets more crowded with tourists.

"Let's give the monsters some water," she says. Both dogs are panting, pink tongues lolling.

"Want to go over in the shade?" Cece suggests. The white gazebo in the middle of the park is a popular site for proposals and weddings, and it's the only patch of shade nearby.

When they reach it, Vi pulls out a bottle of water and the collapsible dog bowl. The dogs take turns lapping up water, nudging each other out of the way. She can't imagine being furry in this heat.

"Can we talk for a minute?" Cece asks.

"Sure." Vi's heart starts to hammer in her chest. She's suddenly unsure what to do with her hands. She gulps the last of the water from the bottle, swallows wrong, and starts coughing.

"Are you okay?" Cece asks.

Vi nods, red-faced and sputtering.

Cece sits on the grass with her long legs stretched out in front of her. Vi sits next to her, cross-legged, leaving enough space for Juno to plop down between them. Cece laughs, swats Juno's fluffy white tail away from her face, and then fiddles nervously with the silver cross she wears around her neck.

"There's something I want to tell you." Her dark eyes meet Vi's.

Vi nods encouragingly. Cece looks so serious. Is this what she thinks it is?

Cece takes a deep breath and then says it fast, in a rush: "I think I like girls too. I mean…I do. I like girls in addition to boys. I think maybe I'm bi." She stares down at the grass, then darts a glance at Vi. "You don't look surprised."

Vi smiles. Tries to look calm and reassuring, even though

inside she is *freaking out*. Cece likes girls! That means it is not impossible that, someday, Cece could like *her*.

"Reading every bi and lesbian YA book at Arden was kind of a big clue," she admits. "But thank you for telling me."

Not that this is about her—it's not—but it makes her so happy that Cece trusts her enough to share this with her.

Cece smiles back. "You're the first person I've told. I wanted to tell you last week, actually, at the Daily Grind. But I got nervous and chickened out."

"You don't have to tell anybody unless you want to," Vi reassures her.

"I haven't told my parents yet. I'm scared how they'll react." Cece tugs on the cross around her neck. "I'm scared what my abuela will say. But I did tell them Ben and I broke up."

"I'm really proud of you," Vi says, and then she winces, hoping that doesn't sound too presumptuous or patronizing. "I mean, I know you were worried about it. How did they take it?"

"It was hard. They really love Ben, and they've been friends with his parents for years. They were so excited when we started dating. I think they were planning our wedding and naming hypothetical future grandchildren," Cece admits. Juno, maybe sensing her distress—dogs are awesome like that—puts her furry white head in Cece's lap.

"You're fifteen," Vi says. "They shouldn't put that kind of pressure on you."

Cece pets Juno. "I know. I just hate feeling like I disappointed them somehow."

"You're smart and kind and thoughtful. What more could they want?"

"Straight?" Cece jokes, giving Vi her most genuine, dimpled grin. She is quiet for a moment, thoughtful. "Do you think your parents would have cared?"

"That I'm gay? I don't think so." It's impossible to know for sure. Would her mom have gotten a rainbow bumper sticker and taken her to DC Pride? Helped her make LGBTQIA book displays at Arden every June? Would her dad have made a rule that if her sisters couldn't have boys in their rooms with the doors closed, she couldn't have girls in her room with the door closed, because fair is fair? "Gram says they would have wanted me to be happy."

Cece sighs and redoes her ponytail. "I'm worried what people will think. What they'll say about me. You're so brave."

"I'm not that brave." Not brave enough to tell Cece how she really feels. "And remember, you don't have to tell anyone till you're ready."

Cece hugs her knees to her chest, dislodging Juno from her lap. "I'm not sure when that will be."

"There's no time limit. I knew for a couple of months

before I told Des. I was super nervous, even though I was pretty sure she'd be okay with it. When she was cool, I told Kat and Bea, and then Gram. You don't have to tell everybody all at once."

"But they were all supportive? Your whole family?" Cece asks.

Vi nods, remembering. Des illustrated a quote with dancing rainbows as a coming-out present. Bea did research on how to be a good ally and then printed it out at Gram's request. Kat joined the GSA for a hot second, till she got too busy with the spring musical and tried to convince Vi to join the drama club instead because it was very gay-friendly.

"You're lucky," Cece says. "Abuela Julia...I don't want her to think I'm going to hell, Vi."

"You're not going to hell. That's ridiculous," Vi says firmly. "Look, maybe she won't know what to say right away. Maybe she'll say the wrong thing at first. But she loves you. I don't think that will change. If she wants advice, she knows she can ask Gram."

"You won't tell her, though, right? Or your sisters?" Cece's shoulders tense.

"Of course not," Vi says. "It's not mine to tell."

Cece slumps back on her elbows and stares up at the cloudless blue sky. "Thank you. I'm so grateful for you, Vi. I kind of don't know what I'd do without you anymore."

"Me too," Vi says. Only she thinks she means it differently. Is it possible that her feelings *aren't* written all over her face? That Cece still doesn't know Vi is crazy about her? Or if she does know and hasn't said anything, what does *that* mean? What if Cece is attracted to girls, but not Vi, and doesn't want to hurt her feelings by addressing the elephant in the room that is Vi's crush?

Slow down, Vi reminds herself. *This is still really new for Cece. She's still figuring things out. Maybe she just needs time. It's not like you've told her how you feel.*

Vi looks down at her green Chucks, her freckled legs, her cutoff shorts, and her blue *Destroy the Patriarchy, Not the Planet* T-shirt. She knows she's kind of weird. Awkward, sometimes. Cece is gorgeous and popular. But they have so much in common. They never run out of things to talk about. And she's honored that Cece confided in her first. She is happy to be able to help her through the coming-out process, however long that takes. She wants to be Cece's friend, and she is trying so hard not to be selfish or make any of this about herself.

But she can't help wondering if maybe, someday soon, Cece might see her as something more than a friend.

CHAPTER TWENTY-ONE

DES

"I love it," **Des says,** staring down at the words freshly inked across her left forearm.

"Let me see!" Paige bounces up from her chair across the room. "Are you sure you don't want to add a little color? Some flowers or something?"

"It's perfect exactly the way it is," Des says firmly. She smiles up at Lola, the pink-haired tattoo artist. "Thank you so much."

"You're welcome, sweets." Lola gives her instructions on how to care for a new tattoo as she covers her forearm in plastic wrap. Des can't stop grinning. She wrote out the quote last night in one of her favorite styles, the letters swooping and curling. Lola traced it and then copied it onto Des's skin in blue ink. And now it's there on her forearm. Forever. After the blue hair fades, after Paige goes back to Baltimore in August, the tattoo will still be there. Maybe the thought should daunt her, but it doesn't.

Des isn't squeamish, but she didn't watch the actual tattooing process. There was plenty to look at around the room, which is decorated with strange tchotchkes and pop art and pin-up photos of Lola and her girlfriend, Grace. It's the perfect aesthetic for Lola, with her pink curls and 1950s-style pineapple-print halter dress.

"It barely even stung, right?" Paige crows. "I told you so. I told you Lola was amazing!"

"She is. This place is incredible." Des is still a little starstruck as they clatter downstairs.

"Right? Worth getting up early," Paige hands Grace her credit card.

Grace runs the card through the machine and then tucks her dark, pin-curled hair behind her ear. "Those are really cute earrings," she says to Des.

Des touches the blue and silver wire tangles. "Thank you. Paige made them, actually."

"Yeah?" Grace looks at Paige with interest. "Do you sell them? I'd love to buy some."

"Oh, thank you, but—I just make them for myself. Sometimes for friends," Paige says. It's the first time Des has ever seen her flustered. "Mostly I do sculptures. I go to MICA."

"You should think about selling them." Grace frowns at the card reader. "I'm sorry, your card was declined."

Paige cusses, then fumbles in her wallet and hands Grace another card. "Here, try this one."

"Sure." There's an awkward pause. Des stares at the pop art Marilyn Monroe on the wall behind the counter. "That was declined as well," Grace says, her voice a little chillier.

"Oh my God. I'm so sorry." Paige's porcelain skin is flushed. "This is really embarrassing. I don't have any cash on me. I'm, like, dead-ass broke right now."

Des looks at her, perplexed. How can that be true? Paige has picked up tons of hours at Tia Julia's over the last few weeks, and yesterday, she was crowing about getting great tips even though she's new and works mostly weeknights.

Regardless, this is super awkward. They can't stiff Lola for her work. Des reaches into her bag. "I'll pay for both of us."

"You sure?" Grace asks.

"Really? Thank you so much, Desdemona." Paige hugs her. "You're the best. *Thank you.* I'll pay you back as soon as I get paid on Friday, I promise."

"Thanks, sweetheart." Grace rings them up, and Des tries not to wince when she sees the total. Paige's tattoo—a gorgeous tangle of skulls and roses, a Day of the Dead design based on something Paige saw at Tia Julia's—is twice as expensive. It took almost two hours for Lola to ink it on her right shoulder blade.

"Want to get coffee? My treat, if I can scrounge up enough quarters," Paige jokes as they walk, blinking, back into the bright sunshine of Fell's Point.

Des checks her phone and groans. She's supposed to work at four, but it's already almost three. It will take at least two hours to drive from Baltimore back to Remington Hollow. "I can't. That took way longer than I estimated. I'm going to be so late. I've got to text Gram."

"Can't she cover for you?" Paige leans against her car. "We could go to the Visionary Art Museum. It's for self-taught artists. Outsiders. Have you ever been?"

Des tugs her red Curious George T-shirt down over her hips. "No. I really can't, though. Gram has physical therapy."

"Desdemona. Come on." Paige levels her with a stern, gray-eyed stare. "She totally takes advantage of you. You know that, right? You've been working ten-hour days, six days a week. Half the time, you don't even get a real lunch."

Des shakes her head. Paige doesn't understand. Gram's done *everything* for them. Not every grandparent would raise four orphaned girls and take on a small business that was barely in the black. "She's not taking advantage! She had major surgery. She's still recovering."

"And your sisters can't help out? There are four of you, aren't there? How come you're the only one I see working her ass off at the store? And at home too. Has anybody else been pitching in to cook and clean, or is it all you?" Paige asks.

"I don't clean that much." Des bites her lip. "I *should*, the house is a mess, but—"

"Des, stop it. You're not fucking Cinderella."

Paige has a point. Why should Des be the one to cook and vacuum and dust and scrub the bathtub and do everybody's laundry? Okay, maybe the bathtub is on her, because she stained it blue when she dyed her hair. But it's *still* blue, two weeks later. None of her sisters has thought, *Hey, Des is busy working ten hours a day at Arden and then cooking us dinner every damn night. Maybe I could at least scrub the bathtub for her.*

She thought they would step up more after school was out, but they haven't.

"Well, they're all really busy," she says. "Bea has her internship, and she's working on a raft for the race." Still, Bea has enough time to stay out until midnight lately and then stress bake until two a.m. "Kat has rehearsal every night, and she's been working at your grandma's place during the day." Des is still annoyed that Kat got a job somewhere else—conveniently, where her new boyfriend works—and that Gram *let* her. "And Gram doesn't want

Vi working alone yet. She's only fifteen. So, like, theoretically she worked with me the other day, but mostly she and Cece sat in the pirate ship and talked about books for two hours."

Paige puts her hands on her skinny hips. "Let's be real, okay? You're making excuses for them. Fine, they have lives; whatever. You deserve to have a life too. You're letting them walk all over you. It's not cool."

"I have a life!" Des snaps, wounded.

"Do you? How much time have you had to work on your art this summer?" Paige asks.

"My art?" Des blushes. The other day, Paige stopped by Arden on her break, and Des showed her two potential lettering options for the tattoo. While she was helping a customer, Paige flipped through her sketchbook and saw some of the quotes Des has been illustrating lately.

"Yes. Your *art*," Paige says. "You are an artist. You're really talented, okay?"

"I thought you were just high," Des admits.

Paige cackles. "Nah. I mean, I was, but I wouldn't say it if it weren't true. You should be doing something with your work."

"Oh, you're one to talk." Paige looks blank, and Des tugs on her earring. "You heard Grace. You could sell these. Start an Etsy shop, or"—Des thinks for a minute—"sell them at the farmer's market. People sell all kinds of stuff there: handmade candles, soap, fancy wooden cutting boards, photographs—"

"I'll do it if you do it," Paige interrupts.

Des twirls the turquoise ring on her finger. "What? No."

"Yes." Paige is nodding, her purple ponytail bouncing. "Yes! People would absolutely buy your quotes. They would probably buy them even if you weren't very good, because you're Desdemona Garrett, and everybody loves you and your whole crazy family. But you *are* good, so you'll sell twice as many. Let's do it. Let's get a table at the farmer's market. Do you think we could get one for Saturday? There'll be a billion tourists in town for Tea Party."

Des's eyes go wide. "That's in *four days*. I can't have anything ready in four days!"

"You could if you took some time off work," Paige says.

"I can't." It's automatic.

"You can. You just have to tell your gram and your sisters what you need from them."

Des twirls the ring around her finger faster and faster. "But it's not really—I'm not really—"

"I mean this in the nicest possible way, but if you say that you're not a real artist one more time, I'm going to punch you," Paige says. "I'm not fucking around, okay? I'm telling you, those quotes are rad, and people will pay money for them. I'm not suggesting you quit your day job, but if you love doing this—"

"I do." Des is nodding like a marionette. "I really do. I just—I've always thought of it as this nerdy hobby." *Practicing your handwriting*, Em said.

"Look, you have to take yourself seriously if you want anybody else to." Paige pokes her in the shoulder. "I want you to say it out loud. Say, 'I am an artist and my art is rad.' Say it!"

"Ouch!" Des ducks away, but she's laughing. "Okay! I am an artist and my art is rad."

"Hell yeah, it is." Paige slings an arm around her. "All right. Let's go home, Desdemona."

⁓ဪ⁓

Three hours later, Des rushes into Arden, the bell clanging above her. Gram sits in the flowered armchair near the counter, her leg propped on a red tasseled footstool. A mom with two kids is browsing in the children's section. Mr. Dixon, Des's eighth-grade Maryland history teacher, is scanning their nonfiction shelves.

"I'm sorry I'm late!" Des texted Gram to let her know she would be an hour late and then texted her again when they got stuck in traffic. "I'm sorry you had to reschedule your physical therapy. Bea couldn't leave the paper early?"

"She had an interview with Lydia about the grand reopening," Gram says.

Des can't read the look on her face. "What about Kat?"

"Kat was rearranging furniture so the photographer could take pictures to accompany the article. Vi was out with Cece. And it wasn't *their* responsibility." Gram's blue eyes are narrowed behind her glasses. "Des, this isn't like you."

"I'm sorry. I said I was sorry." Des drops her bag behind the counter and tucks the telltale edge of plastic wrap beneath the sleeve of her black cardigan. Her tattoo is starting to sting like a bad sunburn.

"What's that?" Gram asks.

Des wasn't planning to hide the tattoo exactly, but she was hoping to find the right moment to reveal it. Preferably a moment that wouldn't involve arguing in front of customers.

"I got a tattoo," she explains, carefully pulling off the cardigan and holding out her plastic-wrapped forearm.

"You did what?" Gram's feathery eyebrows, identical to Des's, shoot up so high, they disappear beneath her bangs. "You didn't think this was something you might mention?"

"I'm nineteen," Des says. "I don't need your permission."

Gram purses her lips. "Was this Paige's idea?"

"It was, but I love it. I really love it. Look. It's an Agatha Christie quote." Des gingerly unwraps the plastic. "I did the lettering, and then Lola traced it. It's kind of swollen right now, but—"

"Lola? Did you research this place first and make sure it was safe?" Gram asks.

"Paige has gotten all her tattoos there," Des says. "And Lola explained the whole process before she even touched me. She was great. We were supporting an awesome, woman-owned small business."

"*We?* So Paige got a tattoo too? How on earth did she pay for that? Every dollar she makes this summer is supposed to go toward repaying her mother!" Gram's voice is getting louder. Mr. Dixon peeks around the nonfiction display and then makes his way toward the door.

"Gram. I don't want to argue about Paige." Des is not about to confide that she paid for Paige's tattoo. It's only a loan, after all. "I need to talk to you about something else. I would really like to take some time off this week. Do you think Bea or Kat could work for me Thursday and Friday?"

Gram rises from her chair, still a little wobbly, and grabs her cane. "You were two hours late because you were off getting a tattoo, and now you're asking if you can take two days off with no notice? Your sisters are busy, Des. There are two issues of the *Gazette* this week. The café's grand reopening is Saturday, and Kat has been working very hard to help Lydia get ready."

Kat has been working very hard? What about all Des's hard work over the last month? Hell, over the last *year?* Des tries to control her twitching temper. "Maybe you and Vi could work together? She can run upstairs for anything you need. I could help for an hour or two while she's walking the dogs. I just—I really need some time off."

"For what? Are you and Paige taking a trip? I have to tell you, Des, I really do not approve of this friendship." Gram sighs.

"Excuse me." It's the woman with the two little boys, balancing the baby in one arm and a teetering stack of picture books in the other. "I'm ready to buy these."

"Great. Thank you so much." Des compliments the baby, asks how old he is, and hands the toddler a bookworm sticker while she rings up the purchase. She waits until they're gone before she turns back to Gram. "I want to sell my art. Some of the quotes I've been working on. There will be so many people in town on Saturday for the parade and the reenactment and the fireworks. It would be the perfect time to try this, but I need to make more prints. Please, Gram."

"Does that mean you want Saturday off too?" Gram shakes her head. "That's one of the busiest days of the year for us, honey. You know that. I need you here."

Des's mind spins. She hadn't thought that far ahead yet, but there has to be some way to make this work. She's willing to compromise. "We always have a couple of tables on the sidewalk for Tea Party, right? What if you let me and Paige take one of them? She's going to sell her earrings too. Then she can handle our table and I'll handle the books. You'd need somebody outside anyway."

Gram pulls off her glasses and cleans them on her white linen pants. "I don't know. I don't trust her, Des."

"Then trust me," Des says. "Please, Gram. This is important to me."

Gram puts her glasses back on and looks at Des for a long minute. "All right. And if you can get one of your sisters to work for you, you can have Thursday and Friday off. But they have their own responsibilities, honey. They might not be able to accommodate you last minute like this."

Des wants to remind Gram of all the times that Kat or Bea have flaked on their hours at Arden because they had rehearsal, or had too much homework, or had to work late at the paper, or wanted to see Erik's tennis match. Des always covers for them. *Always*. Did they get lectures from Gram too? Why is Des's time less valuable?

She doesn't say any of that. Not now. The timing isn't right. Instead, she nods. "Thank you, Gram. I'll work it out with Vi. You won't regret this. I promise."

CHAPTER TWENTY-TWO

BEA

On Wednesday night, Bea's team gathers at Sierra's house. They always work on the raft in Sierra's backyard; her dad has all the tools they need and a shed big enough to store the raft. Their design is pretty simple this year: logs tied together with rope and a plywood platform on top. Their theme is *Star Wars*, so they're building BB-8 and R2-D2 to accompany them. They'll all be dressed as *Star Wars* characters: Sierra as Rose, Drew and Faith as Han and Leia, Erik as Poe, Bea as Rey, and Chloe in a C-3PO dress with gold body paint. Erik had wanted him and Bea to be Han and Leia, but Bea had pointed out that her hair isn't long enough for Leia's iconic buns.

Really, she doesn't want to dress as a couple. It feels too much like a lie.

Sierra, who knows her way around power tools like a boss, is working with the boys to assemble the raft. Faith and Chloe are attaching Styrofoam legs to a trashcan R2-D2 they've already painted silver and white. Yesterday Bea spray-painted an exercise ball white and attached a half sphere of Styrofoam as BB-8's head. Now she's trying to paint the droid's distinctive orange and silver markings.

She glances at the pictures she printed. She isn't great at painting, and she doesn't like doing things she isn't good at. It's her team's fourth and probably final race. When they were freshmen, their *Jurassic Park* raft was a stylish disaster. It sank halfway through the race because they hadn't properly accounted for the weight of their dinosaur props, but it won the Kitchen Sink Award for Most Impressive Failure. Sophomore year, they did a Captain America theme and won the Junior Cup for best raft with a crew mostly sixteen and under. Last year, their theme was *Guardians of the Galaxy*. Chloe dressed up as Gamora with green body paint, and they carried a stuffed raccoon and a Baby Groot. They blasted the soundtrack using Sierra's waterproof speakers. And they won the coveted Tea Cup, the Best of Show. Bea is determined to win again this year. She can't screw this up too. She dips her paintbrush in the orange paint can.

A gray pickup rattles by in the crumbling brick alley behind Sierra's backyard. Bea glances up and freezes, her heart plummeting to somewhere around her bare feet.

It's Gabe. He sees her, stops the truck, and leans out the window. "Hey!"

Oh no. Oh *shit*.

Bea dashes to the truck, trampling through Mrs. Alvarez's pink and white impatiens. She still has the paintbrush in her hand; it's dripping orange paint onto her bare knee.

"Hi, Gabe!" She glances over her shoulder. Everyone is watching. *Erik* is watching.

"Hey. What are you doing?" Gabe grins at her, pushing his sunglasses to the top of his head. "Is that going to be BB-8?"

"Uh-huh. Yeah. The other one's going to be R2-D2. It's for the raft race on Sunday. Our theme is *Star Wars*. Obviously," Bea explains.

She's been down at the marina, hanging out with Gabe, almost every night for the past week. There have been more kisses—a lot of kisses—but she's stopped before things went further.

It's not just about kissing either. At least she doesn't think so. They've talked about their families. Their lives. How he's in his third year at Vanderbilt, studying musical arts and teacher education. How much he loves Nashville. Bea told him how her parents died. About her internship at the *Gazette* and how she wants to be a journalist. But she hasn't told him about her team for the raft race. She hasn't told him anything that involves Erik. She has left out huge, gaping swaths of her life.

"What are you doing here?" It comes out sort of accusatory.

"I was at Memaw's place." Of course. Miss Amelia's backyard backs up to the alley too. "Uncle Matt and I took out the carpet in the living and dining rooms, and there was this gorgeous old hardwood underneath. You should come by and see it sometime."

Bea bites at her fingernail. "I'd like that." She looks back at the others. Chloe and Faith have abandoned all pretense of attaching R2-D2's second leg to stare at her and Gabe. Sierra is focused as always, attaching the plywood while Drew holds it steady. Erik's hands are on the raft, but his eyes are on Bea.

"This is cool. You didn't tell me you were doing this." The way he smiles at Bea makes her melt, but right now, she needs him to quit it. It's not a just-friends smile. "You guys need any help? I'm pretty good with this stuff."

"No. We're good. I mean, thank you." Bea blushes. "This is kind of—our thing. Our team. This is our fourth year. We won last year, actually. Our theme was *Guardians of the Galaxy*." She can't stop talking. "I should probably get back to—"

"Hey, Bea. What's up?" Erik is suddenly next to her. Jesus, this is bad. This is so bad. She shifts away from him.

"Hey, Erik. This, um. This is Gabe. You remember Miss Amelia? This is her grandson. He's in town fixing up her old house. Gabe, I should get back to painting the—"

"Hey. I'm Erik." Erik reaches out to shake Gabe's hand and slips his other arm around Bea's waist. What is he, a fucking octopus? "I'm Bea's boyfriend. Nice to meet you."

Oh shit oh shit oh shit oh shit.

Bea wants to sink through the ground and disappear. She stares at Gabe, trying to apologize without words.

"Oh." Gabe looks—surprised. He shakes Erik's hand quickly. "Hey."

He could say so many snarky, awful things right now. But he doesn't.

Unlike Bea, he is a good person.

"I'll let y'all get back to painting," he says, sliding his sunglasses down over his eyes. Bea can't tell what he's thinking. Is he mad at her? He must be mad at her.

She shrugs away from Erik, but he keeps his hand on the small of her back, possessive. He's making it clear that she belongs to him. He might as well pee on her.

Normally, this would infuriate her. Jealousy is stupid. If you can't trust the person you're with, why are you with them? Back in May, Kat got her heart broken by her first serious boyfriend. They could all see it coming a mile away. Bea tried to warn her that if she didn't trust Adam, if she had to snoop through his phone, if she was that jealous when he was around other girls, maybe her gut was telling her something important.

Right now, maybe Erik's gut is telling him something important.

Bea never, ever thought she would be this person.

"Bye," she says faintly after Gabe's already driven off. She starts to walk back to BB-8.

"How do you two know each other?" Erik asks.

"We met at the Daily Grind," Bea says. "I ran into him. Literally. Spilled coffee all over him."

"I think he likes you," Erik says. *He knows.* He is not the irrationally jealous type.

"What? No!" But her voice doesn't sound believable even to her own ears.

She can't keep doing this. She's lying. Not only by omission, but straight out lying to his face now. Yeah, Gabe likes her. And she likes him.

How did she become this person—someone who is cheating on her boyfriend of five years because she's too much of a coward to break up with him?

But how can she break up with him before Sunday? She looks over at their friends. This is their last Tea Party. Chloe's going to Penn, Sierra's going to Villanova, Drew and Faith are going to Carnegie Mellon. Erik will be at Georgetown. Bea will be...

Where? She doesn't have a plan. She still doesn't have a plan.

Chloe must see her panicking. "Hey! Get back to work, you two! It's going to get dark in an hour, and we still have a lot to do."

Bea kneels and dips her paintbrush back into the orange paint. Erik hesitates and then goes back to the raft.

After she tells him the truth, he won't want to see her. He won't want to stay friends. He won't want Bea on his team for anything, ever again.

She'll tell him after the race.

~~

Sierra and the boys finish assembling the raft, and Faith starts painting the assembled R2-D2. Chloe takes pity on Bea and helps her with BB-8. When it gets dark, they haul everything into Sierra's shed. Their life jackets and paddles from previous years are piled in a corner. Seeing them makes Bea's chest ache.

Once her friends find out, they won't want her on their team anymore either. Drew and Faith have always been closer to Erik. Sierra will follow Faith's lead because they're best friends. Maybe Chloe will still be her friend. But Bea has no illusions that she's anything besides the villain in this breakup story.

She can't stop thinking about the surprise that flitted across Gabe's face.

She owes him the truth too. Maybe he won't want anything to do with her now. She wouldn't blame him for that. She's a damn mess. But she has to at least try to explain.

Erik offers her a ride home, but she tells him she wants to walk. It's a nice night. She and Chloe walk downtown together. When they part to go their separate ways, Chloe hesitates, flipping her dark braid over her shoulder.

"Is there something going on with you and that guy?" she asks. "The one in the truck?"

"No. What? No." Bea is not a very good liar.

Chloe rolls her eyes. "Bea. Come on. Breaking up with Erik, Georgetown—is this all about some other guy?"

"No. I felt this way before Gabe. I just—I'm surer now."

"But not sure enough to break up with Erik?" Chloe asks. "I'm sorry, but—"

Bea winces. "No, I deserve that. I'm going to break up with him on Sunday. After the race. After we win."

Chloe nods. "I'm going to hold you to that."

Bea hesitates at the next corner. Turning right will lead her home. Going straight will take her down to the marina. She should go home. She shouldn't see Gabe again until she's broken up with Erik. It's not fair to anybody.

She goes to the marina anyway. The lantern is on inside the *Stella Anne*. If Gabe were really mad, he would have gone out, right? He had to know she'd come by. She steps onto the deck of the houseboat, hope buzzing along her skin.

He meets her in the doorway, dressed in a black T-shirt and jeans. He smells spicy, shower gel or cologne or something, and his hair is down around his shoulders, still wet. She's never seen it down before. It hits her suddenly, how much she still doesn't know about him. How much she wants to know.

"You shouldn't be here," he says.

"I want to be here. I want to explain."

"Explain what? That you have a boyfriend?" Gabe shakes his head. "I got that."

"Can we go inside and talk? Please? I'm sorry. I'm so, so sorry." Her voice breaks, and she blinks back tears. She won't cry. She won't use tears to make him feel sorry for her. That's not fair.

"Sorry that you were lying to me this whole time? Or sorry I found out?" His Tennessee twang gets more pronounced when he's mad. "Nah. I'm done hiding. We can talk about this right here, out in the open."

"I'm sorry that I lied. Although—we never said we were exclusive. We never said what this was." Bea knows that's a weak argument. "You could be seeing someone else." She imagines Savannah kissing him, and she wants to punch things.

"I'm not, and you know it," Gabe says. "I don't operate like that. You're right. We didn't talk about it. Hell, I knew there was stuff you weren't telling me. But I thought it was about Georgetown, not that there was somebody else." He sighs. "I like you, Bea. I like you a lot. But I'm not going to be the guy you cheat with."

"I like you a lot too," she says. He raises his eyebrows. "I do! This is just—it's complicated, okay? Erik and I have been together since we were thirteen. We're supposed to go to Georgetown together. That's—it's not what I want. It hasn't been since before I met you. I know I haven't been honest with you. But being here, with you—it's the only time I don't feel like I'm falling apart. I am such a damn mess right now. I don't know how you can like me. I don't like myself very much, honestly."

He rubs a hand over his stubbly chin. His shoulders relax a little. "You're not so bad."

She looks at him, hopeful, and takes a step forward. "You think?"

"Yeah." He reaches out and then seems to rethink it. He takes a step back. Away from her. "But I can't do this. Not till you figure out what you want."

"I want *you*." Her answer is immediate, unhesitating. It feels like the only solid ground beneath her feet. "Erik and

I had this whole plan; we had our future all mapped out. It wasn't mine or his; it was *ours*. And I don't want that future anymore, but I don't have a new plan yet, and it's really scary. I thought I had everything figured out, and I was so damn smug about it. Now I look at next week, at next month, at August when I'm supposed to be leaving for Georgetown, and it's all a big question mark. And I don't do uncertainty well. That's…kind of an understatement, actually." Bea takes a deep breath. "But I'm going to break up with him. I am. After the race on Sunday. I can't do it till after the race, okay?"

Gabe is quiet. She can hear the water lapping against the dock, against the boat.

"Okay," he says finally.

"Yeah?" What does that mean? Does that mean he forgives her?

Gabe takes another step back. "We'll talk about it more on Sunday."

And then he goes back inside, and he shuts the door in her face.

CHAPTER TWENTY-THREE
KAT

On Thursday night, Kat is the first one in the rehearsal room. It's rare that she's early for anything. She prefers to make an entrance. But she's been trying to be more responsible lately, to show people that they can count on her, and that includes being on time.

Also, she was hoping Mase would be early too, and they would have a chance to talk.

Things have changed between them since Brandon's text. Mase called out sick the next day. He tried it the day after that too. Kat was ninety-nine percent sure he was avoiding her, but she went to the Kims' house with chicken noodle soup, saltine crackers, and ginger ale like some kind of pissed off Little Red Riding Hood hedging her bets. When Mase answered the door looking rumpled but perfectly healthy, she shoved the basket at him and told him to get his ass back to work because she needed him.

Kat is worried that she needs him.

She waited downstairs while he changed out of his boxers and wrinkled T-shirt into jeans and a less wrinkled T-shirt. While he did his eyeliner and made his hair swoopy. The fauxhawk is growing out into more of a pompadour, which Kat really digs.

Mase came back to work with her Friday, but he's been strictly hands off unless people are watching. No holding hands. No cuddling. No flirting even. When they're at rehearsal or at work, they're an adorable couple. They've taken dozens of carefully curated selfies with the cats. But now that the café's reopened and Miss Lydia is there during the day, they're almost never alone. Mase bolts the minute that work or rehearsal is over.

And he hasn't kissed her once.

Kat's slumped in one of the ugly, high-backed armchairs in the rehearsal room when the door opens and Pen, Jillian, and Hannah—who plays the fourth March sister, Beth—come clamoring in. All three girls have wet hair, and Jillian's carrying a Vera Bradley beach bag stuffed with magazines. As Kat watches, Jillian paws through it and grabs a water bottle.

"Swimming always makes me so thirsty," she says.

Hannah pokes at her pink forearm. "I think I got sunburned."

"I told you to wear sunscr—" Pen stops when she sees Kat peering out from behind the chair. "Hey, Kat."

It hits Kat like a slap in the face: They all went swimming at Pen's. Without her.

"Hi." Kat unfolds her long flamingo legs and stands up, ready for battle. How could Pen do this to her? She's been Kat's best friend since *kindergarten*. How could she betray her like this?

"Let's go get sodas from the machine," Hannah suggests, grabbing Jillian's arm and towing her away.

Pen rushes to fill the silence. "It was cast bonding. We're supposed to be sisters, right?"

"Last time I checked, there are *four* sisters," Kat snaps.

Pen grabs the whiteboard eraser and starts clearing notes from the French class that meets there every Thursday afternoon. "I invited you over. You said you had to work."

"The grand reopening is in two days. And you didn't tell me it was a cast-bonding thing! I'm busy, so you decide to hang out with *Jillian*? Of all the people in the entire world, you had to pick *her*? There are easier ways to tell me you're mad at me, Pen."

"The entire world doesn't revolve around you, Kat!" Pen is still furiously erasing French.

"What. The. Hell." Kat shakes her head. "What's going on with you?"

"What's going on with me? What's going on with *you*?" Pen drops the eraser and turns to face Kat, planting her hands on her hips. "You haven't had any time to hang out with me for weeks. Ever since you started dating Mase. Since when is a guy more important than our friendship? And since when do you even *like* Mase? Three weeks ago, you were still chasing after Adam!"

Kat glances over her shoulder, but the door to the hallway is closed. "First of all, I was not and never have been 'chasing after' anyone. That is beneath us. And no guy, Adam or Mase or *anybody*, is more important than our friendship! Sorry if I thought it was strong enough that the minute you got mad at me, you wouldn't decide to be BFFs with Jillian."

Pen rolls her brown eyes. "I'm not BFFs with Jillian. I had her and Hannah over *once*." She pauses. "And we all got ice cream Tuesday after rehearsal."

Kat's stomach twists. Or maybe it's her back. From the *knife* Pen just stabbed her with. "Why didn't you invite me?"

"I *did* invite you!" Pen protests. "You said you were tired, and you left with Mase. What am I supposed to do, wait around till you find time in your busy schedule to hang out with me?"

"No! But you're not supposed to hang out with *Jillian*! You said she was a basic Abercrombie bitch," Kat reminds her. "You said Adam would cheat on her too, and that she'd deserve it."

"Well, that was before I knew her," Pen mutters. "She's nice."

Kat stares at her. "I can't believe this! You're supposed to be my best friend."

"It goes both ways. I *know* there's something you're not telling me," Pen says.

Kat covers her face with her hands. Why does everything feel like it's spinning out of control? Why can't anyone follow the script in her head and do what they're supposed to do?

She has to give Pen a piece of the truth. She owes her that. "You're right."

"I am?" Pen worries her lower lip between her teeth. "I knew it. Are you okay? Are you relapsing?"

"What? No!" Kat says. "It's Mase. Brandon texted him last week. He's coming home for Tea Party, and he wants to talk, and I don't know what that means. For Mase and me." She takes a deep breath. "I...I really like him, Pen."

Pen searches her face and then, apparently satisfied that Kat is telling the truth—or at least *a* truth—rolls her eyes. "Obviously. Since you've been so busy that you—"

"Pen. Come on." Kat bends one long leg against the wall. She gets that she hasn't had much time for Pen this summer. She gets that maybe Pen is scared she's dropping their friendship for a boy. But that would never happen. "This job is really important to me, okay? Miss Lydia's wanted to redecorate for a while because their sales and adoptions were down, but when I told her my ideas, she totally ran with them. This has been her business for twenty-five years, and she trusted me to redo it. She says I have a great sense of style. And she trusted me to get everything done on time for the grand reopening and to use her business credit card and...I didn't want to screw that up. No one has ever had that much faith in me. I'm the *dramatic* one, you know? The diva. And maybe I play into that sometimes, but—it means a lot to me that Miss Lydia took me seriously. Nobody ever takes me seriously."

"I do," Pen says quietly.

"And that's why you're my best friend." Kat smiles at her. "I'm sorry if I've been taking you for granted. Do you have plans on Saturday?"

Pen runs a hand over the long side of her blond hair. "Besides watching reenactors dump tea in the river? No."

"Will you come and take pictures during the grand reopening? You're the best photographer I know," Kat says. "And it would mean a lot to me if you were there. But Monday's my day off, and I was thinking—if you're free—we could go swimming and read some romance novels and eat Popsicles? Please? Pretty please?"

Pen gives her a slow smile. "All right."

Kat sinks back down in the armchair. "Excellent. You're the best."

Pen perches on the arm of the chair. "I'm not finished. I'll take pictures on Saturday if you promise to be nice to Jillian from now on."

Kat scowls. "Do I have to?"

"Yes. It's not her fault Adam is an asshole. Better women have fallen for those eyes, you know?" She pokes Kat in the shoulder.

"Truth." Kat smirks. "Fine. I'll try. No promises."

The door to the hallway inches open, and Mase's pomaded hair peeks in, followed by his forehead and his dark eyes. "Hey, can the rest of us come in? Are you two done fighting?"

"We're not fighting," Kat says, wrapping an arm around Pen's waist.

Pen pokes Kat in the shoulder again as Mase gives the all-clear. "You should talk to him," she hisses.

Kat shakes her head. "They were together for two years. I can't compete with that."

"Yes, you can. You're *here*, and Brandon's not. And you're amazing. Mase is lucky to have you as his girl-friend."

"I guess," Kat says. Is that what she wants? To be Mase's girlfriend for real?

She watches him come in and settle his stuff on the beat-up sofa nearby. She misses him. They've seen each other every day between work and rehearsal, but it's not the same. They were inseparable for two weeks, and she didn't get bored or annoyed with him at all. They had so much *fun* together—not just kissing, but joking around, singing show tunes, painting, playing with the cats, having picnics in the empty café. They were supposed to be pretending, but somehow she was more real with him than she's ever been with anyone except Pen and her family. She didn't worry about being too dramatic or too loud or too much. She was herself. And Mase liked that.

Or she thought he did, anyway.

She looks at Adam, whose popped-collar dude-bro attitude doesn't seem appealing at all anymore. She knows that the dimples and stormy gray eyes and warm brown skin create an attractive package, aesthetically speaking, but somehow, sometime in the past two weeks, she's stopped being hyperconscious of where he is in the room, so aware of his voice that she could follow the thread of it even when the whole cast is chattering on break. She doesn't watch Adam to see whether he's watching her or whether he's holding Jillian's hand.

She watches Mase instead.

Mase, with his mustard-yellow hipster-grandpa cardigan and skinny jeans and wingtip shoes. Mase, with his perfect black eyeliner and obscenely long lashes and dark-chocolate eyes. Mase, who makes her laugh and sings *Hamilton* to the cats and gives shoulder massages that rock her world.

She's actually falling for him.

This definitely wasn't part of the plan.

CHAPTER TWENTY-FOUR
VI

Vi skips family dinner for the first time ever on Friday night.

Cece and her abuela have plans to make Julia's famous chicken and tomatillo tamales, which, Cece explained, is a time-consuming, whole-afternoon process and one of her very favorite things. She was appalled that Vi has never had tamales. That had to be rectified *immediately*, she insisted, and she gave Vi her most winsome, dimpled smile as she invited her over for dinner. Vi would have agreed to almost anything for that smile. Fortunately, Gram took one look at Vi's pleading, puppy-dog eyes and conceded.

Now, as she stands on the Pérezes' front porch, Vi wishes Gram had said no. At home, she would be wearing shorts and her *Girls Just Want to Have Fun(damental Rights)* T-shirt instead of a knee-length black dress with a bumblebee print and a Peter Pan collar plus a pair of pinching black flats, both borrowed from Kat. At home, she wouldn't worry about whether she was talking too much or not enough. She wouldn't worry whether she likes tamales. She definitely wouldn't wonder if anyone in the room thought she was going to hell.

Vi takes a deep breath, then reaches out and rings the doorbell.

The door flies open almost instantly. "You're here! Hi!" Cece is wearing shorts and a black tank top, and she's barefoot, with her hair pulled into a ponytail. Vi immediately worries that she's too dressed up.

"Hi," she says.

They've seen each other almost every day since Cece announced she was bi. On Saturday, Cece asked if Vi wanted to go to the movies; the Remington Theater was showing an Anne Hathaway double feature of *The Princess Diaries* and *Ella Enchanted*. Vi said yes, of course. The theater was crowded with tons of tween girls, but they sat in the back and shared a bucket of popcorn, and every time their hands touched, Vi felt like she'd been electrified. They started off sitting rigidly in their own seats with their hands in their laps. But by the end of the first movie, Cece's leg was pressed against Vi's, and her hand rested on her knee, only inches away. Vi had wanted to reach over and take it. Did Cece want her to? Had Cece moved closer on purpose? What if she was misreading the situation, and that wasn't what Cece wanted at all? In the end, Vi just sat there, yearning and confused.

This week, they had walked Juno and Athena in the park on Monday and Wednesday. Cece worked the lunch shift on Tuesday, but afterward, they grabbed fraps at the Daily Grind, where Cece convinced Vi to share one of her Beronica fics. Blushing furiously, covering her eyes with both hands, and squirming in her seat, she had handed Cece her phone and practically held her breath while Cece read. Cece had said she loved it. And then yesterday, she had swung by Arden and invited Vi to dinner.

They texted all the time now. About everything. Cece had started watching *Riverdale* and texted Vi her reactions. She sent her selfies with funny filters. She complained about her brothers and fangirled about the books Vi lent her. It was amazing, a total dream come true, and Vi was so grateful—but she was also confused. Was this what having a best friend was like? It felt like more than that, intense and intoxicating. But maybe it only felt like that to her?

In the Pérezes' front hall, there's a crucifix and half a dozen framed photos of Cece and her brothers. Vi pauses in front of a picture of Cece in her middle-school soccer uniform, posed with a soccer ball on the athletic field, her dark hair a riot of curls, her smile full of braces.

Cece cringes and pulls her away. "No, don't look. Those are so embarrassing!"

"Please." Vi rolls her eyes. "Like you ever take a bad picture."

Cece laughs her fizzy laugh. "I do too. I just use filters."

Cece always looks adorable, even if she's vomiting a rainbow or sporting red-laser robot eyes or koala ears. Vi doesn't understand how she does it. It takes Vi ten minutes to get a flattering selfie. She always has an initial moment of disorientation, as though the girl staring back into the camera isn't really her. There's something off about her eyes or her smile or the way she carries her shoulders. *Is that how I really look?* she thinks, and she feels disappointed.

"Filters don't help with my innate awkward," Vi says.

"You're not awkward! Well, you are sometimes, but…" Cece touches the shoulder of Vi's dress, her fingertips brushing Vi's neck. It's the latest in a series of increasingly familiar gestures, like tucking her shirt tag in yesterday or touching her hand to get her attention. "Don't you know how pretty you are?"

Vi feels helpless, caught in an invisible current between them. How can she be the only one who feels it? They stand there, Cece's hand lingering on her shoulder, her brown eyes staring into Vi's blue. Vi takes Cece's other hand, twining their fingers together.

It feels like the most natural thing in the world.

It feels like the most awkward thing in the world.

Cece squeezes her hand. Then she drops it and hurries down the hall.

Vi bites her lip. What is happening between them? What does it all *mean*?

She straightens her collar and follows Cece, nervous about meeting her abuela in this context, even though she has already met her dozens of times. She's grateful that Cece's parents are working at the restaurant tonight and won't be joining them.

"Miguel! Danny! Vi's here, and dinner's almost ready," Cece says. Two of her brothers are sprawled on the carpeted living room floor, playing some football video game. They grunt in acknowledgment and continue wrestling with their controllers.

Cece leads the way into the kitchen, which seems bigger and newer than the last time Vi was here. "Abuela and Luis and I made tamales! Some of them are chicken in tomatillo sauce and some are poblano and cheese. You're not vegetarian, right? I should have checked."

"I'm not. It smells amazing," Vi says. Like chicken and onions and garlic and tomatoes and spices. Cece's littlest brother, Luis, is stirring a big skillet of refried beans while his abuela supervises. Julia Pérez is a short woman with a wrinkled brown face and iron-gray hair pulled into a bun.

She likes Agatha Christie, and sometimes she attends Des's mystery book club. Also, she is apparently homophobic.

Vi isn't sure how to cope with that.

"It's nice to see you, Viola," Mrs. Pérez says.

"Vi," Cece corrects. "Nobody calls her Viola!"

"Thank you so much for having me, Mrs. Pérez," Vi says.

"You're welcome any time." A timer beeps, and Mrs. Pérez switches off the stove and reaches for the big steamer pot. It looks like the one Gram uses to steam crabs. "Everything is nearly ready. Cece, will you call your brothers?"

"Danny! Miguel!" Cece shouts.

"I could have done that," Mrs. Pérez scolds. "Go and tell them. You wash up, Luis."

Cece gives Vi an impish grin and darts off to call her brothers. Vi stares down at the red-tiled floor. She's run into Mrs. Pérez on the sidewalk outside Arden, at middle school graduation, at the farmer's market and bluegrass concerts in Bishop Park. But it feels different now. There is so much Vi wants to say and can't. She wants to tell Mrs. Pérez how much Cece loves her. How much Cece is afraid of disappointing her. She wants to ask whether Mrs. Pérez ever misses her estranged brother. Whether she would do it differently if she could do it all over again. Whether she believes Vi is going to hell. Whether she would condemn her granddaughter for being bi.

The silence grows and stretches between them, sticky as pulled taffy.

Vi looks around at the granite countertops and the shining wooden cabinets. There's a double oven and a farmhouse sink and a subway tile backsplash—terms Vi only knows because Gram has been watching a lot of HGTV since her knee replacement—and a big wooden table already set for six. "This is a beautiful kitchen."

"Thank you. My son had it renovated last year," Mrs. Pérez says.

"Papi had an extension put on the back so Abuela could have a bigger kitchen and Miguel could have his own room," Cece says, reappearing with her brothers in tow. "The construction was such a pain. We had to either eat down at the restaurant or microwave everything and eat on TV trays in the living room."

"But now I have the kitchen I've always wanted," Mrs. Pérez says.

"Before, she had to use the kitchen at the restaurant when all our aunts and uncles and primos came." Cece helps her abuela transfer the tamales from the steamer into two different wide pans, then carries the pans and a dish of refried beans to the table. Mrs. Pérez sits at the head of the table, while the boys sit on one side and Vi sits next to Cece on the other.

Danny starts ladling refried beans onto his plate, but

Miguel smacks him in the back of the head. Cece grabs Vi's hand beneath the table, and for a moment, Vi is confused... until she realizes that everyone is joining hands and bowing their heads. Mrs. Pérez begins to pray over their meal. Vi hopes that her downcast face hides her blush as Cece's fingers twine through hers. When everyone echoes the "amen," she drops Cece's hand and picks up her water glass so fast, she almost spills it.

"Do you have to say grace at your house?" Luis asks Vi.

"No." They don't even go to church. "But it's a very nice tradition."

"I wasn't sure if you like spicy food," Cece explains. "So we made these with serranos and these with jalapenos. And these are refried beans, obviously, and—"

"It all looks delicious," Vi assures her. She watches Cece's brothers unwrap the corn husks surrounding the tamales, and then she does the same.

Little Luis eats a big piece of jalapeno and then starts coughing and guzzling water. His brothers tease him and suggest maybe he was adopted. Luis punches Danny in the shoulder, near tears. Mrs. Pérez reminds them that they have company and if they want brownies for dessert, they ought to behave. Then she asks about everyone's day. Miguel tells them stories from soccer camp, Danny boasts about how he beat Miguel in Madden football, and Luis says he can swim the whole length of the pool now.

"You're awfully quiet, Vi," Mrs. Pérez notices after a while. "What are you doing this summer, besides helping Helen at Arden? Any summer camps for you?"

Vi panics. What does she do besides working at the bookstore? She daydreams about Cece, and she writes Beronica fics and... *Oh my God, what do I do that isn't gay?*

"I walk dogs," she blurts, and then she feels absurd.

"She walks Athena and Juno. And she's a writer," Cece brags.

Vi's eyes widen. She thought Cece understood that was a secret!

"Really? Helen's never mentioned that," Mrs. Pérez says. "What do you write? Are you a journalist, like Bea?"

"No, it's...it's just short fiction," Vi says. Which is true.

"It's not 'just' anything. It's so good," Cece says, and Vi's face flames. She adores Cece, but she wishes she would shut up before Mrs. Pérez starts asking more questions. What if this gets back to Gram? "She let me read one of her stories, and I was super impressed."

"Cece," Vi says warningly, shifting in her wooden chair.

"What? It is good! You should be proud. You're talented," Cece says, touching her forearm. "Vi's always on the honor roll too."

"Like someone else I know," Mrs. Pérez says, and Cece practically glows with happiness.

"Nerd," Miguel coughs.

"Hush. You could stand to follow your sister's good example," Mrs. Pérez says.

"I don't need good grades to be a famous fútbol player," Miguel argues, which sets off Cece *and* his abuela. Vi smiles and eats her tamales, relieved to be rid of the spotlight.

After dinner, they all help clear the table, and then Mrs. Pérez serves warm chipotle chocolate brownies and big frosted glasses of milk while the six of them play Canasta. The sliding glass door is open, letting in a soft summer breeze from the backyard, and the rich scent of chocolate fills the kitchen. Overhead, a ceiling fan whirs lazily. Gram taught Vi and her sisters how to play Canasta when they were littler than Luis, and they play after Friday night dinner too. It feels so homey that Vi relaxes, trash talking and teasing the boys as though they're her own little brothers.

Danny is the first one to reach five thousand points. He does a ridiculous victory dance that makes them all laugh, except Luis, who got bored a few rounds ago and is curled up snoring on the sofa in the corner.

"All right, I need to get this one to bed. It's past your bedtime too, Danny," Mrs. Pérez says as she wakes Luis.

"It's summer!" ten-year-old Danny protests. "There shouldn't be bedtime in summer."

"I guess I should get home," Vi says reluctantly. "Thank you so much for dinner, Mrs. Pérez. It was delicious."

"You're very welcome. I put some brownies in that blue

container on the counter. They're for you to take home. Tell Helen she has to share with you and your sisters, okay?" Mrs. Pérez says.

Cece gets the brownies and walks Vi to the front door.

"I have to work tomorrow afternoon," Cece says, "but do you want to watch the fireworks together tomorrow night?"

Vi gapes at her. Cece doesn't know it, but this is kind of a big deal. One year ago, the night before the Tea Party, Gram asked Vi to pick up Friday night dinner from Tia Julia's. Vi had run into Cece—almost literally run into her in the crowd of customers waiting to be seated or pick up takeout orders at the bar—and noticed her quick dimpled grin. Noticed how super pretty she was. The next night, Vi had watched the fireworks from a picnic blanket in Bishop Park with Des and Em. She had watched as Bea snuck off with Erik and Kat with Adam, and for the first time, she had felt jealous. She had wondered when she would have someone to sneak off and kiss. As golden fireworks shimmered and crackled and streaked across the sky like falling stars, she had made a wish: that next year, she'd have someone special to watch the fireworks with.

Now, *exactly* a year later, Cece is asking her to do just that.

It's only as friends, Vi reminds herself. It's better, smarter, not to get her hopes up.

But they already are. She doesn't know if she can reel them back in. The truth is, she doesn't want to be just friends. She wants more. And what could be more romantic than watching the fireworks together?

"I would love that," she says.

CHAPTER TWENTY-FIVE
DES

"This is amazing!" Des says early Saturday afternoon, flipping through her illustrations to see how many are left. She and Paige have been selling their art since nine a.m. at a card table on the sidewalk outside Arden.

The parade is just finishing—Des can still hear the high school drummers down by the river—but she's already sold twenty of her illustrations. She worked like crazy on her days off to finish five different hand-lettered quotes by Shakespeare, Edgar Allan Poe, L. M. Montgomery, C. S. Lewis, and Jane Austen. Last night, she had ten eight-by-tens printed of each. She's selling them for ten dollars apiece, which means—she does the math quickly in her head—she's made two hundred dollars so far!

"I told you so, didn't I?" Paige says, slumped in the folding chair behind the table.

"You did. Hey." Des takes in her friend's purple-lipped frown. Paige didn't even bother with her fake lashes this morning. "Is everything okay?" Des asks, taking advantage of the momentary lull in customers. Most of the tourists are rushing down to the river to watch the reenactment aboard the *Abigail*. "I texted you a couple times last night. Not that you have to text me back right away. It's okay if you were busy. I was just kind of worried."

Paige tugs on the end of her messy purple braid. "Yeah. Sorry about that. My mother"—her voice goes icy on the word—"canceled my cell phone service."

"What? Why would she do that?" Des asks.

"Apparently, she doesn't think I'm paying her back fast enough." Paige taps her shiny silver nails on her jean-clad knee. "I kind of owe her some money. But don't worry. I'll pay you back for the tattoo, I promise."

"I'm not worried about the money." Des isn't sure if she is or not. "I'm worried about *you*."

Paige buries her face in her hands. "I didn't want to have to tell you; you're, like, the *one* person who still thinks that I have my shit together, but...look, Desdemona, everything I've told you is a lie."

"*Everything*?" Des asks, alarmed. She knew there was stuff Paige wasn't telling her, like whatever's going on between

Paige and her mom. But they've only known each other for a couple of weeks, and Des didn't want to pry.

"Not everything," Paige concedes. She avoids Des's eyes, rearranging her earrings on the rack. She's made dozens of them in different colors, all intricate knots and tangles of wire. "But I'm not a student at MICA…at least not anymore. I got kicked out. Not invited back for the spring semester. Same difference."

Des tries to swallow her shock. MICA was one of the first things Paige told her. It's one of the first things Paige tells *everybody*. Like it's some badge of honor that made her legit.

"I was pretty messed up, and getting kicked out…it made it worse. I was so excited when I got accepted, you know? I was never very good at school. Not like you, I bet." She gives Des a half-hearted smile. "I made it work for a while, but when I got kicked out, I felt like there was no more point in trying. Like I might as well live down to my parents' terrible expectations. I got a job waitressing at this dive bar, and I met this guy who was—he was not a good guy, Desdemona. I did some really stupid shit when I was with him. Like stealing money from my mom. She was so mad that she threatened to call the cops. I was sad and scared and—" Paige swallows. "I took some pills."

"Oh shit." Des grabs Paige's hand. "Why would you do that?"

"I guess I felt like I'd screwed everything up so bad, I could never fix it. Mom found me and called an ambulance, so I got my stomach pumped and spent a couple of days in the psych ward. When I got out, she just stared at me all day. It was like living under a microscope. We got into a big fight about me not wanting to see that therapist anymore, and she threatened to kick me out of the house. I said she was a terrible mother for not noticing I was depressed until I tried to kill myself. That's when she sent me here."

Des bites her lip. "That sounds really hard."

"Yeah. So I'm not some kick-ass art student. I'm just a fucked-up waitress."

Des pokes Paige in the arm. "That is not true. Repeat after me: I am an artist, and my art is rad."

Paige doesn't even smile. "I'm pathetic is what I am. I can't even sell these stupid earrings."

"That's not true. You've already made… How much have you made so far?"

"Not enough." Paige sighs and adjusts the display again. "Maybe I should have priced them lower. What do you think? Is twenty dollars too much? You're selling way more than me."

Des shrugs. "People know me. They're being nice."

Paige rolls her gray eyes. "Stop. They are not."

"Maybe we need to make a sign advertising that you're

Miss Lydia's granddaughter. Hey! Maybe she could sell some at the Tabby Cat Café," Des suggests.

Paige purses her purple lips. "Grandma and I are not on speaking terms right now. I wore a halter top yesterday, and she saw the new tattoo and she was *pissed*. She said all my money should be going straight to my mom, not to tattoos and weed. I didn't want to tell her that you paid for the tattoo, so…she called Mom and snitched, and that's probably why my phone got disconnected." Paige sighs. "I think it might be time for me to leave town. I can couch surf with some friends in Baltimore if I have to. Maybe I could get a job waitressing over in Fell's Point. That'd be cool, right? I could hang with Lola and Grace."

"No!" The word bursts out of Des's mouth. "You can't leave yet. It'll be so boring here without you."

"Aw, Desdemona." Paige wraps an arm around her shoulders. "I'd miss you too."

"You already have a job here. What if you got your own place?" Des suggests. "Hannah Adler's parents are renting out their garage apartment. It used to be a carriage house, so it's small, but it's super cheap."

"I'm super broke, babe. I can't swing a security deposit and first month's rent."

"What if you sold your car?" Des suggests. "The apartment is right over on Petunia. You could walk to Tia Julia's."

"The car's in my mom's name. I don't see how it could work, unless..." She eyes Des. "Unless I had a roommate."

"I don't know anybody who's looking, but I could ask around," Des offers.

"I meant *you*, silly." Paige pokes her in the arm. "Have you ever thought of moving out?"

Des looks over her shoulder, as if Gram and Vi—working inside—can somehow hear. "I can't. They need me."

"They would manage," Paige says. "And maybe...maybe they're not the only ones who need you, you know?"

Des hesitates. Asking for two days off was a big deal for her. She can't imagine telling Gram and her sisters that she wants to move out. Although...it would be kind of cool to have her own apartment. She has the money. Aside from her phone bill, her art supplies, and a large collection of Out of Print book T-shirts, she hardly spends anything she makes working at Arden. She could pay for the security deposit and first month's rent on the Adlers' apartment, no problem.

But is that a good idea? Right now, she and Paige are cool. She doesn't want to become the buzzkill roommate, nagging Paige about chores and her half of the rent. That would only exchange taking care of her family for taking care of Paige.

"I don't know," Des says uncertainly.

"It's okay. I'll figure something out," Paige says.

There's a boom from one of the cannons on the *Abigail*

and then clapping and cheering from the crowd down by the dock. The reenactment has started. "I'm going to run inside to the bathroom." Des kicks the cash box out of sight beneath the long red-and-white checkered tablecloth on the nonfiction table. "Can you keep an eye on things?"

"Yeah, of course," Paige says. "No worries."

The next few hours are busy. Vi watches their table while they take a quick lunch break, grabbing barbecue from one of the vendors in Bishop Park. After the reenactment and the mayor's speech, the crowd floods back up Main Street. Paige volunteers to tend the front tables while Vi takes lunch and Des helps Gram inside.

When Vi returns, Des goes back out to find Dylan in her chair. "Hey," she says.

"Hey, do you mind if I go down to the park?" Paige asks. "I want do some market research. See how jewelry is priced and how it's set up and how it's selling, that kind of thing."

"Yeah, no problem." Des promises to meet up with them later for the fireworks, and they stroll off hand-in-hand.

Vi pokes her head out a few moments later. "Did Paige leave? You want to switch places? I think you're getting sunburned."

Des smirks. Cece is working the hostess stand in the

courtyard next door, and she strongly suspects Vi is motivated by that, not by genuine concern for Des's sunburn. It's stupid hot outside, though, and working in the air-conditioning would be nice.

"Sure, thanks." She goes over the prices with Vi and hands her the iPad they use to process credit cards.

Gram is in her armchair near the counter, wearing a Hillary Clinton-esque red pantsuit. Like half the town, she's also wearing a souvenir pin bearing the likeness of the USS *Abigail*. Despite her festive attire, she looks tired, her mouth pinched, and Des wonders if her knee hurts.

Des wanders around the store, picking up books that have been dropped or misshelved, making small talk with customers. She helps a young mom find the new *Smitten Kitchen* cookbook, recommends the Miss Fisher mystery series to a middle-aged woman, and locates some board books about trucks for an excited toddler with a face covered in chocolate. Gram rings them all up.

Then Vi rushes in. "Des, where's the cash?"

Des looks up from reshelving some graphic novels. "In the cash box?"

Vi flips one red braid over her shoulder impatiently. "No, it's not."

"What do you mean 'No, it's not'? Yes, it is." Des strides toward the door, but Vi is already holding out the metal cash box, its lid flung open to reveal the empty interior.

"Shit," Des mutters. The money was there an hour—
maybe an hour and a half?—ago. She made change for
a twenty for a middle-aged man who bought a book on
colonial ships.

"I need change, like, *now*," Vi says, heading to the register.

Gram looks at Des. "Where did the money go?"

"I don't know. It was there when I came in for Vi's
lunch." Des sets her armful of graphic novels down on the
nearest table.

"It was there before you left Paige in charge of it," Gram
says as Vi rushes back outside.

Des puts her hands on her hips. "Paige didn't take it."

"No? That money just happened to walk off while she
was watching it? I told you I didn't trust her, Des. I told
you she—"

"She didn't steal it. She wouldn't do that," Des insists.

"Honey. She stole from her own mother." The way
Gram looks at her, blue eyes pitying—it feels like she's
been waiting for this to happen.

"That's different. Paige was seeing this guy who was
awful, and she did some stupid things because of him, but
she didn't do this, Gram. Maybe—maybe she wasn't paying
close enough attention. Maybe she was on her phone or—"
Too late, Des remembers that Paige's phone is disconnected. "There are so many strangers in town. You don't
know who—"

"I know exactly who," Gram interrupts. "I know you don't want to think—"

"You're not listening! I'm telling you, Paige didn't do it!" Des never raises her voice. Never. She's certainly never yelled at Gram like this.

Gram is quiet. "I hear you, honey. But I think you're wrong."

Des starts for the door. "Dylan was there too. Maybe it was him. Maybe he took it when she was helping a customer. They went over to the park. I'm going to go ask if she saw anything suspicious."

"Des. You can't go chasing after her. You're in the middle of a shift. I need you here till eight. I'll send Vi over to the bank to get some change; we don't have much in the register. *Desdemona!*" Gram's voice is like a whip. It stops her at the door. "You can find Paige when your shift is over."

"You *want* it to be her. You want her to be guilty so you can say *I told you so. I only wanted what's best for you.* Well, if you want what's best for me, maybe you should consider that I've been working my ass off for the past two months. I never complained about working ten-hour days six days a week or cooking dinner every single night or doing everything around the house. Why would I complain? I don't have a life, right? Bea and Kat and Vi, they get to have lives, they get to have fun, but not me. I'm the oldest.

I'm the responsible one. I can't complain. I have to set a good example. I'm supposed to take care of everybody else and never be selfish and never put myself first." The words tumble out of Des, faster and faster. "Well, you know what? That's bullshit!"

"Where is all this coming from?" Gram looks at her over her glasses. "If this is really how you feel, Des, let's talk about it. But there's no need to yell."

"I'll yell if I want to!" she yells. "I'm going to go find Paige. And I'm moving out. I'm tired of being goddamn Cinderella." She storms out and slams the door behind her.

She doesn't think she's ever slammed a door in her life.

It is supremely satisfying.

CHAPTER TWENTY-SIX
BEA

On Saturday afternoon, Bea and Erik walk hand-in-hand through the farmer's market in Bishop Park. Vendors sell bright bouquets of flowers, scented soaps and candles, wooden cutting boards, cheese, fruits and vegetables, jewelry, and all kinds of art. A bluegrass band plays on a wooden bandstand with a Remington Hollow Tea Party banner fluttering above them. Some of the restaurants in town have set up food tents. At Mama's BBQ, old Miss Evie is selling her mouthwatering pulled pork and her sons are working the smoker. At Captain Dan's Seafood Shack, Captain Dan himself is handing out crab cakes and coleslaw and fries dusted with Old Bay.

"Hi, Ms. Smith!" Bea calls to the red-haired newspaper advisor, who's watching her granddaughter get her face painted like a lion. Ms. Smith waves.

Erik tugs Bea toward a nearby table. "There they are!"

"Bea!" Heather and Hailey, Erik's ten-year-old twin sisters, rush toward her.

"We haven't seen you in forever," Heather says accusingly. Her face is painted like a cat.

"Forever," Hailey adds emphatically, elbowing her twin out of the way to hug Bea. Her face is painted like a bumblebee. "Look! I'm a bee today too!"

"It's beautiful," Bea says.

"When are we going to bake cookies?" Heather asks. "Your cookies are better than Momma's. No offense, Momma."

"None taken. The student has surpassed the teacher." Mrs. Frazier puts down her basil lemonade and wraps Bea in a warm hug. She's the kind of mom Bea hopes she'll be someday, patient and loving: knitting mittens and scarves for her kids, baking delicious pies, refereeing the twins' squabbles, cheering Erik on at all his debate meets and tennis matches.

It hits Bea all over again: she isn't just breaking up with Erik. She's breaking up with his family too. This wonderful, kind, welcoming family that she loves. She will miss them so much.

Bea sinks into the hug, blinking back tears. "How have you been, honey? The girls are right. We've hardly seen you since the graduation party."

Erik's family threw a joint graduation party for him and Bea. Mrs. Frazier gave her earrings made from pen nibs and a new cookbook.

"I'm fine." Bea is on the verge of sobbing. "I'm sorry. I've been so busy with my internship and the raft and..." And Gabe.

"You eat yet?" Mr. Frazier pulls a twenty out of his wallet and hands it to Erik. He has Erik's kind blue eyes. "Go get your girl some lunch."

"Thanks, Dad." Erik grins. "What are you in the mood for, Bea? Mama's or Captain Dan's?"

Bea doesn't deserve this. She can't let them buy her lunch and smile at her. She does not deserve their love.

The panic rises up, choking her. The sun feels too hot on the crown of her head, on her ears, on her bare arms and legs, on the part of her chest exposed by the round neck of her sundress. Her pulse starts to race. She feels sick and dizzy, and she can taste the sweet–tart strawberry lemonade she drank earlier.

"Bea? Are you okay?" Erik looks at her with concern.

She is not okay.

She can't lie to him anymore. Not even one more day. This is unacceptable.

Bea shakes her head. Her chest hurts. Maybe she's having a heart attack.

"Is it the heat? Here, sit down. John, get her some water," Mrs. Frazier says. "Did you eat breakfast?"

"No, I—" Bea wets her lips and tries to speak around the knot in her throat. "I need to go home."

"Now?" Erik's face falls.

"You can't go home yet!" Heather complains.

"Are you going to throw up?" Hailey asks, interested. Mrs. Frazier swats at her shoulder.

"Walk me home?" Bea asks Erik. "Please?"

Eric takes her hand. "Of course."

"I'm sorry," she says to his family. "I'm so sorry."

"It's okay, sweetheart. Feel better," Mrs. Frazier says. "We'll see you soon."

Erik threads his warm fingers through hers. The gesture makes the knot in her throat pull tight. She's been taking this for granted the past few months. Maybe it was easier that way, to try to convince herself she wouldn't miss him. That he was too clingy, too insufferably patient. The truth is, he's kinder than she deserves, and she will miss this. Miss *him*.

They're quiet as they retrace their steps back to her house. Does he know? Does he suspect?

Bea pauses on the front porch. No one else is home. Kat is at the café for the grand reopening. Des and Vi and

Gram are at Arden. The whole street is quiet, nothing but sunshine and insects buzzing and red rosebushes blooming in the drowsy July heat.

"What's going on, Bea?" Erik asks.

He's still holding her hand. He hasn't let go. That's who he is. He won't let go, no matter how snappish or standoffish or selfish she is.

She has to be the one to do this.

Gently, Bea lets go of his hand. She looks up at him and he takes a step back. His spiky brown eyelashes, darker than his hair, are already wet with tears.

Maybe he's known all along but hasn't wanted to see it, to say it out loud, to make it true.

"I'm sorry. I'm so sorry. I can't go to Georgetown with you," she says.

It's the wrong way to start. He looks confused, his forehead rumpled. Then hopeful.

"I'm breaking up with you," she clarifies, and the hope drains out of him. His shoulders, strong from all that tennis, strong from five years of being her rock, bow.

"Why?" Erik bites his lip. "Is it that guy? The one in the truck?"

Bea shakes her head. She's crying now, quiet tears slipping down her freckled cheeks. "It's me. I'm a mess. I'm such a mess. I don't know what I want, but it's not Georgetown. It's not any of the things we planned." *It's not you.*

"That's okay." Erik reaches for her even as he's blinking back his own tears. "We can figure it out. You can defer for a year. I can come home on weekends. It's not that far; we can—"

"No." She collapses into one of the porch chairs. "We can't."

"Bea." Her name is a plea.

"I love you; I will *always* love you, but I need to figure this out on my own," she says.

Erik shakes his head. "I don't understand. I've been giving you space. I've been giving you a *lot* of space."

"I know," she says. "You haven't done anything wrong. You're amazing. It's not about you."

"How can it not be about me? I'm the other person in this relationship. We're a team."

"I haven't been a very good team player lately," she says. "It's not fair to you."

"Don't do that. Let me decide what's fair to me." Erik sits next to her and puts his hand on her knee. "We can fix this."

"You can't fix it," Bea says. "You're not *listening*."

She feels like she is doing this terribly. Would there be any way to do it well?

She covers his hand with hers. She doesn't want to hurt him, but she has to be absolutely clear. "Erik, I don't want to fix it. I'm sorry."

His hand slips out from beneath hers. He shifts away,

and despite the July heat, the air feels cold and new without him right next to her. His blond head bows.

"Why?" he says again. "Are you *sure* this is what you want?"

She nods and then realizes he isn't looking at her. He's staring at his own sandaled feet, at the warped gray floorboards of the porch. "I am. I really am."

"What are you going to do? If you're not—" His voice breaks, and her heart catches on the jagged edges of it. "If you're not going to Georgetown?"

"I don't know," she confesses. "But I have to figure that out myself."

"I don't understand. Georgetown, the *Hoya*, DC—it's what you wanted. I never pressured you. We decided *together*. What about our five-year plan, and our ten-year plan, and… You're supposed to be my *whole future*, Bea." He leans forward, propping his elbows on his knees, and buries his face in his hands. "We had it all planned out."

"I'm sorry." She doesn't know what else to say. She starts to reach out, to rub his back, to comfort him, and then lets her hand fall into the empty space between them.

That isn't her job anymore.

She isn't his girlfriend anymore.

His shoulders are shaking, and she realizes with horror that he's crying. She's only seen him cry once, two summers ago, when his grandfather died. She went to the funeral with him and held his hand.

"What can I do?" she asks.

"Just go," he mumbles.

She stands and then hesitates. She doesn't want this to be their last memory. It's so awful.

He raises his head and looks at her with red-rimmed eyes. She wonders if he'll resent her for seeing him like this. "You don't know what you want, but you know it's not me, right? So just *go*, Bea."

"Okay," she says quietly. "If that's what you want."

"None of this is what I want," he snaps.

She fumbles with her keys, unlocks the front door, and slips inside. She can see him through the living room windows, still sitting on the porch, his shoulders bowed. If he turned, he would see her. Bea stumbles into the kitchen and slides down the striped wallpaper to the floor.

It's over. She's not Bea-and-Erik anymore, only Bea.

She thought maybe she'd feel relieved, like some weight had been lifted. But she doesn't. She feels sad.

She thinks she'll stay on the kitchen floor for a while.

Bea stares at the blue-and-white-striped wallpaper and then at the cookbooks across the room. She presses her hot, teary face against the cold tile floor. She cries.

Ultimately, she is not very good at wallowing. She gets

antsy. But she's not sure how much time has passed, and she's afraid to go into the hall, to peek out the window and see if Erik is still crying on the porch. She listens, half waiting for him to knock on the front door with some new plan, determined to fix everything. He's such a fixer.

He doesn't knock.

Eventually, she climbs to her feet and goes to the refrigerator. She pours herself some iced tea and gets out the strawberries and blueberries. She retrieves sugar and baking soda and flour from the cupboard. Tomorrow's the Fourth of July. She has to make a flag cake.

She's finished combining all the rest of the ingredients in the chipped green mixing bowl when she realizes she doesn't have enough vanilla. Only a trickle. A frustrated breath hisses out between her teeth, and she throws the empty glass bottle across the room. It misses the trashcan and breaks on the tiled white floor.

Bea swears.

She's so stupid. She should have put it on the grocery list. She can't make a vanilla cake without vanilla. And it *has* to be a vanilla cake, with vanilla buttercream frosting, with strawberries and blueberries arranged like a flag across the top. It started off as a Frazier family tradition, but it's become hers too.

Why can't she do anything right?

Why can't she want what she's supposed to want?

She dumps the entire mess into the trash and sinks back onto the kitchen floor, crying.

∽

"Bea? Honey, what are you doing?"

Bea blinks awake. The kitchen is dark and shadowy around her till Gram flips on the overhead light. Bea can't believe she fell asleep on the kitchen floor. The berries are still out on the counter. She gets up and puts them in the fridge.

"I fell asleep," she says. For a minute, she can't remember why. Then it comes rushing back to her—what she did, Erik's *face* afterward—and it's awful. She's awful. She inhales, sharp, and turns away from Gram.

"Were you waiting for your flag cake? How did it turn out?"

"It didn't. I threw it away." Bea turns to the sink and washes out the green mixing bowl. The batter has clumped to the sides. She gives it a vicious scrub with the sponge.

Gram comes closer, her cane thudding against the tiled floor. "Were you crying?"

"I ran out of vanilla and I broke up with Erik." She says it fast, as though they are somehow connected. She concentrates very hard on wiping down the flour-dusted counter with a wet paper towel.

"Oh, Bea." Gram puts a hand on her arm. "Come here."

Bea keeps attacking the counter. "Don't hug me. I don't deserve for you to be nice to me."

Gram wraps an arm around her. "Nonsense. You always deserve for me to be nice to you."

Gram smells like violets and lilies and roses and whatever else is in her fancy Estée Lauder perfume. Bea is stiff in her arms for a long minute.

"Do you hate me?" she asks around the knot in her throat. "Everyone is going to hate me."

"I could never hate you," Gram says.

The knot tightens. "I hurt him."

"That doesn't mean you aren't hurting too," Gram says.

Then Bea is crying again, sinking into Gram, trusting that, Gram will hold her up despite her new knee. And Gram does. She holds on to Bea, and she lets her cry, rubbing her back in slow, soothing circles. Bea remembers sitting on her bed, sobbing, on her ninth birthday—her first birthday without her parents—while Gram rubbed her back just like this.

"I love you, sweet Bea," Gram says. "I will *always* love you, no matter what. I will always be on your side."

When Bea stops crying, it's twilight. The fireworks will be starting soon. Everyone in town will be making their way down to Bishop Park to *ooh* and *aah*.

Bea might not have a long-term plan anymore, but she knows where she wants to be when the first fireworks explode over the river.

She tells Gram she's going out and hurries toward the marina. She slinks through alleys and side streets like a skittish cat—not because she has anything to hide, but because she doesn't want to stop and explain her swollen face and red-rimmed eyes to a dozen concerned neighbors.

She breathes a sigh of relief when she reaches the *Stella Anne*. Gabe's on the front porch, stretched out in an Adirondack chair, lifting a tumbler of whiskey to his lips. He stands when he sees her.

"It's not Sunday, Bea," he says, wary.

"I couldn't wait till Sunday," she says. "I'm sorry I lied to you. It was wrong to start something with you before I ended things with him. But I did. I broke up with him."

Gabe looks at her evenly. What is he thinking?

"Are you okay?" he asks.

She shakes her head. "But it had to be done."

"Do you want to come inside?"

Bea shakes her head again. She doesn't have anything to hide. "Can I watch the fireworks out here with you?"

Gabe offers her a hand and helps her onto the boat. "Yeah. I'd like that."

CHAPTER TWENTY-SEVEN
KAT

Everything is perfect.

The Tabby Cat Café has been packed since they opened at ten o'clock this morning. Maybe the free cupcakes with cat toppers (Kat's suggestion) have something to do with it, but customers are sticking around to order drinks. Mase suggested that, in addition to iced coffee and iced tea, they should offer strawberry, chocolate, two-percent, skim, soy, coconut, and almond milk and serve it in mason jars with Krazy Straws. And people *love* it. Everything is adorable and stylish and selfie-worthy.

People are taking *tons* of selfies: in front of the chalkboard wall, playing with the cats, eating cupcakes, and drinking chocolate milk through Krazy Straws. Their new Instagram account—which Kat started last week with Miss Lydia's approval—is getting tagged a lot, and they have a hundred new followers. Pen is here, snapping Polaroids and hanging them on a clothesline to dry so each person gets one when they leave, along with a ten-percent-off coupon for their next visit.

Kat is working the door, greeting people as they arrive, thanking them as they leave, making sure they collect their Polaroids, and preventing any wayward cats from escaping. She's good at this. In the lulls, she answers questions about the individual cats and the animal rescue they partner with. Three different people have already filled out cat adoption paperwork today, and a few more have taken applications home.

Outside, people cluster on the brick sidewalk, peering through the picture window at the cats and the crowd. Miss Lydia wanders around, offering everyone cupcakes and gossiping. Mase and his friend Maxwell—who's helping out for the day—trade off working the register and pouring drinks.

Mase rushes out from behind the counter. "Did you see that blond woman with the little girl who just left?" he asks Kat. "She's interested in Shadow!"

"Oh my God, really?" Without thinking, Kat hugs him. His arms come around her in response, his hand resting on the bare skin of her lower back. She's wearing her white tank with her red maxi skirt and her hair pulled up in a high, flirty ponytail. She worried maybe it wasn't work appropriate, but when she showed up this morning, Miss Lydia just smiled and said she wished she were sixteen again.

Mase lets go, and Kat steps back. He stares down at his wingtips. Is she imagining things, or is he blushing? He clears his throat.

"You look amazing," he says, his dark eyes colliding with hers. "The whole place looks amazing, thanks to you."

"It does, doesn't it?" She takes it all in. "You helped a lot."

He knocks his shoulder against hers. "We make a pretty good team, huh?"

Kat nods, biting her lip. Is it her imagination, or is he looking at her mouth? She's wearing new lipstick. It's very red. Maybe it's too red? Maybe it's on her teeth? She sweeps her tongue over them just in case.

"Yeah, we do," she says, too late. She wants to ask him about Brandon: When is he coming? How does Mase feel about it? What does he think Brandon wants to talk about? She wants to know, and she doesn't. Once he and Brandon get back together—assuming that's what Brandon wants, and he'd have to be silly *not* to want to be with Mase, because Mase is basically the best—Mase won't be her boyfriend anymore. Not even for pretend.

"Mase!" Maxwell hollers. Mase hurries back behind the counter.

A little while later, Hannah and Jillian and Adam come in. Adam pretends to be bored, checking his phone, but he gets an iced coffee and poses with Jillian in front of the chalkboard. He doesn't get on the floor to play with the cats, but the girls do.

"This place is totally different. Did you and Mase do this? You both have such amazing style," Hannah says as she twitches a feather toy that Luna is trying to catch.

"It's so *cool* now," Jillian gushes, darting a laser pointer across the floor for Sassy. Or is that Shadow? "You guys did a really good job."

"Thank you." Kat had promised Pen she would be nice. She looks at Jillian's khaki skirt and her black T-shirt. She is boring and bland and blond, but maybe she's not *totally* evil. "I like your sandals," she says, which she thinks is very magnanimous of her.

"Thanks," Jillian says.

"Are you and Guyliner still together?" Adam asks.

Jillian elbows him right in the gut. "Don't call him that."

"I heard Brandon was coming back to town this weekend," Adam continues.

God, he's such a shit-stirrer. Kat's heart plummets, but she tries to look nonchalant. "Yeah, he's visiting his parents. I think he and Mase might grab coffee."

"And you're totally okay with that?" Adam laughs. "You used to freak out when I even talked to another girl, but you're cool with Mase going out to lunch with his boyfriend? Yeah right."

"Adam, that's none of your business," Jillian says through gritted teeth.

Kat smirks. "His *ex*-boyfriend. And I don't mind, because unlike *some* people, Mase doesn't have a history of cheating on everyone he's with."

She sashays away without looking over her shoulder to see how that landed. Adam wants to stir shit up? Well, two can play at that game. *Sorry, Pen. I tried.*

"Kat, honey, can you grab more cupcakes from the fridge upstairs?" Miss Lydia calls.

Kat nods. "You've got the door?"

"Yes, ma'am." Miss Lydia grins at her. "Look at you. Between you and Mason, you two could run this place yourselves, couldn't you?"

Mase has disappeared from behind the counter. Kat frowns. Is he in the back texting Brandon? She can't complain if he is. He hasn't taken his lunch break yet, even though it's almost three o'clock.

She runs upstairs and almost collides with him in the hall, coming out of the staff bathroom. He's carrying Shadow. "You're gonna get adopted, buddy! That lady seemed suuuuper nice," he's telling the cat, nose to furry black nose.

Kat grins. "Awww. He loves you."

"He's my favorite," Mase says.

"I thought *I* was your favorite," she flirts, reaching up and tightening her ponytail. Her shirt rises just a little, revealing the pale skin of her stomach.

Mase's eyes dart down and then back up to her face. "Kat—" he starts, putting Shadow down gently on Miss Lydia's desk.

Kat steps closer, her heart racing. "Yes?"

"I'm sorry if I've been kind of a dick this week."

"If?" Kat raises her eyebrows. "Kind of?"

Mase shrugs. "I deserve that. I guess…I've been kind of confused about what's going on with us. It got hard to tell what was real and what was pretend."

Kat's heart leaps. She thinks of Ms. Randall's acting advice: *Make strong choices. Be bold, even if you're wrong.*

"This," she announces, leaning in, "is for real."

She winds both arms around Mase's neck, and her mouth moves slowly, sweetly, over his. He tastes like chocolate milk and vanilla buttercream. His hands trace the small of her back, the bare skin above the waistband of her skirt. It's a small thing, but somehow it makes her heart beat a sharp staccato rhythm against her ribs. She opens her mouth, and his tongue touches hers.

"Mase!" Maxwell shouts from downstairs, and they reluctantly break apart.

Mase runs a hand over his swoopy hair. "I'm going to kill him. He has terrible timing."

"I guess we should go back downstairs." Kat sighs, and they clatter down the steps.

"You two! Get over here for a picture," Pen commands, wielding her Polaroid camera.

Kat hesitates, but Mase grabs her hand and pulls her in front of the chalkboard wall. He wraps one arm around her. She puts both arms around his waist and tilts her head against his. When she's in flats, they're the same height.

"You're so adorable, I want to vomit," Pen declares. "I'd tell you to smile, but you already look disgustingly happy."

"Penelope," Miss Lydia chides. She smiles at Kat. "Where are those cupcakes, dear?"

Busted. Kat looks at Mase, and they both start laughing.

"Were you two upstairs making out? Oh my God, you totally were, weren't you?" Pen demands.

"No!" They chorus, blushing and grinning at each other.

This is real. It has to be. Kat doesn't care who's watching or if nobody is at all.

Pen snaps another picture.

"Stop," Kat whines. "You're supposed to take pictures of the *customers*. And I need to go back upstairs and get the cupcakes."

"You need help?" Mase asks, waggling his eyebrows at her.

How is it possible that she's missed his silly suggestive eyebrow waggle?

"Mase!" Maxwell shouts. "Stop flirting and get over here."

"Yeah," a familiar male voice says. "I need coffee. It was a long-ass drive."

The smile slides right off Mase's face. He stares across the room like he's seen a ghost.

Brandon.

He's tall and broad shouldered, with floppy dark hair and blue eyes. He's wearing square hipster glasses and skinny jeans and a short-sleeved blue shirt that shows off the thick muscles of his arms and shoulders. He's got kind of a Clark Kent vibe. Kat can acknowledge that.

And he's Mase's first love. His first *everything*, he said.

"Cupcakes," she says, grabbing Pen's hand and dragging her, stumbling, up the stairs.

"Kat! Hey, slow down," Pen complains.

"Did you know he was here? Is that why you said we looked happy?" Kat demands.

Did Mase see him too? Is that why he put his arm around her and posed with her and looked at her like—

Like it was real?

No. She saw his face when he heard Brandon's voice. He hadn't known.

"You *are* adorable. And you clearly *were* upstairs making

out," Pen says. "Why shouldn't Brandon know he has serious competition?"

Kat starts stacking cupcake cartons on the desk, one on top of the other.

"Oh shit, Kat. You really like him, don't you?" Pen says.

Kat nods. If she had any doubts before, she doesn't now. She wanted Adam back because she didn't want Jillian to have him. Because she didn't like that he chose someone else over her. She wants Mase because he's funny and sweet and he hasn't asked for his cardigan with the leather elbows back and he gives the best shoulder massages and he makes her laugh and he knows her favorite flavor is strawberry and sometimes he sings *Hamilton* with the lyrics changed to be about the cats and—

"I really do," she admits.

But when she goes back downstairs, Mase is gone. And so is Brandon.

CHAPTER TWENTY-EIGHT
VI

As Vi lugs the last box of books inside the store, her phone chirps with a text from Cece. She knows it's from Cece because she's assigned her texts a special tone. Vi sets the box down and pulls her phone out of her back pocket.

> Changing now. You ready? 🎆

Vi's heart races. "Cece's finishing up next door. Do you need me for anything else?"

Gram looks up from unloading the penultimate box. "No, that's okay, sweetheart. You've been a big help today. You go and enjoy the fireworks."

"Are you sure? Des was supposed to help close." Vi peers at Gram. It seems like she gets tired more easily since her surgery, especially when she's on her feet too much. Like today.

"I'm positive. You shouldn't miss out on the fireworks because your sister ran off." Gram tries to smile, but it falls flat.

"Neither should you," Vi says. Des stormed out mid-afternoon, right in the middle of her shift, after Gram accused Paige of stealing money from the cash box. She hasn't been back since. Vi tried texting her and asking what was going on, but Des hasn't responded.

"I'm too tired to walk down and watch the fireworks anyhow. I'm going to go home, put my feet up, have a glass of rosé, and watch some *House Hunters*. Those people make me so mad, but I love it." Gram's blue eyes soften behind her glasses. "You and Cece have been spending an awful lot of time together lately. Anything you want to tell me about that?"

"We're just friends," Vi says, too fast. "I think. For now, anyway." She unpacks some of the books to avoid looking at Gram. She doesn't want to say too much. Cece's sexuality isn't hers to share.

Gram nods, her gray head bobbing. "She's a sweet girl."

Vi can't help the enormous smile that spreads across her face. "She's the best."

"Does she know how you feel?" Gram asks.

Vi ducks her head, mortified. Is it that obvious? Can everyone tell? Can *Cece* tell?

"I haven't told her," she hedges.

"Well, you go around looking at her like that, I don't think she'll be too shocked," Gram teases. "Just remember, baby girl, not everybody is as confident as you are. Or as comfortable in their own skin. If she's still figuring things out, she might need some time."

"Why does everybody think I'm so confident? I don't *feel* confident." There's a huge part of her life—her fandom life—that she keeps a total secret.

Gram points to Vi's tank top, which says *Gay Purride* and features a rainbow kitten. Kat gave it to her for her fifteenth birthday. "You have always been just exactly yourself, Vi. You are who you are, you stand up for what you believe, and you make no bones about it."

"That doesn't mean it's easy," Vi argues. "I feel awkward all the time. I always worry about whether I'm saying the right thing. If I'm too quiet or too loud."

"I don't imagine it is easy. Especially not in our little town." Gram reaches out and tweaks one of her red braids. "But you do it anyway. That takes real strength of character, and it makes it easier for other people to be themselves too. I'm proud of you, baby girl. I know your mom would be too."

"Thank you," Vi mumbles, blinking back tears.

"Vi!" Cece bursts through the door. "Ready to go see the fireworks?"

"Yeah, just a minute." Vi goes around the counter and gives Gram a big squeezy hug.

"All right now," Gram says. She doesn't look old to Vi anymore. She looks serene and wise and *wonderful*. "You girls have fun."

As they join the crowds of people making their way down toward the river, Vi tells Cece how Paige stole the money from the cash box.

"If she really did it—and I think she must have—Des is going to be so hurt," Vi says. "She and Em have been fighting, and I think she kind of glommed on to Paige as her new best friend. Like, she dyed her hair blue, and she got a tattoo, and I'm pretty sure she's been smoking weed. Paige is the one who convinced her to sell some of her illustrations. And they're so good. I'm going to ask her to make me one from *Riverdale*."

"Full dark, no stars?" Cece guesses.

Vi smiles and ducks her head. She still isn't used to talking about fandom in real life. "Maybe. I do love Dark Betty!"

"Me too." Cece knocks her bare shoulder into Vi's. "So, where do you want to watch the fireworks from? The park is always so crowded, I was thinking maybe we could go somewhere else."

"I'm not a huge fan of crowds," Vi admits. Her mind

whirs. Does Cece want to be alone with her? Or does she just find the crowds obnoxious? There are always tons of families with sugared-up, overtired kids camped out in Bishop Park, plus vendors hawking ice cream and cotton candy and glow-in-the-dark necklaces. Bea and Erik will be there, and Kat and Mase, and lots of their classmates.

"Maybe the marina?" Cece suggests. "It'll be quieter there."

As the sky turns from dusky blue to inky black, they make their way down to the end of a pier, to the quiet slip of an unoccupied boat. A few docks away, there's a raucous party, but tucked away between two powerboats. Cece spreads out her picnic blanket, and they lie on the wooden dock, staring up at the sky.

"This is so much nicer than being in the park," Cece says.

She's lying so close that her pinky finger brushes against Vi's. Their shoulders are almost touching. When Vi turns to look at her, their faces are only inches apart. Cece's lips are full and pink and a little glossy, and the air between them smells like cherries.

Do her lips taste like cherries? Vi would like to find out.

Above them, the first fireworks explode in a shower of red and gold. The partygoers on the sailboat cheer.

"Oh," Cece says in wonderment. Her pinky hooks over Vi's.

The fireworks are a colorful, noisy, nonstop succession

of blue and green and purple and orange and red and gold. The gold ones crackle and shimmer like shooting stars and then fizz into stardust. It makes Vi brave, remembering her wish from last year. She threads her fingers through Cece's and then holds still, barely breathing, waiting to see how she responds.

Cece doesn't pull away.

Vi turns her head. Cece is already looking at her. Their eyes meet for what feels like forever.

Vi props herself up on one elbow and rolls onto her side. Cece mirrors her movements. They are so close, their noses are almost touching. Vi can feel Cece's warm, cherry breath on her face.

Cece gives her a slow, sunrise smile. She leans forward, and Vi moves the rest of the way, and then their mouths meet. Their noses bump and adjust as they find the right angles. Cece's lips are soft and a little sticky, and she tastes like Cherry Coke. The kiss is sweet and slow and searching.

They pull back and look at each other. Vi can't believe this is really happening. *I am kissing Cece Pérez.* Overhead, the fireworks are exploding in a steady *boom boom boom* that matches the quick, loud rhythm of her heart. Cece inches closer and rests one hand on the rise of Vi's hip. Vi leans in, and they kiss, and kiss, and kiss.

It is better than any of her daydreams.

She knots her fingers in Cece's dark curls, anchoring

Cece's face against hers. Cece opens her mouth, and Vi tentatively explores it with her tongue. She doesn't know if she's doing it right. She must be doing okay, she guesses, because Cece presses against her, her fingers tugging on Vi's belt loop. Their legs tangle together on the blanket.

The partygoers on the boat start hooting and hollering, and Vi and Cece break apart. In a rush of color and noise, the grand finale begins.

Cece sits up. "Come here," she says with a shy, dimpled grin, and she wraps her arm around Vi, pulling her closer. "You are so amazing, you know that?"

"*You* are," Vi says. She rests her head on Cece's shoulder.

It is better than any wish she ever made.

"Hi, is Paige home?" Des asks.

"Good morning, Des. Come in." Miss Lydia steps back and gestures her inside.

Des scuffs her red Toms against the wooden floor boards of Miss Lydia's porch. "I really need to see Paige. Is she here?"

Miss Lydia shakes her brassy head. "She's not."

"Do you know where she is?" Des is starting to panic. She hasn't been able to find Paige *anywhere*. After she stormed out of Arden, she looked for Paige and Dylan at the farmer's market to no avail. Des spent hours searching all over town: at the Daily Grind, the thrift store she knows Paige likes, the skate park, the library, even down by the marina. They were supposed to meet up for the fireworks, but Paige and Dylan never showed. Increasingly freaked out, Des drove to the Penningtons' farm, but neither Dylan's truck nor Paige's car was there, and it was too late to knock and risk waking his parents. She drove around town aimlessly for a while after that, listening to the playlist Paige made her, and only went home when she was sure Gram would be in bed. She stayed in her room this morning till Gram left for the store, and then she went straight to Tia Julia's, where Paige was supposed to be working the brunch shift. Only, Paige hadn't shown up, and Mrs. Pérez told her Paige hadn't called in either.

Going to Miss Lydia's is the last resort. Des doesn't want to get Paige in any more trouble, but she doesn't know what else to do. She really, really does not want to believe Paige stole the money, looked her in the face and smiled, and then skipped town without saying goodbye. But it's becoming difficult to ignore her growing suspicions.

Miss Lydia plants her hands on her hips. "Honey, I wish I knew. I think she's gone."

"Gone?" Des leans back against the slim white column of Miss Lydia's porch, her mind scrambling desperately for excuses. For ways to make sense of this that do not require believing the worst of Paige. "Where? Did she go visit her mom? Did they work things out?"

"Des, come on. You weren't born yesterday," Miss

Lydia says sharply. "I love my granddaughter, but she's not about to go home and apologize. My guess is that she's probably run off to stay with friends in Baltimore."

Des stares down at her feet. *I can couch surf with some friends in Baltimore if I have to. Maybe I could get a job waitressing over in Fell's Point. That'd be cool, right? I could hang out with Lola and Grace.* Paige had *told* her what she was going to do. Des hadn't wanted to hear it.

"Are you absolutely *sure* she's gone? Maybe she stayed over at Dylan's." Des can't believe this is happening. She stood up for Paige. She defended her to Gram.

She bites her lip, mortified. She was so sure Paige wouldn't steal from them. Wouldn't take the money Des made selling her art for the very first time. She thought their friendship meant more than that. But if Paige left, without saying goodbye, well... It seems like an awfully big coincidence. Too big.

"I stayed late at the café last night, cleaning up after the grand reopening," Miss Lydia explains. "When I got back, all her things were gone."

Des twists a blue curl around her finger. "Did she leave a note?"

"No." Miss Lydia's mouth is pressed into a thin pink line. "Honey, did she borrow money from you?"

Des nods miserably. She doesn't want to break the news that Paige stole from Arden too. She feels like she might cry, but it's not about the money. Not really. She trusted Paige. Confided in her. She thought they were friends... best friends, even. Paige was helping her take herself and her art seriously.

If Paige is gone...where does that leave Desdemona?

"Let me go get my checkbook," Miss Lydia says. "How much was it?"

"No." Des puts out a hand to stop her. "Gram warned me that Paige stole from her mom, and I—I didn't listen. This isn't your responsibility."

Miss Lydia sighs. "Don't beat yourself up, honey. Paige can be real charming when she wants to be. You're not the first person to give her a chance and regret it."

Des clasps her hands together behind her back. Her tattoo is healing, and it's itchy. Without Paige, she never would have gotten the tattoo. She never would have been brave enough to sell her art. She wouldn't have gone to farm parties or dyed her hair or seen the town from the church cupola. And while she feels bad that she yelled at Gram, she doesn't necessarily regret what she said.

"I'm still glad I met Paige," she says.

Miss Lydia nods. "I'm glad to have gotten to know her a little better myself. I'm never sorry for giving someone a second chance. I sure do regret not locking up that old sapphire ring Henry gave me when we got engaged, though."

"She stole your engagement ring?" Des thought stealing money from Arden was low.

Miss Lydia smooths her purple blouse. "You can give people chances to be better, honey, but they aren't always ready to take them. I'm sorry you had to learn that the hard way."

"Me too." Des's shoulders slump. "But thank you, Miss Lydia. If you hear from her, will you let me know? I just want to be sure she's okay. That she landed somewhere safe."

Miss Lydia nods. "You're a sweet girl, Des."

∽∾

A sweet, *naïve* girl, Des thinks. She is passing the Episcopalian church when someone grabs her wrist and yanks her into the tall bushes along the sidewalk. Des yelps and swings and connects, hard, with someone's shoulder. She kicks at her assailant but only manages to lose one of her Toms.

"Stop! Desdemona, it's me," a familiar voice hisses.

"Paige?" Des steps out of the prickly bush and retrieves her shoe.

"I saw you at Grandma Lydia's. Is she super mad?" Paige's gray eyes are bloodshot, with dark circles beneath them, and her lips are their natural pale pink. It's the first

time Des has seen her without makeup. It makes her look…
young. Vulnerable. Like she's missing her armor.

Des fights against the surge of sympathy. "You stole her
engagement ring and left without saying goodbye. What
do you think?"

"Oh. You're mad too," Paige realizes. "Look, Desdemona,
I can explain."

"That you stole money from Arden? From me?" Des
asks. "Go ahead. I'd like to hear it."

Des expects her to feign outrage. To deny it. But she
doesn't.

"I was desperate." Paige stares down at the church's
bright, manicured grass, evading Des's eyes. "I still owe my
mom all that money, and I owe this other guy too, and he
was getting pretty pissed. I'll pay you back, I swear. I didn't
have any other choice."

"You had choices," Des argues. "Your mom might be
playing the tough love card, but that's because she's worried
about you. Your grandma's worried about you too. You
could have asked them for help."

"You don't understand. They already think I'm such a
screw-up. All they do is judge me," Paige says, flipping her
purple hair over her shoulder.

"Well, maybe they should." Des crosses her arms over
her chest. "I trusted you, Paige. I defended you to Gram,
insisted that you would *never* steal from us. I even put a

down payment on the Adlers' garage apartment. For us to be roommates."

"You did?" Paige finally meets her eyes. "Desdemona, I thought you knew that was just a stupid daydream. It was never going to work."

A stupid daydream. The words cut through Des like a knife. And it hits her that Paige still hasn't apologized. All she's done is justify her mistakes. "You're right. It never would have worked, because you're a liar and a thief. You must have thought I was so stupid. So gullible." She starts to walk away.

"Desdemona, wait!" Paige calls. Des pauses, and Paige gives her a sad little smile. "I do think you're rad. That wasn't a lie. I liked hanging out with you. And your art really is good."

A few weeks ago—hell, even yesterday—Paige's approval, her validation, would have meant the world to Des. Now she isn't sure whether she can believe a single word out of her mouth.

"Whatever. Goodbye, Paige." She walks away, and she doesn't look back.

As Des stalks down to Bishop Park, she feels angry and betrayed and—maybe worst of all—incredibly, incredibly stupid. Gram warned her, but she didn't want to hear it. She's lost what she thought was a good friend. And she's lost the six hundred dollars Paige stole from the cash box—she'll have to repay Gram three hundred of it—plus the four hundred for Paige's tattoo, plus five hundred for the down payment on the apartment. Does she even *want* to move out on her own? She'd never thought about it much before Paige suggested it.

Des blushes as she remembers interrupting the Adlers' dinner, insisting that she give them a down payment right then and there. Mr. Adler had to persuade her to look at the apartment first and make sure she actually liked it. She had been so *angry*, so absolutely determined to prove Gram wrong.

The raft race won't start for another hour, but Bishop Park is already filling up with people. Several of the rafts are lined up by the river's edge. Des spots Erik and Chloe and some of Bea's other friends near a log raft, wearing *Star Wars* costumes and hovering around little BB-8 and R2-D2 props. She doesn't see Bea yet, and she's glad for it. When she crept in last night, Bea was asleep, and then she was still sleeping—or at least pretending to sleep—when Des left the house. Des wonders if her sisters have all heard what she did. How she shouted at Gram and stormed out in the middle of her shift. If she weren't Gram's granddaughter, she would be fired, and she would deserve it.

"Des!" Em jogs toward her. "Is it true?"

"Is *what* true?" Des asks. She and Em haven't texted

since their argument at Arden. It's the longest they've gone without speaking since the fifth grade.

"That you rented the Adlers' garage." Em is grinning. "I didn't think you'd *ever* move out."

"Well, I am," Des says.

"That's really cool. Your own place." Em brushes her long, asymmetrical bob out of her face and, for the first time, Des can admit that the new style looks good on her. "You remember how we used to talk about being roommates someday? How I'd get a job at the county coroner and you'd run the bookstore and we'd solve mysteries together?"

Des smiles, but she feels close to tears. She honestly thought she and Em would be friends forever. And then she tried to replace her with Paige, and look how *that* turned out. Em is worth ten Paiges.

"Hey." Em touches her arm. "Are you okay?"

Des shakes her head. "I'm so stupid," she whispers, brushing away tears with both hands. She doesn't want to cry in front of Em. Em doesn't get to see her like this anymore.

"What? You are not stupid!" Em squashes Des in a big hug. Surprised, Des lets her. Em still smells like strawberry shampoo and peppermint gum.

"I am too," Des cries from the safety of Em's arms. "Paige stole money from Arden yesterday. Gram knew it was her, but I didn't want to believe it. I got so mad, I yelled at Gram and told her I was moving out because I didn't want to be goddamn Cinderella anymore. I left work right in the middle of my shift, and…God, I was such a brat."

"You walked out in the middle of your shift? And you cussed at Gram?" Em draws back and looks at Des, from her tousled blue curls and her red, teary eyes down to her Toms. "Wait, is that—" She leans closer to look at Des's left forearm. "Oh my God, is that a real tattoo?"

Des nods, holding out her arm so Em can get a better look. "Do you like it?"

Em laughs. "I do! I can't believe you got a tattoo." She touches a strand of Des's hair. "And you dyed your hair blue. And you're getting your own apartment. And I didn't know about *any* of it. I miss you, Des. There's so much I wanted to tell you the last couple of weeks."

"I miss you too," Des confesses. "I've wanted to text you so many times. I wanted to tell you about everything: my hair, and the tattoo, and"—she lowers her voice—"I got stoned. A lot. And I sold some of my illustrations. I think, if Gram ever forgives me, I might start selling them at the store. And maybe set up my own Etsy."

"Wait, seriously?" Em grins. "That is so cool!"

"I haven't changed my mind about getting my BFA," Des warns. For a while during their senior year, Em had tried to persuade her to go to the University of Maryland too and study fine arts and business, so she could run the bookstore *and* be an artist. And for a little while, Des had been tempted. But she hadn't felt like she could leave Gram and her sisters. She hadn't been ready. She still isn't.

Baby steps.

Like her own apartment.

"Hey, you do you." Em shrugs. "Look, I'm not happy that you lied to me about having the flu. But I talked to my mom, and she pointed out that I was kind of insensitive about the frat party. I know you don't drink because of what happened to your parents. I'm sorry I didn't think about that."

"I should have said I was uncomfortable instead of lying to you," Des admits. "I'm sorry too. I don't want us to lie to each other. I just…you were off having all these new adventures and making new friends and changing your hair…"

"Well, now we both changed our hair." Em tugs on one of Des's blue curls. "So…can we be friends again?"

"Yes, please," Des says. This time, she's the one who moves to hug Em.

Em stiffens in her arms, staring over her shoulder. "Uh-oh. That is not good."

"What? Is it Paige?" Des spins around to see Bea heading toward her raft and Erik intercepting her, waving his phone and yelling. "Why does he look so mad?"

Em pulls her phone out of her pocket, brings the browser up—it's on Savannah Lockwood's blog—and hands it to Des. "You should read this."

CHAPTER THIRTY

BEA

The race starts in half an hour, and Bea is late. She texted Chloe that she would meet everyone at Bishop Park instead of at Sierra's.

She didn't tell Chloe that she broke up with Erik. She hasn't told anyone except Gram and Gabe.

She almost told Kat while she got into costume. "Bea? Are you okay?" Kat had asked as she wrapped each of Bea's arms in white gauze.

"What? Yes," Bea had lied automatically. She'd straightened the long, sand-colored vest she wore over her sleeveless white shirt. Then she'd opened her mouth to correct herself. To be honest. But Kat had already turned away, and Bea had looked in the mirror and seen the photos hanging over the desk behind her. So many of them were pictures of her and Erik: at the eighth-grade Homecoming dance, in their Halloween costumes freshman year (Bea had been Nancy Drew; Erik had been Sherlock), at the Valentine's Day dance sophomore year, at junior prom, and holding the Tea Cup last summer. It had hit her: she'd have to take them all down. Switch her profile pictures on social media to photos of her by herself, instead of her with Erik. Change her Facebook status from "in a relationship" to "single." The idea of it—of everyone knowing, of all the questions coming her way—was daunting.

Last night, after the fireworks, she'd come home and watched *Tiny House Hunters* with Gram. While she was out, Gram had made a fruit crisp with the strawberries and blueberries Bea had been planning to use for her flag cake. It had felt nice to have someone else bake for her. Like comfort in a bowl.

Now her feet drag along the sidewalk in Kat's clunky black boots. She dreads seeing Erik. What will he say? What will *she* say? Has he told their friends yet?

As Bea cuts across the grass, she spots their raft. It's already lined up near the dock with the droids on board. It looks fantastic, and all her friends' costumes are amazing, and Bea allows herself a moment of satisfaction. Then Chloe spots her and starts shaking her head frantically. What's going on? What's wrong?

Then *Erik* looks up and sees her and—

Bea has never seen him look so mad. Not at her or at anybody else. His lips are pressed together so hard, they've gone white. He stalks across the grass toward her, waving his phone.

"I don't want you on the raft," he says the minute he reaches her. His broad shoulders are set in a tense line, his square jaw clenched. "In fact, I think you should leave. I don't want you here at all."

"What?" Bea shrinks from the anger in his voice. He's never spoken to her like this. "Erik, it's our last Tea Party. I don't think it's fair to—"

"Fair?" He barks out an unfamiliar laugh. "Oh, that's funny, *you* talking about what's fair. Was it fair when you cheated on me?"

"I…what?" Her stomach drops.

How does he know? *What* does he know?

"This!" He waves the phone right in her face, almost smacking her with it, and Bea takes a step back. "You and Miss Amelia's grandson. I knew it! I knew he liked you."

Oh no. "Erik—" she starts, but what can she say? It's true.

Around them, everyone is staring.

His face twists. "I don't want to hear it. Five years, Bea. We were together for *five years*! We had our whole future planned out! I thought I was going to marry you someday, and you couldn't show me enough respect to break up with me first?" He shakes his head, blond hair falling across his rumpled forehead. Bea thinks of all the times she's pushed that wayward strand of hair back. Of how she'll never have the right to do that again. "How long have you been sleeping with him, huh? Is that why you haven't wanted to—-"

"That's enough." She says it firmly. "I don't know where you got your information, but I am not sleeping with *anybody*, okay?"

"Why should I believe that? I asked you if it was because of him. I asked you, and you lied right to my face," Erik reminds her. "I had to go and read about it in the damn paper!"

"The *paper*?" Bea snatches the phone from his hand. The browser is open to Savannah's *About Town* blog. Oh no. Oh *shit*.

She scans the blog. *Move over, Ann Shirley, because we've got gossip on all four of Remington Hollow's favorite redheaded orphans. We hear one of them is going through a rebellious stage. First that blue hair, then a tatoo, and now moving out! One just broke up with her longtime boyfriend and was already spotted locking lips with the handsome not-quite stranger in town. What a busy little bee! Almost makes you wonder how long it's been going on, doesn't it, Dear Reader? Meanwhile, looks like the poor kitty cat got dumped again. We spotted her new boyfriend kissing his not-so-ex at the fireworks. Claws are sure to come out when our favorite diva hears about that.* Meow! *As for the littlest orphan, Pride Month may be over, but we hear she and the girl from the restaurant next door are just heating things up.*

Bea tosses Erik's phone back at him, spitting mad. It is one thing to talk shit about *her*—she knew Savannah was interested in Gabe, knew Savannah would be angry and jealous when she found out. But it is another thing to drag Bea's sisters into this. Especially her *underage* sisters.

"Tell me that's not true," Erik says. "Tell me you weren't with him last night."

"I watched the fireworks with him, but it wasn't like that," Bea says. He makes it sound so…lurid. Gabe kissed her goodbye before she went home, but that was it. He seemed to know she needed a little time. That she was there, with him, but she was still really sad. And of course Savannah had seen that one, sweet moment and twisted it. She had probably been watching the boat with fucking binoculars.

"Like what? Like you're a lying *bitch*?" Erik's voice cracks, and Bea wonders, in a sort of detached way, if he's ever said that word before. He doesn't usually swear.

Kat stomps up out of nowhere. "I don't know what's going on, but you'd better not call my sister a bitch again."

"It's okay, Kat," Bea says quietly.

"Calling you names is *not* okay!" Kat argues.

"But cheating is okay?" Erik asks, and Bea shrinks into herself.

"What?" Kat looks at him like he's being ridiculous. "Bea would never cheat on you!"

Bea's heart sinks at her sister's absolute faith. At having to disappoint her. "I didn't sleep with him. I swear to God, Erik, I didn't sleep with him—and I didn't break up with you because of him. I've been unhappy for a long time. All spring. And there are lots of reasons for that. But..." She takes a deep breath. "I did cheat. I did kiss him before we broke up. I wasn't honest about that yesterday. I'm really sorry."

"If you were really sorry, you wouldn't have gone over there last night. How can I believe a word out of your mouth? God, Bea, do you ever think about anybody besides yourself? You're so *selfish*," Erik says.

Bea closes her eyes. She hates this. Hates the way he is looking at her, but it's her own damn fault. "I am far from perfect."

"That's an understatement. Stay away from the raft, okay? And stay away from me," Erik says. Then he stalks back to their friends.

Bea's arms and legs are shaking, adrenaline racing through her veins. She can't believe that just happened. Her neighbors and classmates, gathered on picnic blankets and folding chairs to watch the raft race, are still staring. How many of them overheard? How many have read the blog? She might as well be wearing a scarlet letter A pinned to her vest.

Kat wraps an arm around her shoulder. "Are you okay?"

"No," Bea says truthfully. Every time she meets someone's eyes, they quickly avert theirs. Like she's a human car wreck. Bea feels hot and panicky, like she might throw up right here in front of everyone.

"So...you broke up with Erik? And you're hooking up with some other guy?" Kat asks.

Bea nods, breathing deeply. She should ask Kat about Mase. She should ask Kat if *she's* okay. Has she read the blog? Does she know about Mase and Brandon?

Then Bea sees *her*.

Savannah is standing with her father right down by the edge of the river. She's wearing a striped red-and-white maxi dress. Her brown hair cascades down over her slim white shoulders. She looks tall and willowy and beautiful, belying the fact that she is bitter and vindictive and *evil* on the inside. It has been a long time since Bea has hated anyone so much.

"I'll be right back," she says to Kat, and then she marches across the grass toward Savannah and Charlie.

"Bea!" Savannah says, her red lips curling into a venomous smile. "I hear you've been very *busy* lately." She puts an emphasis on *busy*, and Bea knows she's proud of her stupid *busy little bee* line.

There are many things Bea wants to say, but they all involve four-letter words, and she doesn't want to be that unprofessional in front of her boss. Instead, she pulls out her phone and starts to bring up Savannah's blog. "Did you approve this, Charlie?"

"Approve what?" Charlie raises his thick brown eyebrows. "Is everything all right?"

He doesn't know. *Of course* he doesn't know. Charlie is a genuinely nice guy, even if he's clueless where his daughter's concerned. Savannah didn't get his approval before she published the blog, even though it's linked on the *Gazette*'s homepage.

"No, everything is *not* all right. Are you okay with your daughter outing a fifteen-year-old girl in her column? Is that the kind of journalistic standard the *Gazette* wants to be associated with? Here, read it for yourself." She hands Charlie her phone. "In addition to being incredibly irresponsible and just plain mean-spirited, you'll also notice there are not one but *two* typos. Anne Shirley is famously Anne-with-an-e. And 'tattoo' has two t's, Savannah. Sending your columns to the copyeditor is important."

Savannah turns to her dad. "I'll fix the typos. Bea's only mad because now everybody knows she cheated on her boyfriend. She's embarrassed. As she should be." She turns to Bea and mouths *slut*, and Bea thinks of a few things that might be worth getting fired for.

Behind his glasses, Charlie's blue eyes are narrowed. "Savannah, you know I had misgivings about this column. One of my conditions was that you refrain from featuring anyone under eighteen. You cannot publish gossip about *children*."

"Dad, people post *everything* online," Savannah argues.

He waves the phone at her. "This is not the blog I signed off on yesterday, which means you went behind my back to publish it. You knew I wouldn't approve. You've hurt the paper's reputation with this nonsense. You've hurt *my* reputation. This is inexcusable."

"Inexcusable? Are you firing me?" Savannah gasps.

"I understand if you need to fire me too," Bea says.

Charlie frowns at her. "Why would I fire *you*?"

"Because of this." Bea reaches out and pushes Savannah sideways. Hard.

Savannah makes a nice splash.

The river isn't deep on the other side of the bulwark, maybe three feet. There's no danger of Savannah drowning. She flails for a minute but pops right back to the surface, sputtering. Her hair is plastered to her face. Inky black trails of mascara weave their way down over her cheeks.

"You say whatever you want about me," Bea tells her, "but you leave my sisters the hell alone."

Later, on the *Stella Anne*, Bea recounts the awful events of the afternoon to Gabe.

"You pushed her into the river?" Gabe shakes his head. He's wearing his dark-blond hair loose, down to his shoulders. "Remind me never to make you mad."

"You'd better not," Bea teases. They're sitting curled up next to each other on the gray futon. "So...there's something I've been wondering, and I can no longer contain my curiosity. Who is *Stella Anne?* Is she an ex?"

"Uh. No." Gabe ducks his head, blushing. "The boat's named after my moms: Stella Beauford and Anne Stewart."

"Seriously? That is *adorable!*" Bea squeals. "I've been jealous of your moms for weeks!"

"Well, they are pretty rad," Gabe says.

"Were you ever into Savannah?" she asks. "Like, even a tiny bit?"

He shakes his head. "I have been raised never to speak ill of a lady, but...you have nothing to worry about there. Seriously, nothing." He grins and curls his hand around her ankle. "I was thinking...you want to take the boat out tonight? We could go down the river."

Bea's phone beeps with a text from Gram.

Family meeting at 6. At home. Expect you all to be there ON TIME.

Uh-oh. Bea is guessing that some nosy neighbor showed Gram the blog.

"I would love to, but I can't. We're having a family meeting. It's nonnegotiable. My sisters are going to have a million questions about my breakup and about you. And I still have to tell them I'm not going to Georgetown."

"You start looking at any other schools yet?" Gabe asks, his thumb tracing circles on the thin skin of her ankle. "You could come visit me this fall at Vandy. See how you like Nashville."

Bea looks up at him, startled. Is he already thinking that far ahead? Does he think they'll stay together after he leaves Remington Hollow?

Gabe laughs, low and rumbly. "The look on your face! I freaked you out, didn't I? I freaked you out so bad."

"No, you didn't!" she protests. He stares at her until she relents. "Okay, yeah. Maybe a little. I'm sorry. I just...I need to take this slow."

"All right." Gabe slides across the futon toward her, scooping her legs into his lap, giving her a wicked grin. "Slow it is." He bends his head and presses a soft kiss to her collarbone. Slowly, maddeningly slowly, he kisses his way up the pale, freckled line of her throat. When he reaches her ear, he proceeds to do incredible things with his lips and teeth and tongue. Bea melts. By the time he lowers his mouth to hers, she is ready to devour him whole.

Half an hour later, she untangles her fingers from his hair and climbs out of his lap. "Slow," she reminds herself out loud.

"Slow is gonna kill me," he groans.

Bea tucks her hair behind her ear. "Are you complaining?"

"I am not." He grins and goes to sit at the table. "Come on. I'm going to teach you how to play poker."

She remembers the first night she came on board the *Stella Anne*. It feels like ages ago. "I am not going to play strip poker with you."

"We'll see about that." He pulls off his heather-gray Henley, revealing the muscles of his shoulders and chest and abs. All that construction is doing excellent things to his upper body. Really excellent things. "What if I give you a head start?"

Bea's mouth goes dry. "That is not fair."

CHAPTER THIRTY-ONE

KAT

"Oh wow," Kat says as she watches her sister push Savannah Lockwood right into the river.

She didn't think Bea had such a diva gesture in her. Bea looks flushed and victorious as she pokes her glasses up on her freckled nose, snatches her phone from Charlie, and marches back to Kat. She does all of this while wearing her Rey costume and holding her head high despite the staring eyes of nearly everyone in Bishop Park.

"Are you okay?" she asks Kat.

"Better now," Kat says, eyes wide. "That was *amazing.*"

"She deserved it," Bea mutters darkly.

"I am so proud of you." Kat gives her sister a high five. She can't believe Bea and Erik broke up. And that Bea is already seeing somebody else. Apparently Kat isn't the only Garrett sister who's been keeping secrets this summer. "So...tell me about this mysterious new guy!"

Bea gazes down at the grass, shifting her feet in Kat's clunky black boots. "You're not mad?"

Kat tugs at the hem of her blue romper. It's not like she *approves* of Bea kissing someone else before she broke up with Erik, but Bea is her sister. Kat's always going to defend her. That's what sisters do. "Mad that you cheated on Erik? I mean...that's not really my business, is it?"

"Oh. Well. That's very enlightened of you," Bea says, but Kat can tell she means *unusually forgiving.* "I know he was practically part of the family. Like a big brother to you and Vi. I thought maybe...I don't know...you liked him better than me."

Kat shakes her head, her high ponytail swinging. Bea is being way too hard on herself, as usual. "Look, you're my sister. Maybe I don't always *like* you, but I love you. And it's bullshit that girls are always expected to be *nice* and *cute* and *likable.* So you're kind of snappish and impatient and self-absorbed sometimes. So what? You're also super smart and ambitious. I...you know...admire that. I admire *you.*"

Bea looks like she might cry. "Thank you. That means a lot. I've been so scared everybody would be mad at me... especially you."

"Why?" Kat knows she can be melodramatic sometimes, but this is really not about her.

"Well, I mean…given what happened with you and Adam, and now Mase. I'm really sorry about that. And I'm sorry that Savannah posted stuff about you to get back at me."

Kat's stomach plunges down around her wedge heels. "Wait…what happened with Mase, exactly?"

Bea's face falls. "Oh shit. Kat."

Kat grabs for Bea's phone. "Let me see that."

Bea hands it over, and Kat scans Savannah's blog till she gets to the part about her: *Meanwhile, looks like the poor kitty cat got dumped again. We spotted her new boyfriend kissing his not-so-ex at the fireworks. Claws are sure to come out when our favorite diva hears about that.* Meow!

Mase and Brandon kissed.

Mase didn't come back to work after his lunch break, even though they were open for another three and a half hours. Miss Lydia was understandably pissed. Kat stayed past closing, helping her clean up. Hoping futilely that Mase would come back and apologize. That he'd tell her he and Brandon had a long talk but ultimately decided their breakup was for the best. That *she* was the one he wanted to be with.

Kat had looked at the pictures Pen took of her and Mase—the posed one and then the second one, where they were blushing and grinning at each other after Pen busted them for making out upstairs—and she had felt temporarily buoyed. Whatever she and Mase had, it felt like it was worth fighting for. The pictures were proof.

Mase is a good actor, but he likes her. She *knows* he likes her. The way he kissed her yesterday, the way he looked at her...that wasn't pretend.

But whatever is happening between them is just beginning. How can she compete with Brandon? She and Mase were only supposed to be a ruse, a scheme to get their exes back. Brandon was always supposed to be his endgame.

Kat feels small and silly and sort of crushed for ever thinking otherwise.

Then, slowly—more slowly than she would like—anger starts to burn through her veins. Even if Mase doesn't like her back—or if he decided he likes Brandon more—they have an agreement. Even if he can't face her, he could text. He should have respected her enough to tell her their fake relationship was over.

How could Mase let her find out that he and Brandon were back together by reading about it in the newspaper? What a *coward*.

And now everyone's going to read Savannah's blog and know that Kat got dumped *again*. It reinforces everything Adam says about her. That she's crazy and jealous and so much *drama*.

Kat lowers her angry blue eyes to her sister's anxious ones.

"Do you want to talk about it?" Bea asks, hovering.

"Not with you," Kat snaps.

Bea takes a step back. "Kat, you said you weren't mad at me."

"That was before I read this. God, why can't everyone just be *honest*? Why is that so hard?"

"You're right." Bea's shoulders droop. "I don't know."

Kat's anger dims. She wants Bea to argue, not agree with her. To fight back, so she can stay angry instead of giving in to the sadness lurking around the edges.

"Erik was right," she says. "You should get out of here. And I guess since you're not in the raft race after all, I'm going back to the café."

Kat stalks toward the entrance of Bishop Park. God, what if Mase is at the café? What if he's there *with Brandon*? He wouldn't do that, would he? Bring him to the place he and Kat worked together, where they started to fall for each other?

Kat *knows* he was starting to fall for her.

"Hey, kitty Kat," a familiar male voice says.

Kat looks up to find Adam and Jillian entering the park, hand-in-hand. Adam is doing his popped-collar strut, new Jordans on his feet. Jillian is wearing a black cold-shoulder sundress and flat black sandals. Kat wonders if Adam makes her wear flats so that she's not taller than him. He used to do that with Kat too. His masculinity is pathetically fragile.

Kat lifts her chin. Better to get this over with now, she guesses.

Adam doesn't waste any time getting right into it. "So much for Guyliner not having a history of cheating, huh? For being someone you could really *trust*?"

"Adam." Jillian elbows him, hard, and he makes a little *oof* noise.

"Mase is twice the guy you are. In *every* way," Kat says, smirking suggestively. Going for the small penis joke is low, but so is Adam throwing this in her face.

"Like you'd know, virgin," Adam says. "You talk big, but—"

"Adam! Shut. Up," Jillian says, raising her mirrored sunglasses to glare at him.

"Mase probably got tired of being bossed around," Adam mutters. "Although, I don't know, maybe faggots like—"

Kat doesn't wait for him to finish. She's already grabbing the bottle of Diet Coke from her bag, unscrewing the cap in one quick twist, and tossing the contents right into Adam's face.

She has always wanted to throw a drink in somebody's face.

"What the fuck!" he gasps, soda dripping down his polo shirt and onto his precious white sneakers. She bets they were expensive.

"You know my sister's gay, right? I am not here for your homophobic shit," Kat hisses. "And you keep Mase's name out of your mouth. If I hear you call him that ever again, I will kick your ass."

"Jill, are you going to let this crazy bitch attack me?" Adam asks, wiping off his face with the hem of his blue shirt.

"No." Jillian smiles at him beatifically. "I'm going to congratulate her."

"What? Baby, I—"

"Don't call me 'baby,'" Jillian snaps. "You're *gross*, Adam, and I'm breaking up with you for being a misogynistic, homophobic *jerk*. You've been talking shit about Kat ever since we got together. You're the one who broke up with her, remember? To be with me? If you're so threatened by your ex being happy with some other guy who happens to be bisexual then maybe you need to spend some time alone figuring that out."

"Alone? You think I can't get another girl like that?" Adam snaps his fingers.

"Good luck with that." Jillian rolls her eyes. "Come on, Kat. Let me buy you another Coke to replace the one you threw on that loser."

"Loser? I..." Adam starts ranting, but Kat doesn't hear him. She's walking away. With Jillian.

People are surprising her all over the place today.

"That was amazing," Kat says, looking at her former archnemesis. "And I owe you an apology. It was cool of you to stick up for me after the way I've treated you."

Jillian shrugs. "I did kiss your boyfriend. I kind of deserved it."

"Still," Kat says as they walk past the big old houses on Water Street. "I should have blamed him, not you."

"He can be really charming," Jillian says. "But, oh my God, he's so insecure. He needs every girl in the room to be in love with him. He's been pressuring me to have sex, but he's already been flirting with Cassidy. And I'm tired of wearing flats just so I'm shorter than him. It's ridiculous. Like, nobody cares that you're short, dude."

"I know, right?" Kat laughs. It feels good to laugh.

"I'm sorry about you and Mase. You guys seemed really happy."

"Yeah." Kat's smile fades. "I thought we were."

"You should talk to him. I mean, who am I to give you advice, right? But maybe it's not true. Maybe Savannah got it wrong."

"Maybe." Kat doubts it. But maybe it's worth at least talking to Mase before she goes all scorched earth on him. He's not Adam. Not the kind of guy to hurt her on purpose. "Can I take a rain check on the Coke? I'm going to go see if Mase is at the café."

"Yeah, of course." Jillian hesitates, scuffing one sandal

against the brick sidewalk, and then looks at Kat shyly. "So...friends now?"

"Friends," Kat agrees. "And thanks again for having my back."

"Chicks before dicks," Jillian says, and Kat gives a startled laugh. "That's what we say in field hockey. I'm sorry I broke the girl code."

"It's forgotten," Kat says. "Honestly. I know I have a reputation for holding grudges, but we're cool now."

"Thanks." Jillian grins at her. "Go get him, tiger! Fight for your man."

Kat nods. If there's one thing she knows how to do, it's fighting for what she wants.

❦

When Gram texts about the family meeting, Kat is upstairs at the café.

Specifically, she is moping on a flowered love seat—a throwback from before the renovation which is ugly but super comfortable—and petting Sassy. Sassy licks Kat's hand with her rough sandpaper tongue and purrs when Kat scratches her ears. Kat is now positive, thanks to the telltale pink collar around the cat's neck, that this is Sassy and not Shadow. Shadow has a blue collar because he's a boy cat.

Downstairs, the café is already closed. All the shops in

Remington Hollow close by five o'clock on Sundays. But Miss Lydia took one look at Kat's sad face and told her she could stay as long as she wanted if she promised to set the alarm when she left.

Maybe I'll swear off boys, Kat thinks. *Maybe I'll become a famous eccentric actress with a mansion full of cats.*

The front door slams, and then footsteps trudge up the stairs.

"Hello?" she calls. "Miss Lydia?"

A familiar swoopy black pompadour comes into view, followed by a pair of earnest brown eyes with obscenely long lashes. *Does* he use mascara? Kat still isn't sure. Her traitorous heart races, and Sassy paws at her arm, utterly forgotten.

"Hi," Mase says. "I've been looking everywhere for you."

"You didn't look very hard," she says glumly. "I've been here for hours."

"I thought you'd be at the race cheering Bea on." He sits backward in Miss Lydia's desk chair, facing Kat.

"What do you want, Mase?" She's been hoping he'd show up. That she could convince him to choose her. She had this whole monologue all planned out. But she's been waiting for *three hours.* While he was…where? With Brandon? All the fight drained out of her while she sat here, petting cats and picturing Mase kissing his ex-boyfriend. She doesn't want to fight for somebody who doesn't want her back. She's done doing that.

"You saw the blog," he says. "Savannah's column."

"Yeah." Kat traces one of the flowers on the love seat.

"I can explain," he says. "Brandon and I—"

"You don't have to explain," Kat interrupts. "I think it's pretty obvious. The two of you are back together. That was always the plan, right? The point of this whole charade? Well. Congratulations. I'm happy for you."

"You are?" Mase runs a hand over his pompadour, frowning.

For a minute, Kat is tempted to tell him that Jillian and Adam broke up. To make it sound like she got what she wanted too. But Adam is so far from what she wants now, she can't bring herself to lie about it. Not when the person she does want is sitting right across from her in skinny jeans and wingtip shoes and an obscure band T-shirt, staring at her with puzzled kohl-rimmed eyes.

"No, I'm not," she admits, burying her face in her hands. This is so embarrassing. "I hate it. I hate him and his stupid Clark Kent style and his stupid shoulders that you massaged and his stupid face that you kissed."

Mase rolls the desk chair across the floor toward her. It startles Sassy, and she leaps off Kat's lap and runs down the hall.

"Hey." Mase touches Kat's arm. "Kat. It's not what you think."

She peeks out from between her fingers. "You didn't

kiss Brandon last night at the fireworks? Savannah made that up?"

"Well, okay, maybe it's a little bit what you think," Mase says. "We did kiss."

"You tripped and fell on his mouth?" Kat asks scornfully.

Mase gives her a long-suffering look that she might deserve. "Would you please shut up for two minutes and let me explain? It was this, I don't know, moment of nostalgia. We never had a chance to do a real postmortem. He told me he hooked up with somebody else, and we broke up over text message, for God's sake. So yeah, there were a lot of big feelings when we saw each other yesterday. We walked all around town and talked. And we did kiss, but we both knew right away it was stupid. We're not getting back together."

Kat sits up a little straighter. "Why not?"

"Because none of the reasons we broke up have changed. He's in Virginia. I'm here. He wants to be able to date other guys. And I…" Mase trails off.

"And you?" Kat prompts, leaning forward, full of hope.

"And I feel like maybe I'm starting to fall for somebody else, and I want to see where that goes," Mase says in a rush.

Kat bites back an enormous grin. "Somebody else, huh? Do I know him?"

"Her," Mase corrects. "I don't know; you might have

heard of her. She's a real diva. I heard she threw a Coke in some asshole's face this afternoon, defending my honor."

Kat flushes. "You heard about that?"

"Gossip travels fast." Mase scoots the chair closer, till his jean-clad knees bump against hers. "Let's see, what else. She's smart. And funny. She makes me laugh all the time. She has all these crazy plans, but some of them turn out to be kind of brilliant. Oh, and she's really bossy. And hot. Actually, it's kind of hot that she's so bossy."

"Is it?" Kat asks, inching forward on the love seat. "You don't think she's too much? Too, I don't know, sensitive? Too dramatic?"

Mase leans over the back of the desk chair. His breath smells like chocolate. "Nope. I like her just the way she is."

It is the most perfect thing he could possibly say.

"Kiss me," Kat commands. "For real."

Mase reaches out and cups her cheek. "Kissing you has always been for real."

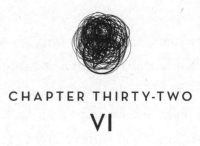

CHAPTER THIRTY-TWO
VI

"Hey," Vi says, hurrying up to Des and Em in Bishop Park. The raft race has just started. Vi sees Bea's *Star Wars* raft with BB-8 and R2-D2 and Erik onboard, but Bea isn't there. Which is strange, because Bea loves winning things, and unless it somehow sinks, her raft is a shoo-in for the Tea Cup. "What's going on? Where's Bea?"

Des and Em exchange a look. It is the kind of look that says they know something they don't want to tell her. "Bea isn't on the raft," Des says.

"Yeah, I can see that." Vi rolls her eyes. "How come?"

"She and Erik broke up," Des explains.

"What?" Vi gasps. Erik and Bea have been dating since Vi was ten years old. Erik is the big brother she never had. He helped her get the hang of algebra and corrected her Chinese pronunciation because her sisters all took Spanish. Vi adores Erik. But she'll never forgive him if he hurt her sister.

Vi has only been dating Cece for one day (*Are* they dating? They haven't quantified what happened last night yet.), but she would be destroyed if Cece broke up with her. She can't imagine how devastated Bea must be.

"Do we hate him now? Is Bea okay?" she asks.

"I think," Des says slowly, "that Bea is the one who broke up with *him*. I'm not sure. It seems like maybe she was hooking up with somebody else?"

"What? *Who?*" Vi gasps, scandalized.

"Remember old Miss Amelia? She made those spritz cookies for the fire hall bake sale," Em says. "It's her grandson. I've seen him. He's hot."

"What…how…" Vi sputters. She can't believe this is happening. She knows Bea and Erik are only eighteen, but they were supposed to be together forever. He was practically part of their family.

"I know. I can't believe she didn't tell us," Des says. She and Em exchange another look, and Vi frowns. They seem to be friends again, which is nice, but why are they treating her like a little kid? Like someone who needs to be shielded from bad news?

"Is there something else?" she asks.

Em nudges Des with her elbow, and Des glares at her.

"Vi, have you read Savannah's blog today?" Des asks.

Vi shakes her head. "No. Ew."

Em hands Vi her phone. "You need to read this."

She needs to read it? Why?

Vi's breath catches. No. No, no, no, no, no. Savannah couldn't. She *wouldn't*.

She scans the screenshot Em took, her hands shaking so much that the words blur together.

As for the littlest orphan, Pride Month may be over, but we hear she and the girl from the restaurant next door are just heating things up.

"How dare she," Vi seethes. "How *dare* she."

"Bea pushed her in the river," Em volunteers. "It was kind of awesome."

"She should have drowned her." Vi hands the phone back. "I'm going to call the editor and complain. I'm going to have them print a retraction!"

"Charlie already deleted the post," Des says. "But once something like this is out…"

"She's not," Vi says. "Cece, I mean. She's not out."

"But something happened? Between you two?" Des asks.

"Do you want me to give you guys some space?" Em asks.

Vi shakes her head, remembering last night. She was so happy sitting on the dock with her head on Cece's shoulder, with Cece's arm around her, watching the fireworks finale. And then—as they heard people leaving the party boat and coming down the pier—they scrambled up. Cece walked Vi home, pulled her into the little alley between the Garretts' row house and the Mitchells', pressed her up against the brick wall, and kissed her till they were both breathless. Vi blushes, thinking about it. The whole night felt like a dream. Like it was too good to be true. Do girls like her—weird, bookish, queer girls—get to have happily-ever-afters?

What if it's already turned into a nightmare for Cece?

Vi was so happy this morning that she didn't stop and think about whether she and Cece are on the same page. They didn't hold hands walking through town. Cece didn't kiss Vi on her front porch, where anyone could see; she pulled her into the alley. Maybe those kisses didn't change anything for Cece. Maybe she still wasn't ready to tell her family. Now that choice has been taken away from her. They'll hear about it from a customer who read Savannah's blog.

Vi is furious. When and how and to whom she came out should have been Cece's decision. No one else's. Certainly not Savannah's. How will the Pérezes react? Will this make Cece regret everything? What if they forbid her to see Vi? What if they send her away?

"I have to go," Vi says grimly. There are a lot of things

she wants to ask Des—did she ever find Paige and did Paige steal the money and is Des really moving out—but that can wait. First she has to talk to Cece.

"Maybe you should give her some time to figure things out," Des says.

That might be the sensible thing, but Vi doesn't feel very sensible right now. She has to find out what's going on. She and Cece sent each other funny selfies with dog filters this morning, but she hasn't heard from her for a couple hours. She thought it was because Cece was working the brunch shift. But maybe that's not it. Maybe her parents saw the blog and they took her phone away.

Are you okay? She texts Cece as she hurries back through town. **Did you see Savannah's blog?**

There's no answer by the time she reaches Tia Julia's.

She finds Cece behind the hostess stand in the courtyard. When Cece turns around and sees Vi standing there, flushed and panting, her hair falling out of its braids, she gives her the slow sunrise smile that makes Vi's breath catch. "Hi!"

She doesn't know, Vi thinks. Cece hasn't read the blog yet, or she wouldn't smile at her like that for everybody to see.

Vi hates Savannah Lockwood with her whole heart.

"Can you take a break?" she asks.

"It's pretty busy, but...let me see if I can get Elena to cover for me." Cece's hair is wound up in a braid around the crown of her head, leaving the nape of her neck bare, and Vi wants to press a kiss right there. The thought makes her miserable. What if she can never kiss Cece again?

Cece whispers with a middle-aged waitress, then comes back and gives Vi a dimpled grin. "Okay. I've got five minutes. How are you? I thought you were going to the raft race. Is it already over? Did Bea win?"

Vi draws her down the brick sidewalk between a tree box and a trashcan. She wishes there were somewhere more private for them to have this talk, but they only have five minutes, and Gram is at Arden. She hands Cece her phone. Em texted her the screenshot. "You have to read this."

"Savannah's blog? Why?" Cece scrunches up her nose adorably. As she reads, her scowl deepens, and then she looks at Vi with panicky eyes. "Did you tell someone?"

Vi shakes her head. "She must have seen us down at the marina."

"No one else was around," Cece insists.

"There were the people on the party boat. Maybe she was there," Vi says, trying to stay calm.

"You didn't tell anyone? Not even your sisters?"

Why is Cece interrogating her? This is not Vi's fault.

"I didn't tell anyone," Vi says. "But I'm happy that we're...whatever we are. I like you, Cece. I don't regret kissing you."

"*Shhhhh*," Cece hisses. She takes a step away, and the empty space between them cracks Vi's heart open like a clam.

"You're not ready for this, are you?" Vi wants to cry. She should have known better. She should have given her more time. Maybe this *is* kind of her fault. "Do you want me to deny it? Pretend nothing happened? I could say it was just me, having a pathetic unrequited crush on the straight girl next door."

Her voice is bitter despite herself. She does not want to lie about this. She has never had to lie about who she is. She knows that is a privilege. She would lie, for Cece, if Cece asked her to. But she hopes Cece won't.

"Vi. Stop." Cece covers her face with both hands. Her nails are painted a bright glittery pink. "I'm trying not to freak out, okay? If my parents don't know yet, they're going to know by the end of the dinner rush. Things never stay secret in Remington Hollow."

"Is that what you want? To keep us secret?" Vi keeps her voice low. "*Is* there an us?"

Cece drops her hands to her sides. "I don't know, okay? You knew that I wasn't out. You told me I should wait till I was ready, remember?"

"I did say that." Vi feels stupid for assuming they were dating. For assuming a few kisses had erased all of Cece's doubts and fears. "I guess I thought that maybe...after last night...you would feel differently."

"This is not about you!" Cece snaps.

Vi reels back, stung. She doesn't say anything for a long moment while Cece paces back and forth. Then she takes a deep breath. "I'm sorry. The thing is...abandoning all pretense of being cool here...I have liked you for a really long time. But it's not fair that Savannah stuck her nose into this. It should be up to you when to tell your family. Just let me know what you want me to say. Or not say. It's your decision."

CHAPTER THIRTY-THREE

DES

Midafternoon, Gram sends a group text to all four Garrett sisters.

> Family meeting at 6. At home. Expect you to all be there ON TIME.

Des slinks back toward the house right before six. She is mortified by her behavior yesterday. She told Em all about it, painting a vivid picture of how she yelled at Gram so loud, the customers on the sidewalk could probably hear every single word, how she stalked out like a brat and slammed the door. Em reassured her that Gram would forgive her and that everyone their age fights with their parents.

Em said this with the world-weary attitude of someone who has been away at college for a whole year. It was a little annoying, but Des has missed her a lot. They had so much catching up to do. It turned out that at Em's roommate's house party, her friend Lauren—the blond with the nose ring—had hooked up with Em's crush, Hunter. Em is still pretty broken up about it. Des feels bad that she wasn't around when Em needed her.

And apparently she hasn't been there for her sisters either. All four of them have been keeping secrets, big and small.

How can she move out? They need her.

Bea is walking down their street from the opposite direction, and they step onto the front porch at the same time.

"You're moving out?" Bea asks. "Since when? Why didn't you tell me?"

"You broke up with Erik and have a new boyfriend?" Des counters, pushing open the front door. "Since when? Why didn't you tell me?"

Bea frowns at her. "He's not my boyfriend. We're just… hanging out. Having fun."

"In the living room, girls!" Gram hollers. Her mobility and her eyesight aren't what they used to be, but her hearing is excellent. Annoyingly so.

In the living room, Kat is stretched out facedown on the soft striped rug, doing some kind of hip-opener stretch. Vi's curled up in her favorite oversized armchair, nervously playing with her braids. Gram sits in the other armchair, her knee propped on the ottoman, holding what Des suspects is a printed copy of Savannah's blog. Des and Bea glare at each other and sit on opposite ends of the couch, a wide gulf between them.

"It has come to my attention," Gram says, rustling the paper theatrically, "that each of you has some things you might like to share with the rest of the family. Some things that perhaps we ought to have heard from you, instead of that little snake Savannah Lockwood."

Kat lifts her head. She really is amazingly bendy. "At least her dad fired her."

"Was that before or after Bea pushed her into the river?" Gram asks, looking at Bea sternly over her glasses. "You're lucky you aren't fired yourself, after a stunt like that. Charlie called me, you know. He apologized for Savannah—he already made her take that post down—but I had to promise him you'll be on your best behavior and let bygones be bygones."

"Bygones?" Vi shoots out of her chair like she's been fired out of a cannon. "She outed Cece. That is not okay. What if Cece's abuela kicks her out of the house? I told her she could come stay with us if she needs a place to go. That would be all right, wouldn't it, Gram?"

"Of course it would, but I don't think that will be necessary," Gram says.

Vi's blue eyes are owlish with worry. "Cece says her abuela thinks we're going to hell."

Gram clucks. "Vi, sweetheart, stop and think for a minute. Would I be friends with someone who believes you are going to hell?"

Vi hesitates. "No, but…what about her abuela's brother? Cece says he got disowned for being gay, and her abuela never talks about him."

"Ernesto? Honey, that was back in the sixties. Things are different now for a lot of folks. Not everybody, unfortunately. But Julia probably doesn't talk about him because she regrets not standing up to her father back then. Cecilia is her only granddaughter. She loves that girl more than life itself. I assure you, she does not think either of you are going to hell. Now." Gram draws a baton out from behind her back and raps it on the coffee table. "Let this family meeting begin. You all remember the rules, don't you?"

"Oh noooo," Vi moans. "Not the talking stick!"

The talking stick is a sparkly blue relic from Kat's brief stint in the elementary school color guard. It has white streamers on each end, as befits the navy-and-white of the Remington Hollow Buccaneers. They used the baton for family meetings when they were younger, so that everybody had a fair chance to talk without being interrupted half a dozen times. It has been resting in peace in the hall closet for the past few years.

"I *love* the talking stick," Kat says, reaching for the baton.

"You love it when you're holding it," Vi mutters.

"Oldest first," Gram says, handing the baton to Des.

"Whyyyyy?" Kat complains, just as Vi says, "No fair!" Bea only scowls.

Des stands up. She doesn't know why. She shifts the baton nervously from one hand to the other and stares down at her red Toms. She takes a deep breath.

"First, I'm really sorry that I yelled at you, Gram," she says, meeting Gram's eyes. "I didn't want to believe you about Paige, but you were right. She did take the money from Arden and from me. I saw her today on her way out of town, and she admitted it. She took Miss Lydia's engagement ring too. And she didn't even seem sorry." Des shakes her head. "I trusted her with the cash box, and I shouldn't have. I'll pay you back."

"That's not necessary," Gram says.

"Please let me pay you back," Des says. "I have the money in my savings. And I was so awful. I left in the middle of my shift. I was irresponsible and disrespectful, and I displayed bad judgment, and I understand if—if you want to fire me." She holds her breath. She would deserve it. But she doesn't know what she'll do if she can't work at Arden anymore. She *loves* being a bookseller, and she loves the connection it gives her to her mom.

Gram shakes her head, her silver earrings dancing. "I'm

not going to fire you, honey. But I appreciate the apology. And I admit, there was some truth in the things you said. I've relied on you an awful lot lately. Maybe too much. And you haven't exactly gotten a lot of help from this bunch."

Gram sweeps a stern eye around the room, and all three of Des's sisters shrink into themselves. Des purses her mouth. Paige wasn't a good friend to her, but she wasn't entirely wrong about *everything*. Des should have spoken up sooner, when she started feeling so overwhelmed and unappreciated.

"As you girls get older," Gram continues, "there will be times I don't agree with your decisions or like your friends. And maybe sometimes I'll meddle a little too much. Mostly that's me trying to protect you and keep you from getting hurt, but sometimes…well, sometimes I am a little old-fashioned. To tell you the truth, Des, I don't care for your tattoo or that blue hair, but it's your body, and it's your right to do whatever you want with it."

"Thank you." Des shifts awkwardly. "So…the other thing is that Savannah was right. I am moving out."

"What?" Kat gasps, popping up from her yoga stretch. "When?"

"Where?" Bea asks.

"Who's going to run the store? Who's going to cook dinner?" Kat demands.

"Maybe some other people will have to learn to cook

dinner. And do their own laundry," Gram suggests, with a pointed look at Kat.

"Are you going to art school?" Vi looks worried. "Will you be far away?"

"No. Oh my God, *chill*," Des says, waving the talking stick at them. "I'm moving into the Adlers' garage apartment. I'll be all of five blocks away."

Vi turns to Gram, bouncing in her seat. "Does that mean we can get a dog?"

"No! A cat!" Kat crawls across the floor to lean on Gram's good knee and look up at her with pleading eyes. "There's the sweetest little black cat at the café. Her name's Sassy. Pleeeeease, Gram?"

"What about *both*?" Vi suggests. "You know *I'm* responsible. I walk Juno and Athena all the time."

"I've been super responsible at the café! Ask Miss Lydia. She said I could practically run the whole place," Kat says, glowing with pride.

Great, Des thinks. *I am being replaced by a dog and/or a cat. I can't believe I felt so guilty about this.* "So…you're all okay with me moving out?"

"I think it's excellent!" Kat crows. "Does this mean I can have your room? Since Bea will be at Georgetown?"

"Actually," Bea says quietly, curling into herself, "I'm not going to Georgetown."

CHAPTER THIRTY-FOUR

BEA

"Actually," Bea says quietly, curling into herself, "I'm not going to Georgetown."

This time, the living room doesn't explode into a flurry of questions. Four heads swivel to silently gape at her. Des hands her the baton without a word.

Bea wishes she could disappear into the couch cushions like she used to when she was little. She used to make great pillow forts.

"I'm deferring my acceptance for a year," she explains. "To figure some things out. I, um, assume I can live here for another year?"

"Of course you can," Gram says, but there's a big furrow in her forehead. "Why, though? Is this about

Amelia's grandson? I thought he was only here for the summer."

"He is," Bea says, exasperated. "I am not postponing college for a cute boy. Although he is. Cute. Very, very cute."

"Do you have a picture?" Kat asks, interested.

Bea shakes her head.

"But you are seeing him," Gram says.

Bea nods, fighting against a blush. She is seeing a *lot* of him. She's better at poker than she expected.

How can it be possible to feel so many different things at once? She remembers all the ugly things Erik said to her in the park. He wasn't wrong. She *was* selfish. She was more worried about what people would think of her, about disappointing her family, than about hurting him. She regrets how badly she handled this. It wasn't fair to him or to Gabe.

But for the first time in months, she's not filled with dread when she thinks of her future, all neatly mapped out before her. Bea is not a spontaneous person. She likes routines and schedules and rules. Now her future is a question mark, and that's scary. But last night, she finally slept. For eleven hours straight.

"Why did you break up with Erik?" Vi asks.

Bea pushes her glasses up her nose and draws on Chloe's inspirational speech. "We've been together for so long, you know? Since I was thirteen. I'm not the same person now that I was at thirteen. I don't want the same things. And trying to *make* myself want them, to convince myself I was still happy and in love with him and couldn't wait to go to Georgetown…I've been having panic attacks. I haven't been sleeping."

"I noticed you've been stress baking a lot," Kat says.

"Actually, I was thinking…" Bea hesitates. "Maybe I could go see Jenna? Maybe she could help me with my anxiety. Teach me some coping strategies or something. You liked her, right?"

"Jenna, my old therapist?" Kat twirls a red curl around her finger. "Yeah. I mean…I resented that Gram made me go, at the time, but Jenna was actually pretty great."

"I'm so tired," Bea says, near tears. "I'm anxious all the time, and it's *exhausting*. I get mad at myself for the tiniest mistakes. The mean way I talk to myself…I would never talk to anybody else like that. I feel like if I'm not perfect, everyone will be disappointed in me. And then this summer, I've made so many mistakes. I know I should have broken up with Erik months ago, but I was afraid you'd all be mad. That maybe you like him better than me. I know I'm not always easy."

"What? That's dumb." Kat leans her head against Bea's leg. "You're my *sister*."

"We're Team Bea," Vi says. "No matter what."

"Always," Des adds.

Bea blinks back tears. "You're not mad at me? I'm sorry I let you down."

"You didn't let us down, sweet Bea," Gram says. "I think maybe you let yourself down a little. Maybe that's something you and Jenna can talk about."

"I have a question," Vi says. "What are you going to do this year, if you're not going to Georgetown?"

Bea chews on one of her already-ragged fingernails. "I'm still figuring that out. I'm going to ask Charlie if I can keep interning at the *Gazette*. I really like working for a small-town paper. I know it's not exactly hard-hitting, Pulitzer Prize–winning reporting," she says apologetically and then wonders why she feels the need to apologize. "But I love my women entrepreneurs series. It's really inspiring to see how many women in our community have started their own businesses. I'd like to interview you later this summer, Gram."

"Now you're just buttering me up," Gram jokes, but her cheeks go pink with pleasure.

"I was also thinking I could pick up some of the slack around here, if Des moves out. *Some* of it. You two have to help out more," she says to Kat and Vi. "We'll make a chore chart!"

"Can it have stickers?" Kat asks.

"It can definitely have stickers." Bea looks at her older sister. "Des, I'm sorry. Gram's right, we all took you for granted, and that's not fair. You've been working so much overtime at Arden since Gram's surgery. Maybe I could take some of those hours? I was thinking…I'd kind of like to start a nonfiction book club."

"That would be rad," Des says. "I would love to have more time to work on my art."

"I guess this means I can't have your room, huh," Kat pouts.

"Nope. Not for at least another year," Bea says.

Kat bats her eyelashes. "How would you feel about getting a cat?"

"Don't you spend all day with cats? Isn't that why you took that job working for Lydia?" Gram asks.

"Actually…" Kat grabs the baton from Bea and starts twirling it through her fingers. "Since we're all being super honest today, I took the job because Mase and I had this plan to make our ex-boyfriends jealous by fake-dating."

CHAPTER THIRTY-FIVE
KAT

*"Actually..." **Kat grabs the baton*** from Bea and starts twirling it through her fingers. "Since we're all being super honest today, I took the job because Mase and I had this plan to make our ex-boyfriends jealous by fake-dating."

"What? I thought you really liked him," Bea says. "I know you're a good actress, but..."

"No, I did. I do." Kat jumps to her feet and twirls the baton faster and faster, till it's just a flash of navy blue and white. "It got complicated."

"Why would you take Adam back after how he treated you? He was a jerk," Vi says, uncurling herself from her armchair. "He cheated on you! No offense, Bea."

"None taken. I was a jerk too," Bea acknowledges.

"Adam gaslighted you all the time. He'd flirt with another girl right in front of you and then tell you that you were being crazy and overdramatic when you got mad. He didn't respect your feelings at *all*," Vi says, clearly outraged. Kat had no idea that her little sister felt that strongly about it. "You can do so much better."

"You're right," Kat says.

Vi's eyes go wide with surprise. "I am?"

"Yeah. It took me a while to figure out that I only wanted him back because Jillian had him. You may have noticed I'm a little competitive sometimes. Just a teeny-tiny bit," Kat says, and all three of her sisters and Gram burst out laughing. "Okay, it's not *that* funny."

She isn't *that* bad. Is she?

"Kat, we couldn't play Monopoly for *years* because of the epic tantrums you threw when you lost. Epic," Des reminds her. "Do you guys remember that?"

Bea nods. "You are the second most competitive person I have ever met, after myself."

"I think I might actually be even more..." Kat starts and then trails off as she sees the smile twitching at Bea's lips. "Oh ha ha. I see what you did there."

Gram is shaking her gray head. "So this was all some kind of act?"

"No," Kat says, pacing and twirling the baton. "Mase

and I were pretending at first, but then we ended up really liking each other. We talked this afternoon, and he explained what happened with Brandon, and now we're going to try dating for real."

"So nothing happened between them?" Bea asks.

"No…he and Brandon did kiss. But it was a goodbye thing." Kat drops the baton, and it crashes to the hardwood floor. "I'm still a *little* mad about it. But love is complicated."

"You didn't cuss him out?" Vi asks.

"Of course not!" Kat bends and scoops up the baton. "I would never."

"You," Bea pronounces, "have grown as a person this summer, Kat."

"Well, thank goodness," Gram says. "I never really liked that Adam boy."

"None of us did," Des admits, twirling a blue curl around her finger.

"What? Why didn't any of you tell me?" Kat demands. She didn't know they'd come to a whole *consensus* about it.

"Because that would have only made you like him more. You would have thought it was some kind of star-crossed Romeo and Juliet thing," Bea points out.

Kat puts her non–baton hand on her hip. "I would not!" she protests, but she has to admit it is possible. The quickest way to get her do something is to tell her she can't.

"He's so cocky. He walks like he's trying to show everybody how big his…well, you know," Vi says, blushing.

"We know." Kat looks at her younger sister. "So…you and Cece, huh?"

Vi smiles. Actually, she kind of *glows*. Kat has never seen her look so happy. "I don't know. I think that depends on her family."

"No other deep, dark secrets? Do you even need the talking stick?" Kat jokes.

Vi grabs the baton and then curls back up in her armchair, clutching it. "Actually. You know how I'm always writing in my journal? It's not really a journal. I write fan fiction, and I love it, and if any of you laugh at me, I'm going to beat you with this baton."

CHAPTER THIRTY-SIX
VI

"Actually. You know how I'm always writing in my journal? It's not really a journal. I write fan fiction, and I love it, and if any of you laugh at me, I'm going to beat you with this baton." Vi glares at her sisters preemptively.

"Why would we laugh at you?" Kat asks, flopping back down onto the rug.

"What is fan fiction?" Gram asks, peering at Vi over her glasses.

"It's when you write stories about characters from TV shows, right?" Bea asks.

"Or books or movies." Vi nods. "How do you know that?"

Bea shrugs. "Chloe went through a big *Teen Wolf* phase."

"Are you serious?" Vi gasps. She doesn't know anyone else

in real life who is into TV fandoms like she is. "Oh my gosh. I want to read her fics! Are they still up? Do you know if she posted them on AO3? What name did she write under?"

"I have absolutely no idea." Bea tucks her hair behind her ear. "You will have to consult with Chloe. But why did you think we'd laugh at you?"

Vi feels suddenly shy. She is fully clothed in her shorts and Ravenclaw Quidditch T-shirt, but she feels like she's sitting in front of her sisters naked, just waiting for them to notice all her flaws and start criticizing her. "Because you've always been the writer. You've been winning essay contests since you were in third grade. And you're kind of a literary and TV snob."

"I am not!" Bea argues, sitting up straighter on her end of the couch.

"All you ever watch on television are those History Channel documentaries, unless you're in a mood," Gram points out.

"You act like Agatha Christie writes for the *National Enquirer*," Des adds.

"Remember that time you caught me reading one of Pen's Regency romances with one of those half-naked guys on the front?" Kat asks. "You said it was *trashy*. But most romance authors—and readers—are women. Did you ever think maybe *that's* why romance gets less respect?"

Vi is pretty sure Kat is parroting things she's heard from

Pen, whose mom teaches gender studies, but she's not wrong. It's the same with most young adult fiction.

"But they're so...tropey," Bea argues, wrinkling her nose. "So cliché!"

"Sometimes you just need a happily-ever-after," Vi says. "That's why I write my fics. Lots of times queer characters still don't get happy endings. That whole 'bury your gays' trope. Remember how they killed off Lexa on *The 100*?"

"Yes, because you ranted about it for *weeks*," Kat groans.

Vi glares at her. "That's because there still aren't that many lesbian and bi characters on TV, and representation is really important. So, in my fics, I give my favorite characters their happily-ever-afters. Or I take characters who might be straight in the canon and make them queer."

Bea smiles. "I like that. Do you think you'd ever write your own original characters?"

"Maybe," Vi says. She traces a flower on the love seat with her fingertip. "I think maybe it would be fun to write a book someday."

"You could be an author–bookseller, like Judy Blume! She runs a bookstore in Key West. And Ann Patchett owns one in Nashville," Des says.

"Nashville, huh?" Bea blushes. "I've heard that's a really cool city."

"You are being so shady right now," Kat accuses her,

and then she turns back to Vi. "I can't believe you thought we'd make fun of you."

"Sometimes I feel like nobody takes me seriously," Vi admits, "'cause I'm the youngest."

"Are you kidding? You are way more confident than I was at fifteen, or than I am now, for that matter. You're so *you*, and you don't care what anybody thinks," Bea says.

"I feel like nobody takes me seriously because I have so many *feelings*," Kat confesses, and Vi has to admit that sometimes that's true. It can be hard to tell when Kat's performing to get attention and when she really means it.

"But all those feelings make you a really good actress," she points out.

"Kat, I feel like you don't take me seriously sometimes because I don't care about makeup and fashion and boys. Or girls," Des complains.

"That's not true! We're going to miss you so much," Kat says.

"Because I cook?" Des jokes. "You will still see me *all the time*. I promise. What about you, Bea?"

"Me?" Bea ponders for a minute. "I guess I feel like everyone takes me *too* seriously. Like I can't ever relax, because I'll never do enough or be enough."

"I think you put that on yourself, honey," Gram says. "As for me…I know you girls make fun of all the HGTV I've been watching."

"I secretly love *Tiny House Hunters!*" Bea says. "Those people are *bananas*."

"Let's watch now. And order pizza," Vi says. She needs to distract herself while she waits to hear from Cece.

The doorbell rings. "Um, did you just make a pizza appear?" Kat asks. "Are you a wizard?"

Des peeks out the window. "It's for you, Vi."

"Ooh, is it *Cece*?" Kat clasps her hands to her heart and pretends to swoon.

"Shut up," Vi says, blushing.

"The family meeting is hereby adjourned." Gram grins at Vi. "And tell Cece she can stay for pizza if she wants."

Vi runs to the front door before one of her sisters can get there first and do or say something mortifying. She was hoping Cece would text her and let her know how things went with her parents. Whether she came out to them or lied. Vi really hopes it's the former, because the cat is kind of already out of the bag with her own family.

"Hi," Cece says. She's changed out of her black hostess dress into short pink shorts and a white tank top that sets off her brown skin.

"Hi." Vi has zero chill right now. "How…um…how are you?"

"I wanted to tell you in person how my talk with my family went," Cece says.

"Okay." Vi gestures toward the chairs on the front

porch, and Cece sits in one, her hands clasped together in her lap. She doesn't look sad. At least Vi doesn't think so. Does that mean Gram was right, and everything went well? Vi sits down next to her.

"Mami was so mad when she saw the blog, she wanted to go down to the newspaper office and give Mr. Lockwood a piece of her mind. But she says she doesn't care who I date, whether it's girls or boys, as long as they treat me well. And Papi said that boys only want to get in my pants so he would rather I date girls. Which is stupid, but it works in our favor, so I let that go for now." She grins, and Vi smiles back.

"I'm so glad." *Our favor*, Cece said. Hope creeps over her like morning glory.

"Abuela was the biggest surprise though, because she *wasn't* surprised. She said she could tell from the way I looked at you when you came over for dinner that I liked you as more than a friend."

"Really?" Vi's heart leaps. "And she's okay with it? She doesn't think it's sinful?"

"She says she is still figuring out where she stands on marriage being only between one man and one woman. So we've got some work to do. But she said God doesn't make mistakes, and no way is anything about me a mistake. She said she loves me and she wants me to be happy. And she said you can come over for tamales and Canasta any time."

Cece wipes away a tear with the back of her hand. "I am so relieved, Vi. You have no idea. I mean…actually, I guess you do. But it's like this huge weight has been lifted. Now I can just be happy. And I can do this."

"Do what?" Vi asks, nervous.

Cece stands, grabs Vi's hands, and pulls her to her feet. "This."

And then she kisses Vi. Right there on the front porch, with Kat spying on them through the window and Mr. Mitchell walking Juno down the brick sidewalk. Gorgeous, popular Cece Pérez kisses strange, bookish little Vi Garrett for the whole world to see.

And it is amazing.

Acknowledgments

Like my character Bea, I love to make lists. Here's a list of the amazing folks who helped turn an idea that started off as "*Little Women* meets *Gilmore Girls* by way of Sarah Dessen" into a real book.

- My agent, Jim McCarthy, who is a constant source of support and reassurance.
- Annette Pollert-Morgan, for her helpful notes and for loving the Garrett girls.
- Sarah Kasman, for keeping things running smoothly and answering all my questions.
- Cassie Gutman, for her fantastic line edits and her patience.

- Copyeditor Kelly Burch and proofreader Sabrina Baskey, for finding all my mistakes.
- Designers Jillian Rahn and Nicole Hower, for making the book look gorgeous inside and out.
- Lathea Williams, Alex Yeadon, and Beth Oleniczak, for helping the book find its readers.
- Robin Talley, Katherine Locke, and Tehlor Kay Mejia, for their insightful early reads.
- Lindsay Smith and Miranda Kenneally, for cheerleading and margaritas the size of our heads.
- Tiffany Schmidt, Lauren Spieller, and Bess Cozby, for Highlights magic.
- Jill Coste, for help with Kat and marathon phone dates.
- Jenn Reeder, for forgiving me all my canceled Tuesdays.
- My husband, for everything. This book would not exist without you.
- Tiffany Schmidt again, for being this book's fairy godmother from start to finish.
- And last but never least, my readers, for picking up this book when you have so many choices. Which Garrett girl are you most like? I can't wait to hear from you.

About the Author

Jessica Spotswood is the author of the Cahill Witch Chronicles (*Born Wicked*, *Star Cursed*, and *Sisters' Fate*) and *Wild Swans*. She is the editor of the feminist historical anthologies *A Tyranny of Petticoats* and *The Radical Element* and coeditor of the feminist witch anthology *Toil & Trouble*. Jess lives in Washington, DC, where she works as a children's library associate for the DC Public Library.

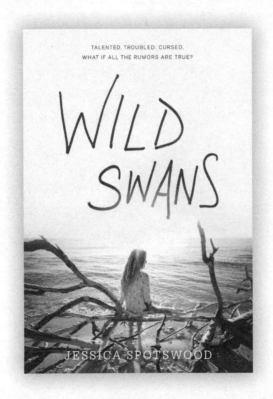

FIREreads

— ⑨ #getbooklit —

Your hub for the hottest in young adult books!

Visit us online and sign up for our
newsletter at FIREreads.com

 @sourcebooksfire

 sourcebooksfire

 firereads.tumblr.com